BRAINSTORM

An Alan Llewellyn Novel

Walt Breede

SIGNALMAN PUBLISHING

Brainstorm
by Walt Breede

Signalman Publishing
www.signalmanpublishing.com
email: info@signalmanpublishing.com
Kissimmee, Florida

Brainstorm is a work of fiction. Names, characters, most places and incidents either are the product of the author's imagination or are used fictitiously. Any resemblance to actual persons, living or dead, events or locales, is entirely coincidental. The reader may recognize some thinly disguised places (Chestertown, Virginia does not exist per se. On the other hand, J. Brian's Pub does exist, but not in Chestertown.) The author had the great good fortune to have lived for 27 years in the Commonwealth of Virginia and, in writing this work of fiction, did play a bit fast and loose with places, pubs and such in the name of telling a story.

Cover design by Rob Cheney

ISBN: 978-1-940145-22-8 (paperback)
978-1-940145-23-5 (ebook)

Library of Congress Control Number: 2014939373

Signalman
Publishing

This story is for Karen, Mark, Anne-Marie, David and Erik.

God bless you all.

Prologue

"Do you understand?" the older man hissed. Spittle flecked the corners of his mouth. His right fist rapped the table between them.

"Yes, yes, Hüsni Baba," the young man answered, respectfully, his eyes down, looking at the tabletop.

"All right. Tomorrow night you will sleep in the ground. In a *tabut*, a coffin. In a grave. An open grave, of course. From which you will be permitted to contemplate the enormity of your heroism. And your sacrifice. Dress warmly. The nights here are getting chilly. After your death, there will be no coffin for you. Allah only knows what the infidels will do with your body parts. There probably will not be enough left of you to bury. But the feasts of Paradise await you. Allah will heal you and cure you and reward you well.

"All you need to do now is pray and walk into that house of sin and pull the cord in your pocket."

The older man stood up and clapped the shoulder of the young man gently.

"Peace, my young friend. May Allah guard your soul and share His peace with you. I'll see you tomorrow."

The young man rose, placed his right hand on his chest, bowed toward the older man and left the room.

WASHINGTON, D.C.
METROPOLITAN AREA

CAMP DAVID

BALTIMORE

SEVERN RIVER

MARYLAND

ANNAPOLIS
(U.S.N.A.)

PENTAGON

WASHINGTON D.C.

VIRGINIA

A. WASHINGTON
HIGH SCHOOL

PATUXENT
RIVER

CHESAPEAKE BAY

CHANCELLORSVILLE

CHESTERTOWN, VA

POTOMAC RIVER

RAPPAHANNOCK RIVER

Chapter One

I walked into Fat Harry's after work on Friday the first day of November, All Saints' Day. November is the month when autumn begins to sink her teeth into northern Virginia. The leaves of the oaks and beeches have dulled from the brilliant crimsons and golds of October to the earth tones of death. And they also have started to fall with a vengeance. The pleasant days and nights of the Piedmont October have given way to the colder temperatures of true autumn. I knew that any one of these nights when I stepped outside to take Cory, our seven-month-old chocolate Labrador, for her bedtime walk, there'd be a bite of frost and the aroma of wood smoke in the air.

Fat Harry's is a pizza-and-sandwich joint just north of Chestertown, Virginia, where I have the pleasure of living with Maria, the love of my life, and Elizabeth, the other love of my life—our daughter—who has just turned thirteen. God help us.

I was in the process of coming home from work and fulfilling our family custom of picking up a "take-out" dinner on Friday evening. I had already called in an order for a sausage-and-artichoke pizza from my office at *BIAS*—Bureau of International Affairs Studies—on the campus of Martha Washington University. *BIAS* was the overt name for a highly classified, deep-cover presidential intelligence fact-checking office. I ran the office at the behest of my high-school classmate and track team running mate, Jim Kehoe, who is now "POTUS," President of the United States. We— the guys and gals at *BIAS*—and by extension, "the man"—Kehoe—had been through a rough few months with the People's Republic of China and their Ministry of State Security recently, but we seem to have put things to rest. At some risk to the life of yours truly and those of a few others. Some of those "risks" had morphed into deaths, but *BIAS* had remained relatively unscathed. More recently, *BIAS* has been humming along, doing what we are supposed to do, gathering information and comparing it with what the "big boys" in the Intelligence Community were giving POTUS.

And we were doing it the way I liked, with no bullets whizzing around and no bombs blowing up. After all, I came to *BIAS*—and *BIAS* came to me—after a short career in the United States Navy, followed by a slightly longer career as a high school math teacher. The craving for order was in my DNA.

Despite the restaurant's name, Fat Harry wasn't a Harry at all—he was a Palestinian Arab named Hafez Abdul-Aziz—and his little dive produced the best pizzas outside the metro New York area. His sandwiches were even better. The "steak bomb"—a salami, steak, ham, pepper, and cheese concoction—was so good it would bring tears to a glass eye. I enjoyed dropping in—not only for the food but also to practice my limited Arabic.

"Es selaamu aleikum," I said as I approached the counter.

"Wa aleikum essalaam, Alan,*"* Harry said with a big grin on his face, showing a gold tooth. Then he switched to English.

"Alan, this is my nephew, Khalil," he said, nodding toward a young man sitting at the counter.

The young man swiveled on the stool, stood and smiled. He was, I guessed, about twenty-four or -five, making me feel ancient at forty. He had a neat haircut and a slightly scraggily mustache, all black, which matched his limpid brown eyes perfectly.

"Es selaamu aleikum," he said. *"Tifham Arabi?"*

"Do you speak Arabic?"

I was quickly running out of gas with my Arabic.

"Laa," I said. *"Ma afham."*

"No. I don't speak it."

"You weren't doing too badly at all," he said, in perfect English, his grin widening. He held out his hand.

"I'm Khalil," he said.

"I'm Alan Llewellyn," I answered, shaking his hand.

"Hafez Bey is my uncle," he said, by way of explanation.

"Hafez is my good friend and is patient with me when I try to practice my broken Arabic," I said. "Plus he makes the best pizza in northern Virginia."

Hafez laughed.

"That's because I started out making pizza in the Bronx," he said. "I learned from the masters."

He hauled a flat box off the top of the ovens.

"Here's your pizza, Alan," he said. "Sausage and artichokes. Seventeen ninety-five."

"Could I throw a dozen wings onto the order without causing a problem?" I asked.

"Of course, of course," Hafez responded. He took a pair of tongs and picked out thirteen chicken wings from a little warming oven and put them into a foil-lined bag.

"Baker's dozen," he said. "That's twenty-two bucks even."

I took out my wallet and extracted a twenty and a five.

"Good to go," I said, handing him the bills and picking up the warm pizza box and the bag of wings.

"Nice meeting you, Khalil," I added.

"Nice meeting you, sir," he said with a smile.

Chapter Two

The pizza box was still warm when I pulled into the driveway of fifteen-oh-six Prince Henry Street in Chestertown. Cold November rain started hammering the roof of the truck as I turned off the engine. The interior of my ancient Explorer contained a mixture of bouquets—yeast and cheese from the pizza and herbal heat and buffalo sauce from the chicken wings plus the more feral aroma of my running gear. When I entered the mudroom of our old-but-charming Chestertown house, I could hear animated female chatter. It had become difficult for me to discern childish female voices as compared to those of adult females in my household. Elizabeth's voice had developed a new, deeper resonance and so had the voice of one of her best friends, Esmé. Esmé was a somewhat short girl—I'd guess her at just under five feet. But her voice was very adult and her brown eyes looked to me like eyes that saw everything—including my innermost thoughts. I found that unsettling, to say the least. Maybe I should stop thinking of her as a little girl despite her short stature. Tala, the other friend, still had a more-or-less childlike-sounding voice, but she was around five-feet, seven inches tall and looked at me almost straight in the eye. Which I found unsettling as well. It's a hell of a thing for a forty-year-old guy to be intimidated by his thirteen-year-old daughter's girlfriends, I reflected. Anyway, the girls were chattering away. Nothing new or different there. I walked into the kitchen with the pizza and the wings. I thanked my guardian angel for tipping me to buy an order of wings back at Fat Harry's. Now we had enough grub if Esmé and Tala wanted to stay for "dinner." I put the unhealthy-but-scrumptious Friday night vittles on the stove top and popped into the living room. Maria was in the recliner, feet up with ankles crossed, and seemingly deeply absorbed in a Michael Connelly novel. She's a freelance writer and historian and damned good at what she does. When she's not researching or writing, she reads various forms of what I call "fun fiction."

We're a black-haired family. The two women are gorgeous. Maria's Italian heritage shows up in her black hair, dark brown eyes, and patrician features. Elizabeth's hair is black as well. She has her mama's features—a good thing—and her dad's green eyes. My black hair is starting to show small incursions of gray around the temples—which I try to camouflage by keeping it cut as short as that of a Naval Academy plebe.

The teenyboppers were sitting on the floor and appeared to be watching some sort of shopping drivel on TV. They were discussing the merits—or lack thereof—of an impossibly expensive diamond bracelet. Cory, the chocolate Lab, was on the floor amidst the girls and looked like she was smiling and thought she was in heaven.

"Hi, ladies," I said.

That got me a smile from Maria and a, "Hi, Dad/Mr. Llewellyn," from the peanut gallery. It also got me a floor-thumping wag of the tail from Cory. I gave Maria a little smooch just as my government-issue cell phone chimed in my pocket.

"Hmm," I muttered, standing up and taking out the phone.

It was a text from a number that I recognized but most people wouldn't. Kehoe. POTUS.

"Uh oh," I muttered and thumbed up the text.

Loose:

Lunch 2morro @ CD? Talk about ME-Euro paper. Chopper ETD 1130 @ Quantico. U'll be home in time for the Navy-Duke game @ 1530.

Keys

Translation. "Loose" was my high-school track team nickname when Jim Kehoe and I ran on the same 3,200-meter relay. That was when we were callow teenagers on the Cardinal Mindzenty High School track team in Clancyville, New York. Now Jim was the President of the United States. He was "inviting" me to lunch tomorrow at Camp David to discuss a point paper that *BIAS* had prepared for him in response to a National Intelligence Estimate on Middle East radicals based in Europe. I had turned it in to him yesterday. The text told me he'd read it. Or someone had. A Marine helo would give me a lift, leaving the Marine Corps Air Facility at Quantico at 11:30 tomorrow. He obviously knew that the Navy-Duke game was on TV tomorrow afternoon. "Keys" was his high-school track moniker.

"What's up?" Maria asked.

"Lunch with the man at Camp David tomorrow," I said, starting to thumb in a reply. "He is sending a chopper, so I don't have to drive. Home by 3:30, he says. And he's pretty good about staying on schedule."

"There he goes, messing up another weekend," she said.

She was getting used to weekend intrusions, what with me being at the beck and call of the leader of the free world. Accustomed to it but not liking it a hell of a lot.

Elizabeth turned and cocked her head.

"Lunch with the president?" she asked.

"Looks that way, sweetie," I said.

"Wow!" said Tala.

Esmé said, "You're the man, Mr. Ell."

No wonder the little weasels have me wrapped around their fingers.

I walked back into the kitchen and Maria followed, her finger tucked into the pages of the Connelly novel.

I sent a text back to POTUS.

Keys,

I'll be there. I'll bring Darps if OK. CU 2morro,

Loose

Darps was Darpley Roentgen Taylor, a Naval Academy classmate of mine, who functioned ostensibly as my deputy but really was my other, smarter half at *BIAS*.

I looked at Maria. She wasn't too happy, but she looked like she understood. I decided to change the subject.

"I think there's enough chow for five," I said. "There's the large pizza plus a dozen wings."

"I'll throw a tomato-and cucumber salad together, so it won't be a total nutrition atrocity," Maria said. "You ask the girls."

I did and they did. They broke out the cell phones and called their parents, asking if they could "have Friday night dinner at the Llewellyns." And that was that.

It was always an experience to break bread with three thirteen-year-olds. Especially these three. All three of them are voracious readers, and they have the robust vocabularies to prove it. On the other hand, there are some pretty wide gaps in their knowledge banks. Maybe it's because they haven't developed any interest in politics or the workings of governments yet. And maybe that's a good thing. It gives them a certain freshness, an innocence that is free of the sour cynicism that will probably come later. Except for Esmé. She's not cynical, but she is pretty tuned in to national politics. Maria and I, on the other hand, share tremendous gaps in our awareness of pop culture. We have zero knowledge of and regard for the so-called celebs of the day and zippo insights into so-called reality TV. Like our daughter and her girlfriends, we do read a lot of fiction and it's no doubt more "pop" than literary. Escapist trash, really. But in our defense, we do read "serious" fiction from time to time and even some non-fiction once in a while. And Maria, for her part, writes serious non-fiction. Mostly historical stuff. For publication. And gets paid for it. Albeit not all that well.

With these girls this evening, we batted around some of the issues from the latest Harry Potter novel. The book, not the movie. Relationships, magic, evil, time travel. It was pretty fascinating and a lot less boring than many adult conversations I'd had over the recent weeks.

One slice of the way through the pizza, the cell phone chimed again. I looked at the text.

Darps is welcome, the b#%&!!d. Keys

Kehoe's nose was still out of joint because, when the rascal tried to hire Darps away from *BIAS* for an "important White House job," Darps turned him down flat. Privately, Darps had told me that he still had too much integrity left to work with "a bunch of broke-dick politicos."

I don't think I'd characterize my old high school classmate—POTUS—that harshly, but what the hey, Darps can be a bit cantankerous at times. I *was* glad he'd decided to stay at *BIAS.*

I sent him—Darps—a quick text about tomorrow's meeting and its logistics. When I got back to the table, the girls were munching on Scottish shortbread cookies and drinking milk. There was a skinny sliver of pizza, one chicken wing and a couple of fragments of salad left for dear old dad. Oh, well. I'd had one slice already.

Chapter Three

Major Faisal el-Shahawi was the Military Attaché of Yemen assigned to the Yemeni Embassy in Havana. As the only officer assigned to his Embassy's attaché office, he had a full plate. His duties included advising his ambassador on military matters, particularly those having to do with the Cuban armed forces. He also was the official representative of the Yemeni military establishment to the Government of Cuba. He collected and reported military and political-military information to the Yemeni Ministry of Defense. And, unbeknownst to both his Yemeni superiors and his Cuban hosts, assisted in *al Qaeda* operations against the United States of America when needed.

Yemen was, ostensibly, an ally of the United States. Major el-Shahawi had other ideas. Although he was not a fervent Muslim and did not consider himself "observant," he was a Muslim. The idea of knocking down the decadent ideas and mores of the West appealed to him as did the notion of revenge for America's slaughter of so many of his fellow Muslims. On the other hand, he knew that some of his cravings for western delights rendered him somewhat hypocritical. But, he was a soldier. He followed orders. One day at a time.

The major had an extremely capable assistant and factotum in the person of one Master Sergeant Tariq, also a soldier in the Yemeni Army. El-Shahawi and Tariq maintained the militarily proper distance between an officer and a sergeant, but worked well together.

Major el-Shahawi was rapier-thin. His complexion was pockmarked Mediterranean, as if he'd suffered from fierce acne as a youth, which indeed he had. His heavy-lidded eyes were a deep brown. He wore a narrow, clipped mustache over his thin mouth. His native tongue was Arabic of course; he also spoke Spanish, Russian, Italian and English.

Master Sergeant Tariq was also multilingual and also wore a mustache, but any resemblance between the two men stopped there. Tariq had a large frame and a barrel chest. His brand of Islam consisted of fasting and refraining from sex and smoking during daylight hours of Ramadan. All bets were off after the sun went down. For the rest of the year, he was a good soldier who knew how to find a good time at any hour of the day or night.

The office phone chirped.

Tariq answered. El-Shahawi heard him say, "Yes sir. One second."

The light on his phone started blinking and Tariq's head popped into the office.

"Ali," he said softly.

The officer reached for the handset.

"El-Shahawi," he said.

"Good afternoon, major. This is Ali," said a silky smooth voice. Ali was a junior intelligence officer assigned by the Yemeni Muhkabaret—Intelligence Department—as a special assistant to the ambassador. The ambassador was a sprightly octogenarian with a surprisingly young wife. The ambassador enjoyed playing tennis on the clay court at his Havana residence.

"Are you available? At three?" Ali asked.

"Tennis?"

"Of course."

Major el-Shahawi glanced at his watch, a gold Movado.

"Of course. I'll make myself available. Three o'clock at the residence."

"You don't want to miss it. He's invited some women. To play. Tennis."

"The old hound! I wouldn't miss that for the world. Will the women wear burquas?"

Ali snickered.

"I think not. They're western women. Cuban, Italian, and Spanish. I expect they'll wear western tennis attire."

"The old hound," el Shahawi repeated. "I'll be there at three. Or a bit before."

Better than his word, Major el Shahawi was at the ambassador's residence tennis court at 2:45. Immaculate in his tennis whites, he took his racket and stepped onto the fence-enclosed court where three other players were warming up. The ambassador was not among them, but his wife Elise, a Lebanese-Christian thirty-five years his junior, was. El-Shahawi joined her on her side of the net.

"Good afternoon, ma'am," he said.

"Hello, Faisal," she said, smiling. "Welcome."

Elise had what el-Shahawi thought of as Cleopatra-league beauty. Her straight black hair was cut short, to mid neck. She was extremely athletic, obvious even in repose, as her arms and legs were well muscled. On the tennis court, she moved with the quickness of a snake and hit solid, whistling shots. Her ass was perfect.

"Have you met Laura?" she asked, nodding toward the other side of the court, which was occupied by Ali and a striking blond woman who appeared to be in her late twenties.

"I've not had the pleasure," he said.

Elise called out the introductions and el-Shahawi and Laura shook hands across the net.

Black or blond? he thought, wondering about Laura's pubic hair. He noticed that she didn't shave her legs. They were even better formed than Elise's, deeply tanned and the hairs on them bleached golden blond by the sun. The effect was quite erotic.

"Laura is a novelist. She's working on a novel that features Ernest Hemingway here in Cuba. And don't try to get her to talk about it. She's very tight-lipped about her work," Elise said. "She has a day job at the Havana office of the World Bank, but it doesn't seem to wear her down all that much."

Laura laughed, showing dazzling white teeth.

"Elise means that I talk my head off about anything except my current novel," she said. "And seldom work nights."

"Shall we play a set of mixed doubles?" Elise asked. "Izzy is inside with a few of our guests. They'll be out momentarily."

They played. El-Shahawi had played with both Elise and Ali numerous times before. Laura was new territory and was very impressive. She patrolled the court like a jaguar.

At fifteen-thirty in the second game, Ambassador Hamdi accompanied by an assistant foreign minister and two women took seats on lawn chairs outside the court. On the court, Ali and Laura took the first set, six-four.

The ambassador made introductions all around. The Cuban from the MFA was one Señor Alejandro Ruiz, and his daughter, Marisa, accompanied him. The other woman was the daughter of someone from the Spanish Embassy. Her name was Astrid. Major el-Shahawi and his fellow players yielded the court to the newcomers, swabbed themselves with fluffy white towels, and helped themselves to bottled water from a small, courtside cooler. Before going back onto the court, el-Shahawi ascertained that Laura's family name was Marino and that she had published a previous novel under her own name. It also featured Hemingway, but was set in Venice. He didn't need to ask her for her phone number. Getting it would be no trouble whatsoever.

Chapter Four

It was drizzly and chilly when I got to the VIP parking area at the Marine Corps Air Facility at Quantico. A Marine MP directed me to a reserved parking space. Darps was waiting, leaning against his Saab convertible in the drizzle. He has been with me since *BIAS* started up last year and I was lucky enough to hire him. He no longer resembles the Midshipman Taylor of old, having lost most of his head hair and has grown a very professorial beard to compensate. Today he wore a New York Yankees ball cap to protect his bald pate from the rain. Plus a tan raincoat. Darps is one of the smartest people I know. Officially, he's the Deputy Director of *BIAS*. In reality, he's my alter ego and is ready to take over if I go down. Darps was chatting with Luke Wallace, one of two Secret Service agents assigned to *BIAS* for security reasons after the Chinese or their minions started shooting at us several months ago. Mike Atwater, Luke's Secret Service "twin" at *BIAS*, had this Saturday off.

The waiting helicopter's rotor blades were chopping and slinging off rainwater as we ran to the hatch. We were barely belted in when the bird lifted off.

At Camp David, the drizzle was about the same as at Quantico, but the temperature was a good ten degrees colder when we climbed off the helicopter. Jim Kehoe was waiting for us at the edge of the LZ. He wore a knee-length Irish Macintosh over olive-green cords and work boots and a purple Holy Cross ball cap as protection from the elements. Sham, his Champagne-colored golden retriever, was at his heel, looking as happy as could be despite—or maybe because of—the chill rain.

"Welcome, gentlemen," said the president. "I know it's only November, but it chills down pretty quickly here in the mountains, so the staff had a fire going when I arrived. Let's enjoy it with a glass of sherry before lunch."

We went inside and stripped off our raincoats.

Kehoe must have briefed the staff before we arrived because a Navy steward bearing a silver tray and three delicate glasses of pale liquid materialized as we approached the fireplace. Luke had peeled off—no doubt to hobnob with some of his Secret Service buddies. The president raised his glass.

"Cheers, guys. And welcome," he said.

Darps and I hoisted our glasses in response.

"Cheers, Mr. President," we chorused.

"Have a seat and enjoy the fire," he said, sitting down in one of the chairs grouped around the fireplace.

Sham had already curled up in front of the grate. Darps and I sat. I could hear Schubert coming from unseen speakers, and I thought about how peaceful it was sitting by the fire in the mountain dacha. I took a sip of sherry and wondered what sort of a bomb Jim Kehoe was about to drop in our laps and shatter the rainy Saturday peace. I didn't have to wait long.

"Your Middle East-Europe paper was first-rate, as usual," he said, putting down his glass. "But—"

"Let me guess, Jim," I said. "You didn't like the addendum. The North American Addendum."

"Whether I like it is not the point," Kehoe said. "And you guys know that. The whole reason for having *BIAS* is to protect me from the clowns that only want to tell me what I *do* like. But I did find your North American Addendum unsettling. An Arab terrorist attack on the United States launched from Germany? If that's accurate, then the whole national intelligence apparatus—except for you guys—has missed it. Including the National Counter Terrorism Center. And that's very goddam unsettling. Plus the additional implications regarding other major terrorist attacks in the United States are also very goddam unsettling. Especially the 'major' part. So talk to me."

He picked up his glass of sherry and took a hummingbird-sized sip.

I took another sip of mine and put my glass down.

"Okay. The main body of the paper said that Europe has its own problems with its Muslim immigrant populations. And they vary considerably from country to country," I said.

"Sure," said the President of the United States. "And the U.S. National Intelligence Estimate said the same thing."

"Yes, sir. I know that," I replied, a little testily. "So did *The Economist*, a few weeks ago. But what I suspect that you don't like is our inference that there's a radical Islamic cabal in Berlin or Vienna or Hamburg that may be planning major terrorist attacks in CONUS."

"Whether I like that or not is beside the point," Kehoe said. "The point is that *BIAS* is telling me there's an active, cooking terrorist plot against the United States, and the rest of the U. S. Intelligence Community is telling me no such thing. All they're telling me is that various nasty, unsavory groups in Yemen, Somalia and Waziristan want to kill lots of Americans. And that's pretty vague, most of the time. Not at all specific."

"I understand," I said. "I thought you hired me to give you alternative views—when necessary—to what you were getting from the Intelligence Community. Not necessarily differing, but red-flagging judgments that might be, uh, specious."

"I did, indeed. But this difference, this departure is so huge. On one hand, the U.S. Intelligence Community describes a nasty stew of European Muslim immigrants who have a highly-refined hatred for their adoptive homelands and Danish cartoonists, but who don't really give a rat's ass about things in the good ole USA. That's obviously an oversimplification, but it's essentially what they're telling me. *BIAS*, on the other hand, says that some sort of Muslim rat pack in Europe is cooking up another nine-eleven."

I swallowed. What the man said was true, more or less. Darps jumped in.

"Mr. President, we don't have any proof. None whatsoever. But we do have field agents on the ground—albeit sporadically—in Europe and the Middle East. They spend time in the cities and the towns, they watch TV, they read the papers, and hang out in bars and coffee shops. They talk to people. And they're getting subtle but strong vibes that there's some sort of radical Islamist group—or groups—that is or are cooking up some sort of wildly violent plot against the U.S. The most and strongest vibrations to that effect are in Germany. The constants are just that—major violence and on U.S. soil. No proof at all. But the hints are there. And there is a phrase. Or a partial phrase. That has cropped up more than once. 'Revenge of—or for—.' We don't have the last part. But it sounds like it might be the name or motto of some group that wants to do something big and bad. Here."

"Jesus Christ! You're not supposed to be eavesdropping on *anyone's* communications. I've got enough trouble with NSA activities that have been okayed by our lawyers and the courts."

I jumped in.

"We're not. Listening to anybody's communications, that is," I said. "Unless they're on the Internet or elsewhere in the public domain. The 'revenge' or 'vengeance' phrase was reported to us from a foreign contact."

"Okay. Foreign contact. Hints. I'll buy all that. You both know what this means, don't you?"

A little *bong!* chimed. The president drained his sherry and stood up. Darps and I did likewise.

"Lunch time," said the president.

We sat down in a surprisingly small dining room. A Navy steward served us steaming bowls of thick lentil soup—perfect for a wet, chilly day. After a few spoonfuls and some oohing and ahing about how it hit the spot on a cold, drizzly day like today, the president put his spoon down.

"As I was saying," he said. "You guys have your work cut out for you. *BIAS*, that is. You've got to have your guys and gals run those 'hints' down. We *must* have more information. More specificity. Note the 'must.' Where, when, who—you know what I mean. And you need to run down this 'Revenge of' title."

He went back to his soup.

Sandwiches of smoked turkey and lettuce, washed down with sweet iced tea, followed the soup. The sandwiches were delicious—they had some sort of delicate, mayonnaise-based dressing that complemented the smokiness of the fowl perfectly. Maybe a hint of pesto in the mayo. Trouble was, under the circumstances, I could barely swallow the first bite, even with a hefty swig of sweet tea. I put the sandwich down.

"Um—Jim," I started. "With all due respect, I think *you* should be the one who runs this stuff down. You've got the heavy artillery. Turn on NSA. Turn the FBI loose here in the states. And CIA and State overseas—they can talk with our allies. Governments. National intelligence organizations. *BIAS* can't do any of that stuff. We just talk to bartenders, barflies, hotel maids, little guys. We gave you the hints. You need the big boys to run 'em to ground."

Kehoe popped the last of his sandwich into his mouth, took a swallow of sweet tea and wiped his lips with a linen napkin.

Then he grinned. The grin was more wolfish than amused.

"Loose, old buddy," he said. The 'heavy artillery,' as you call it, *is* turned on and turned loose. Has been for a long time. There's no way I—or anybody else—can ratchet things up any more than they already are. The machinery is maxed out. That's point number one.

"Point number two is that, even with the U.S. Intelligence Community going at max rpm, the 'heavy artillery' hasn't flushed out a possible terrorist strike or strikes against the U.S. from Europe. Nary a peep. Oh, there are plenty of plots cooking in Somalia and Yemen and most of them are half-assed. A few are real and have to be taken seriously. And there are the occasional American homegrown martyr wannabes. The clowns that spend their time jacking off whilst surfing radical web sites and deciding that they want to blow something up. But they're incompetent, dysfunctional, and catchable, and I think we're on top of them. But we have *nothing* on someone or something serious coming at us from Europe. The intel big boys say that the euro countries have their work cut out for themselves, but they're not saying anything about a toxic plot coming our way from Europe. They're not saying anything about some guys referring to themselves as 'Revenge of the blank,' either. But *BIAS*—your bar maids and barflies and the people who talk to them—have. That tells me that, if anyone can follow up on the leads—or 'hints' as you call them—*BIAS* can. So go for it. That's all I'm saying."

"'That's all?'" I asked in disbelief. "Jesus Christ, Keys. We're small, we're poor as church mice, and we're just nibbling at the edges of the issues."

"Nibble away," said the leader of the free world. "That seems to be working."

The helo ride back to Quantico was even more depressing than the lunch at Camp David. The door of the helo closed, and we took off in the rain again.

"I thought you said Kehoe was your buddy," Darps said as the pilots pointed the nose of the chopper south and east.

"I did," I said. "But he's testing the limits of that friendship. I can't believe what he just laid on our doorstep. The bastard."

"Some friend," Darps said. "You go out on a limb for him and he throws you a chainsaw."

The Marine corporal crew chief sitting across from us looked at us a little strangely. So did Luke. It was their boss we were discussing. And ours.

Chapter Five

By the time we arrived back at the air facility at Quantico, Darps and I had decided to have a major *BIAS* brainstorming session Monday after lunch. We had a number of our key intel analysts in town. My hope was that we'd be able to caucus and figure out when and where to focus our efforts. A spark of an idea flared briefly in my fevered brain, but I didn't mention it to Darps on the chopper, deciding instead to do a little solo brainstorming with the issue before letting it see the light of day. I thought I might run it by Maria as well.

When I got back to fifteen-oh-six Prince Henry Street, the drizzle had stopped, the skies had started to clear, and the temperature had fallen through the forties. The thermometer outside the mud room said thirty-eight. On top of that, the oaks, poplars, and beeches around our white colonial had dropped about half their leaves on our lawn. But the man had spoken the truth. Kickoff was still ten minutes away as I let myself in.

"I think there's time for me to start a fire," I said.

"First one of the season," Maria said. "And I have time to finish this paragraph."

She's writing a book about New York regiments in the Civil War. There were a lot of them.

"It's a fire kinda day," Elizabeth said.

I had the blaze going merrily by the time Navy kicked off to Duke. The Navy players looked to be about two-thirds the size of their Blue Devil rivals, if that.

"Oh by the way," Maria said. "A man called. Strange name. 'Haleel,' I think he said. Sounded nice. Said he'd call back."

"Khalil, by any chance?" I asked.

"Yes," she answered. "I'm sure that's it. It definitely had that *kh* sound at the beginning."

"Did he leave a number?" I asked, wondering what Fat Harry's nephew wanted.

"No. He said he'd call back. But I'm sure the number is on the Caller ID."

Navy stopped a Duke drive on their thirty-eight with a sack of the Duke quarterback. The tiny Navy punt returner was able to run the ball back to the Navy forty for decent field position.

I watched happily for two Navy first downs, and when they took a commercial timeout, I want to the phone. The Caller ID showed a cell phone number for Stafford, Virginia.

"Was that call from Stafford?" I asked.

"Umm, yes. It was," Maria replied. "Cell phone."

I decided to wait and see if he called back and returned to the game just in time to see the Navy quarterback keep the ball in an option to the right and waltz almost untouched into the end zone. Things were looking better than they were when Darps and I left Camp David on the Marine Corps chopper. If only because my savoring of Navy's lead overshadowed the huge challenge President Kehoe had dumped into our laps.

I enjoyed the rest of the game, too. Duke's big guys pushed around Navy's little guys, but Navy stayed in the game and finished with a tough 35 – 31 win. I raked up a fifteen-by-fifteen foot square of wet leaves in the backyard during halftime, but by the time the game ended, the sun was down and Chestertown was dark. Maria had spaghetti and meatballs starting to fire up on the stove and I poured her a dry sherry and a scotch for me.

"So what did the man want at lunch?" she asked.

"Darn," I said. "I'd managed to suppress all thought of our lunchtime conversation during the game. You're not gonna believe this."

And then I told her. And after I told her what the man wanted, I told her of my germ—or spark—of an idea.

"I think he needs to give us a license to hunt—or fish—at home—in CONUS, the continental United States," I said.

"Yikes," she said.

That's when the phone rang. The Caller ID said it was the Stafford cell phone. I picked up.

"Hello."

"Hello? Mr. Llewellyn. This is Khalil Al-Hassani. We met at my uncle's restaurant yesterday."

"I remember, Khalil. And please call me Alan."

"Okay, uh, Alan," he said. "I was talking with my uncle and told him I'm interested in becoming a teacher. A high school teacher. I graduated from George Mason with a master's in retailing a year and a half ago. I've fooled around with a couple of sales jobs since, but I feel like I'm spinning my wheels. Then I got the teaching idea. I bounced it off my uncle. And he suggested that I speak with you. He said you'd been a high school teacher for a number of years. I wondered if we might perhaps have lunch together and I could pick your brain."

"Sure, Khalil. I'd be happy to do that. Although I'm not sure you'll get very much by picking *my* brain. I've been out of teaching for over a year."

"I respect my uncle's judgment on that score, Alan. How about next Saturday? A week from today?"

I glanced at my planner that was lying on the counter next to the phone. Saturday was clear.

"Saturday works for me," I said.

"Good," he said. "It'll be my treat. You can pick a place."

"How about your uncle's?"

"I was thinking of someplace a little more—um—upscale. Nothing against Uncle Hafez, but..."

He let the sentence hang.

"Well then, how about *Teacher Man* here in Chestertown?" I asked.

At least the name of the place was apropos. *Teacher Man* was a nice little bistro that had opened a few years ago. Rumor had it that the owner-chef was a retired physics professor from the university. The menu was pleasantly diverse and the food was excellent. Atmosphere was comfortable, at least to Maria and me. And the prices weren't heart-stoppers.

"Yes," he said. "I've been there before. It's quite good. Shall we meet there?"

"Sounds good. Noon on Saturday?"

"See you then."

We hung up.

"Sounds like you have a date," Maria said as I jotted it down in my planner.

"I do. Fat Harry's nephew."

"Fat Harry? The pizza guy?"

"The same," I said. "That's who Khalil is. His young nephew."

"Does this mean that *BIAS* is going into the pizza business?" she asked in her wise-ass voice.

"No, sweetheart. It means that the pizza man's nephew—whom I met at the restaurant yesterday when I was picking up our pizza—thinks he might want to be a teacher. Fat Harry suggested that he buy me lunch and pick my brain. Not being one to turn down a free lunch, I accepted."

"With alacrity, I noticed," she said. "And at *Teacher Man* as well, you sly devil."

"Hey—my first suggestion was *Fat Harry's*," I said. "His uncle probably would have picked up the tab."

"I know. I'm only teasing."

I reached out and put my arms around Maria.

"Since Khalil is paying for lunch next Saturday, I think I can afford a lunch with you on, say, Wednesday—at *the Teacher Man*. I'd be honored and delighted if you'd accept."

"I accept with pleasure," she said. And planted a lovely wet kiss on my mouth.

When I walked Cory around ten that night, I could smell wood smoke in the air. When I crawled into bed, Maria snuggled in and planted another lovely, wet kiss on my mouth. Elizabeth had gone over to Esmé's house for a sleepover. Things went rapidly downhill from there. It was good. Very good.

Chapter Six

Havana
November 4
Monday

Major Faisal el-Shahawi was "trolling." The Yemeni Military Attaché observed that there were more than a dozen uniformed Cuban officers at the reception hosted by the Russian Ambassador at his embassy in Havana. They wore their "revolutionary" uniforms—jazzed up green fatigues, rather than the dress uniforms worn by the Russians, various military and naval attaches, and el-Shahawi himself.

There was a major general and two full colonels. He would ignore the three of them. They were too far up the food chain for his purposes. Two more were lieutenant colonels. They were also up there in the food chain and hence gravitated to the bottom of his priority list. He would try and talk with them only if there was sufficient time. He would concentrate on the five majors and three captains. El-Shahawi knew that the Cuban military always turned out in force for social functions at the Russian Embassy. He assumed that was because of the Russian vodka and caviar. Or maybe there were standing orders in the Cuban armed forces to maximize participation at Russian diplomatic affairs. El-Shahawi observed that one of the majors was with a tall, attractive woman and no one else. El-Shahawi activated the recorder in his inside pocket and headed in their direction. The officer's nametag read *Ramirez.*

"Buenas noches," he said.

Introductions were made. The men exchanged calling cards. The attractive woman's surname was Sanz—not Ramirez. Neither she nor her escort wore wedding bands. They chatted about the vodka and the hurricane season. Major el-Shahawi took out a pack of Marlboro cigarettes and offered them. Ramirez and Señorita Sanz each took one. The Yemeni put his vodka glass down on a table while he lit their cigarettes with a small silver lighter. He didn't pick the glass up. After a few more minutes of polite chatter, Major el-Shahawi spotted two Cuban captains talking quietly to each other. He excused himself and walked over to the captains.

One was an artillery officer and the other one was an engineer. Their names were Diaz and Trevino. Diaz wore a wedding band; Trevino did not. When a waiter passed with a tray holding little glasses of vodka, all three officers helped themselves. Both Cubans downed their drinks. Major el-Shahawi moistened his lips with the vodka. They talked about the hurricane season and the recent American baseball World Series. In the course of ten minutes of conversation, the two Cubans downed two more shots of vodka.

By the time large numbers of people began leaving the reception, Major el-Shahawi had spoken with four majors and the two captains. He had consumed less than half a shot of vodka. He returned to his apartment via a Yemeni Embassy Mercedes driven by a Cuban civilian. He let himself in. Laura Marino, the novelist from the World Bank, was there. She wore a short, flimsy robe and apparently little else. She was watching a movie and drinking a glass of white wine.

"How was the reception?" she asked.

"Like them all," he said, unbuttoning his uniform blouse.

"I wish you'd take me to one of them."

"No you don't. You'd get in trouble. I would get in trouble. You wouldn't like that. Nor would I. Besides, they're boring," he said, taking off his tie. "Now, if you'll excuse me for a few minutes, I have a bit of work to do. But it won't take long."

He removed the digital recorder from the inside pocket of his tunic, stepped into his small study and closed the door. He removed a small stack of calling cards from a trouser pocket and set them on the desktop. Sitting down at the desk, he took a tiny headset from a drawer and fitted the buds into his ears and connected the headset to the recorder. He then pulled out a wallet-sized checkbook from a middle drawer. He turned to the deposit slips in the back of the book, clicked the recorder on, and began writing. In Arabic.

Ramirez. Roberto. Major. Infantry. Battalion operations officer. Apparently unmarried. Slightly overweight. Doesn't seem political. Accompanied by Srta Dalys Sanz. Hobbies: Unknown. Rating: 4.

Diaz. Antonio. Captain. Artillery. Battery commander. Married (wedding ring) but not accompanied. Drinks quite a bit but doesn't show it. Likes to play tennis. Rating: 7.

He continued with his notes in the order with which he'd had the conversations. When he'd finished, he erased the recorder and put the checkbook and the calling cards in his briefcase to carry to the embassy tomorrow. *It's sparse, but it's a start,* he thought. Back in the sitting room, he poured a large scotch from a 1.75 liter bottle of Johnny Walker Red.

"Would you like some more wine?" he asked Laura.

"Si, per piacere," she said, holding out her glass. He took a swallow of scotch and refilled her glass from a bottle in an ice bucket.

Good, he thought. *The more she drinks, the less inhibited she is.*

Chapter Seven

I walked into the *BIAS* parking lot just as Darps parked his Saab convertible. He got out of the car a little stiffly, I thought. He was wearing a trench coat, even though the sun was shining and the outside temperature was unseasonably warm. But then, Darps is a tad eccentric. We walked together to the front door. Once we were inside, he pulled back the trench coat in a flasher-like movement. There was an upside-down rifle strapped to his shoulder inside the trench coat.

"Whisky-tango foxtrot?" I asked. NATO phonetic for "WTF." You get the idea.

"It's an M-1," he said.

"I can see that," I said. At Annapolis we had been issued M-1 Garand rifles. They were World War Two-Korean War vintage. We drilled with them, marched with them, and fired them on the rifle range.

"An uncle of mine—a Korean War vet—died a few months ago. He willed this rifle to me. Annie is an anti-gun fanatic. She won't allow it in the house. I thought I could stash it here—with our emergency stuff. I've got a bandolier of ammo, too," he said, pulling back the other side of his trench coat.

There was an olive-drab fabric strap of pockets of .30 caliber rifle rounds in clips hanging from his other shoulder.

"Good Christ," I said. "What sort of 'emergency' could we possibly get into that would require using that beast?"

Even with its open sights, the M-1, fired by someone in the prone position, could take down a man at ranges up to six hundred yards. Permanently.

"Hell, I dunno," Darps said. "But I couldn't just shitcan it. Maybe if I do a long, slow, sweet-talking sales job, Annie will relent and let me bring it home. Meantime, I'd like to keep it here."

"No problem," I said. I wasn't worried about the thing getting stolen. Our locks and alarm system had been installed by the Secret Service. Hell, the custodial team that cleans up the *BIAS* office spaces had been cleared by the Secret Service.

After we got Darps's uncle's rifle stowed, I sent an email around the office and around the western world. It went to all of our Middle East, North Africa, and Western Europe people on board. I CC'd it to those who were traveling as well as the Eastern Europe gang. I also sent a copy to Sammy Chen. He's our China guy and theoretically shouldn't be in the loop on this Euro-Arab issue. But Sammy's mind works at warp speed and with deadly accuracy. Hence, if an issue is critical, I unfailingly bring Sammy into the loop. The email announced a meeting at 1330 in the main conference room—known as "The Big Kahuna"—at Ripley Hall on the Martha Washington campus. (The small conference room was nicknamed "Little Paycheck.") Subject of the email was *CONUS Terrorism from Europe*. All action addees were invited.

Judy laid on some extra coffee with the caterer plus a bunch of bottled water in a cooler of ice. There were a couple of jugs of Arizona tea of various flavors as well. We started right on time, which is SOP, standard operating procedure, at *BIAS*.

"This probably comes as no surprise to any of you, but our Middle East/Europe paper has caused a bit of an uproar in our nation's capital," I said, to set the stage.

"Actually, it wasn't the paper itself, but the North America Addendum that caused the stir. And if there's anyone to blame for that, it's me. I should have heeded the advice of those of you who thought it would be smart if we stuck with describing situations of which we're pretty confident. Meaning predictions based on facts, or at least, near-facts. Instead, I decided to paste on that addendum, which we all know is based more on rumor and innuendo rather than facts. Now it's come back to bite us in the ass."

I looked around the room. *BIAS* has a kind of two-track organizational structure. For each region—Central Asia, for example—we have a primary desk officer and a backup. Samantha Jennings is our primary for Central Asia, and she was at the meeting. She is good — very good. She speaks Turkish, Farsi, and a smattering of Arabic, which is growing quickly.

Which is a good thing as she's the backup for the Asian Middle East. Samantha has streaky blond hair that she keeps short and ice-gray eyes that have a permanent glint. Her backup for Central Asia is Sam Halachis, who is the primary for the Asian Middle East. He speaks Arabic, Greek, Farsi, and some Urdu and is working on his Turkish. Sam was on the road somewhere in Syria at the present time.

We try and flip-flop primaries and backups so one is home and the other one is in the target area. That makes for some challenging juggling acts with schedules at which Judy Palladino, our multitalented office manager, is quite adept.

We had the "primaries" for northern Europe and North Africa and the backups for southern Europe on hand. Also in attendance were Darps (of course!) and our lawyer, Ashleigh MacDonald, whom we had just hired. I had been aiming at hiring a part-time retired geezer who knew where all the nation's capital bodies were buried. But I'd tried that once, and the guy we hired turned out to be a mole for the Red Chinese. His body was among those buried. Literally. In the Congressional Cemetery. Ashleigh was young, just out of the University of Miami Law School, spoke seven languages, and could jump in and pinch-hit for half of our desk officers. I was confident that she could give Sammy and Darps a run for the money in the smarts department. Plus, as Darps was fond of saying, "...she can keep our young asses out of jail." Ashleigh looked young and innocent, which was good cover for her cutting-edge smarts. She wore glasses that somehow added to her innocent aura. And as if that weren't enough, she was as pretty as the dawn and had a nice figure. Finally, sitting in the back with Ashleigh, was Sammy Chen.

Samantha spoke up.

"Alan, is there any collateral regarding terrorist attacks on a CONUS target?"

"None. Other than what you guys produced."

"How about here? In the states? FBI, DHS? NCTC? Anything?"

"Not that I'm aware of. And if there *were* something, I'm pretty sure I'd know of it."

"What about the hit on 'Revenge of the Nerds'?" she asked, referring to the 'Revenge' or 'Vengeance' group or motto or whatever.

"Nada," I said. "The boss man was a little spooked about us possibly eavesdropping on somebody to get that little phrase, but I told him it came to us face-to-face overseas. Which is true."

"Is there any reason why *we* don't have a CONUS—or at least, a North American—desk officer?" Ashleigh asked.

"You mean 'we,' as in *BIAS*?" I asked.

She nodded vigorously.

"Probably a ton of them," I responded. "Policy, for one. *BIAS* was set up to deal with international issues. Not domestic ones. I'm sure that the powers that be—the few that know we exist—consider us an unofficial member of the U.S. Intelligence Community. Which collects overseas but not stateside. We leave that to the cops. From the Feebs on down to local sheriffs and police departments. The idea that transnational issues are tending to bleed into domestic ones seems to be lost on the Washington bureaucrats. Then, of course, there's turf. We start poking around stateside, various noses get bent out of joint. Finally, there's politics. If some senator or congressman from a progressive state or district sees a way to raise an issue and gain politically, they'll do it. In a heartbeat. That would apply to *BIAS* activities—especially stateside. National security be damned. They'd shut us down in a New York minute for a handful of votes. Look at the phone-intercept issue after nine-eleven and the howls of sanctimonious outrage that exploded in the aftermath of that."

I paused. Nobody said anything. The silence hung like a lead weight for two or three seconds.

"Nonetheless," I said, "I'm thinking of going to the 'powers that be' to ask for funding for a North American desk officer and a backup. And permission to keep our ear to the ground here in the good ole USA. Not to mention Canada. I don't think that the country or we—*BIAS*—can afford to fiddle-fuck around on this issue. Excuse my French."

That caused a little stir and a little buzz in the meeting. Not "my French," except with Judy who hates the F-word. The idea of putting some assets to work in the U.S. It meant we were intending to jump off the reservation. But only with an "OK" from "the powers that be."

Once the hoo-rah over the possibility of *BIAS* stateside ops died down, we got back to the business of adding to the specificity of our judgments. The "when, where, and who" as Kehoe had put it. And that quickly boiled down to the issue of manpower. Not just a couple of people to do some CONUS-based collection, but a couple of more pairs of eyeballs and ears to add to those already running around Europe and the Middle East. Always conscious of funding constraints, I was starting to see where this was heading. I needed to kick things around with Darps and Judy. And then with Kehoe. The president. *"Cheetah,"* as he was known by the Secret Service.

When I went home around five-thirty, the air was downright cold and there was already a pungent smell of wood smoke in the air.

Chapter Eight

On Wednesday, I walked home to meet Maria for our lunch date, hitting the door at about 11:45. It was a perfect November day—clear air, deep blue skies, and bracing temperatures. Maria was working on her laptop when I walked in the door. But she was ready for lunch, and we walked the five blocks to *Teacher Man* holding hands, talking nonsense and savoring the sunshine and the late autumn air.

At the restaurant, she ordered a glass of sauvignon blanc and I a merlot. When the waitress returned with our wine, Maria ordered a Caesar salad with grilled chicken, and I asked for a Reuben. Nothing fancy, but the sandwich was perfect, my warm German potato salad side was scrumptious, and Maria leaned into her monster salad with gusto. We had a jolly good lunch.

Over coffee—we passed on dessert—Maria cleared her throat. Not a good sign.

"Esmé's mom called me this morning."

"What about?" I asked.

"Elizabeth."

About a half a sip of coffee went down the wrong pipe and I started coughing.

"What about Elizabeth?" I sputtered.

"Nothing really. But apparently Esmé told her that some high school kid 'has a case of the hots' for our daughter. And that 'he's a total sketch ball.' Those are Esmé's words, not her mom's."

I had to chuckle, even though my worry index was in the red zone.

"Did she give you a name?" I asked.

"Yes. Jerrod Skinner. She said he's a football player. A sophomore. He calls Elizabeth on her cell and sends her text messages. A lot. Esmé says that Elizabeth enjoys the attention and is jazzed up by getting phone calls and texts from a football player."

I put down my coffee cup.

"I know that little turd. He was in my algebra one class at Washington last year," I said, remembering a ferret-faced kid with a wispy mustache and an overbite. Who came close to failing algebra one. Algebra one, for Christ's sake! Definitely not a future brain surgeon.

Augustine Washington High School in Stafford, Virginia, was the school at which I used to teach and coach. Before Kehoe and *BIAS*.

"I only bring this up because I think we should present a united front to Elizabeth," Maria said. "If I try to minimize it and you explode—or vice versa—then we'll convince her that we are the idiots that she probably already suspects we are. She's thirteen, after all. We need to be on the same page before we talk to her."

As usual, Maria was making good sense. Also as usual, I wasn't getting it.

"I'll find out who his math teacher is and have him or her fail the little bastard. It shouldn't be difficult. The kid's a fucking idiot."

"Stop it," she hissed. "You'll do no such thing!"

See what I mean.

"Okay. You're right. So what do we do? Take away her cell phone?"

"No. Calm down. We talk to her. About minimizing risk."

"She's thirteen years old. She shouldn't have to worry about 'minimizing risk.'"

"I disagree. She needs to start learning exactly that now. And maybe this 'sketch ball' means that we should emphasize it a bit. Besides, we don't really know he's a sketch ball. That's just what Esmé says."

"Esmé has amazing powers of observation and excellent judgment," I said.

"Yes. But she's the same age as Elizabeth. Thirteen."

I took another swig of coffee.

"So what do we do?" I asked.

"Talk to her. Calmly. Not make a big deal of it. As an eighth-grader, she probably feels kind of pleased and proud that a high-school tenth-grader and a football player is calling and texting her. She already knows the facts of life. School beat me out by about six months in informing her the year before last. I say we—that's you and I—have a little chat with her. Bring up the subject of predatory boys and all the baggage that goes with that issue—and leave it at that."

Once again, I realized that women are smarter than men. But a part of my brain reserved the right to call Mort Jackson, the Washington football coach, and ask him to have a heart-to-heart with Skinner. Mort has a couple of daughters—he'd understand. Perhaps he'd run the little maggot till he collapsed in his own vomit. But I tabled that idea—for the time being, at least. I did resolve to examine our cell phone bills a bit more closely.

"You're right, sweetheart," I said.

We walked back home together, holding hands. I didn't go in, but kissed her in front of the house and then headed back to Ripley Hall. During the walk back, I thought about convent schools in Switzerland. When I got back to the office, the shit hit the fan.

It seemed like all the television sets in the building were on—nothing unusual about that. But the volume was turned up and *BIAS* staffers were clustered together in front of them and appeared to be paying rapt attention.

I hurried down to my office, hearing disjointed phrases coming out of the TV sets on the way. "Eight known dead...," "twenty-two total casualties...." "...Air Force Base...." I wasn't feeling good about this at all. Darps was right behind me as I went through my office door.

"Suicide bomber," he said as I picked up a remote and thumbed off the mute button for the TV in my office. "In Germany. In a night club right outside Ramstein Air Base. Reportedly it's a well-known U.S. service member hangout. Eight dead. Six GI's, one German civilian, plus the bomber. Whose nationality is, as yet, unknown. Sixteen wounded. I would have texted you, but I knew you were having lunch with Maria and I didn't want to screw that up."

By the time he finished with his little summary, the CNN guy was getting an imagery feed that showed a bunch of flashing red and blue lights in the dark and then zoomed in on a guy in a raincoat holding a microphone.

"There is still one corpse and two injured people pinned under the rubble behind me, and I'm assuming the dead body is that of the bomber," the guy said. "First responders are inside working to free the casualties. This is Javier Taylor reporting from right outside Ramstein Air Base in Kaiserslautern, Germany."

Darps grabbed a sticky note off my desk and started writing.

Wilderness at 1700? he scrawled. I nodded. He crumpled his note and stuck it in his pants pocket.

The Wilderness—famous for the Civil War battle fought there—was the location of the *BIAS* safe house. We had acquired the place back in the paranoid days when I'd figured—correctly, as it turned out—that we'd been penetrated by a Chinese mole. Very few people were witting of the existence of a *BIAS* safe house, let alone its location.

I surfed around various news sites and it seemed nobody knew anything more about the Ramstein bombing than what Darps and CNN had told me. Then I wandered around the building, listening to *BIAS* in-house chatter. Nobody here seemed to know anything but the bare essentials. Until I got to Samantha's office. Ashleigh, the multi-lingual lawyer, was there. So was Sammy Chen. The two women were seated on chairs facing a white board. Sammy was half standing, half sitting on the edge of Samantha's desk. They were all staring at the white board on which one word was printed in red: *REHEARSAL???*

"Ahem," I said.

They turned to me.

"Hi Alan," they said.

Samantha stood up and slapped the white board.

"You've got to wonder," she said.

"You mean for here? Stateside?"

She nodded.

"Possibly, but not necessarily. Unfortunately, that's all we can do until more information surfaces. Wonder about it."

I was impressed. And said so.

"Keep thinking," I said. "I'm impressed at the way you're pushing the envelope. And there's bound to be more information coming out in the next twenty-four to forty-eight hours. Has anyone talked to Willi?"

Willi was Wilhelm Praetorious. Our primary guy in the German-speaking countries. Downrange now.

Ashleigh nodded.

"He called Judy. From Vienna. He's probably in Germany by now. I'm sure he'll call as soon as he has something."

Sammy cleared his throat.

"This 'rehearsal' idea isn't totally random," he said.

Sammy uses the word "random" in its accurate, mathematical sense—as opposed to its pop-cultural meaning.

"I know," I said.

The clock said four-forty. Darps was probably hitting the road for the Wilderness.

"Don't let up," I said to the three of them. "You may well be onto something. I gotta run."

Chapter Nine

Major el-Shahawi served on the clay court of Havana's most exclusive tennis club. Even though the years of scotch and Marlboro cigarettes and today's heat were taking their toll, the serve felt good, sounded good, and looked good.

"Out—long!" called Captain Diaz from the far court.

Bullshit! el-Shahawi thought. He had moved Diaz to the top of his list of prospective agents. Today was the first time the two officers had met for tennis. Two days earlier, they had met for a beer after work. They had chatted amiably enough, but it was small talk. Today would be the day when he would put the bite on *el Capitan,* now code-named Agent *Krait. Appropriate enough,* thought el-Shahawi. *A dangerous snake in the grass.*

Whatever Diaz drank and smoked were taking their toll on him as well. A handsome young man, clean-shaven with a child's clear complexion, he was clearly out of shape. Thick around the middle and drenched with sweat he was barely moving and was reduced to cheating on the line calls. Time to put a merciful end to this business. El-Shahawi put the next serve where there could be no doubt—squarely in the middle of the court. But it was a sizzler. Captain Diaz barely got to it and hit a feeble return. El-Shahawi smoked a passing shot down the line out of reach of Diaz's feckless backhand. Game and set. The Yemeni had let Diaz take the first set.

"That's it," el-Shahawi said. "I've had it. Beat. We're even. A set apiece. I'm tired. Let's have a beer."

Both players grabbed towels and sopped up perspiration. They walked over to the tennis club's outdoor bar and sat in the shade.

"Two beers, please," ordered the Yemeni. "The coldest you have," he added.

The bartender complied, pouring parts of two one-liter bottles of *Presidente* into two frosted mugs.

"Salud!" both tired tennis players said together. They drank. Diaz finished half his mug and refilled it with the rest of the bottle. Then he finished half of that.

"Hits the spot," he said. "Nothing like a cold beer after a couple of sets of tennis in the hot sun."

"Yes, indeed," el-Shahawi agreed.

"But there's one thing I don't understand, Faisal," Diaz continued. "You're a Muslim. But you drink beer."

"Yes I do. And I enjoy it. It is the product of human hands working with gifts from Allah. I don't believe seventh-century rules necessarily apply in the twenty-first."

When Diaz was halfway through his second beer, the Yemeni leaned toward him.

"Antonio, I have an extremely small favor to ask," he said quietly.

"If it's possible, I'll do it," Diaz responded.

"As you probably know, my Army is small and under-funded. We are in the Middle Ages in many ways as well. Shit—I exaggerate. But to say we are suited for World War One—and no more modern operations—is no exaggeration. Not at all.

"You, Antonio, are a field artillery officer in a modern army. I was wondering if you could write me a short paper. Say between five and ten pages. On how you solve the gunnery problem in the Cuban artillery. All unclassified, of course. Just stuff that is out in the open. From the forward observer's fire request. His use of Global Positioning System. How the artillery compensates for targets that are at higher or lower elevations than the guns. All unclassified, nothing sensitive," he repeated.

Captain Diaz looked uncomfortable.

"I can't write in Arabic," he said. "Hell, I can't write in English either."

"Spanish is fine," el-Shahawi said. "We can get it translated, no problem. I could probably write the paper myself by reading newspapers and magazines. But I'm an infantry officer and have little knowledge of these things. You wouldn't have to do any research. Just write down what you know. And I'm authorized to pay you five hundred dollars, U.S."

The captain's eyes widened.

"When do you need this paper?" he asked quietly.

"Let's say in a month. A month from today. Can you do that?"

Diaz nodded.

"Easily," he said.

"When we leave, take my towel and I'll take yours."

He nodded at the rumpled towels between the two of them.

"You'll find an envelope folded in my towel. It contains two hundred and fifty dollars. The first half of your fee. You get the other half on delivery."

El-Shahawi finished his beer, took out his wallet and laid two twenties on the table—thirty dollars for the three beers plus a ten-dollar tip. He always paid in dollars and tipped well. He supposed that was why he invariably received exquisite service at the tennis club.

"Shall we go, Antonio?"

The two men stood up.

"And by the way, Antonio," the Yemeni said softly. "Let's keep this little chat between the two of us."

Chapter Ten

The Wilderness
November 6
Wednesday

When I pulled into the narrow, dirt road leading to the little farm-guesthouse shack that was the *BIAS* safe house, I saw that the lights were on. As I swung my battered Explorer around behind the house, I saw Darps's Saab convertible. He was already there. I wasn't surprised. I parked the truck and went in the back door.

The heat was on and the blast of warm air felt good.

"Hey, shipmate," Darps said. He was in the act of pouring Dewar's Scotch into a pair of glasses containing ice cubes.

"Ahoy!" I said. "Aren't we getting fancy? Glasses made of actual glass instead of cardboard. Ice cubes. Next thing, you'll be serving up cucumber and watercress sandwiches."

"A little civilization doesn't hurt," he said, handing me a glass.

He turned on a boom box and started a Mozart CD. Symphony Number Forty-One. "Jupiter." Wolfgang's last.

"Did you have a chance to talk to Sammy and the girls?" he asked.

"I did. That is if you mean Ashleigh and Samantha. And if they ever hear you refer to them as 'the girls,' you're dead meat."

He took a pull of scotch and nodded.

"Then let that be our little secret. But did they tell you what they're thinking?"

I took a nip of scotch.

"I think so. They had the big red word, *'Rehearsal,'* scrawled on the white board in Samantha's office. They suggested that the Ramstein bombing was just that. A rehearsal for another, bigger bombing. Possibly for a stateside bombing. But they said that they were guessing and that detailed info on the Ramstein bombing was still sparse."

"Well, I think they're on to something. Even with the info being sparse," Darps said.

"I agree. History suggests it. Almost every time there's been a major Arab suicide bombing anywhere in the West—there has been a similar, smaller incident somewhere else, two to six months earlier. So the Ramstein bombing could well be a rehearsal for a stateside suicide attack."

"Parameters are a tad different for an attack in Germany as opposed to one in the States," he said, almost to himself. "Getting the goodies into the country, recruiting some poor half-wit to be the trigger-man, getting to the target, all different rules in Germany than here."

"Except that things are, if anything, tighter in Germany than here. According to Willi. Whom I trust completely. And it all depends on what the target is. Getting a bomber into a U.S. military base would be a huge challenge. Unless they recruited a U.S. service member. Like a medical officer. On the other hand, sending a bomb-laden martyr to a soft, stateside target would be a piece of cake. A big mall the day after Thanksgiving, for example. Or a rest stop on the Jersey Turnpike at lunchtime. Moron wearing a C-4 vest wrapped in a bunch of nails rolls in, pulls the cord and boom! Wholesale slaughter! And what a fucking statement!" I said, thinking out loud.

"No kidding," he said. "In less than ten minutes, we could list a hundred or so soft stateside targets."

"What are your thoughts on the issue of putting *BIAS* assets to work here in the good ole USA?"

"The sooner, the better. *If* we can do it. Lackawanna, Erie, Detroit, the Washington D.C. metro area, northern New Jersey, for that matter. Christ, we need a platoon. A company! But good luck in getting your old buddy to buy it. Even if it's only two guys."

"And getting the money for the two guys is probably the easy part. Getting *permission* will be the war-stopper. And for that to happen, I've got to convince *Cheetah* that it's a military necessity first."

"First you need to talk to MacDonald. If it's totally illegal, you've got to know that before you talk to the man. Ashleigh can give you a complete legal picture. If what we're proposing is wildly illegal and you still want to ask Kehoe to approve it, you and he both need to know what you're asking for."

I finished my scotch, stood up and walked over to the kitchen sink. I rinsed my glass and grabbed a dishtowel.

"There's another issue. I think a few more feet on the ground in Germany are needed for a bit. But we don't have any spare bods. I'm thinking of going over and spending a little time with Willi myself," I said

"I can go with you and watch your back," Darps said.

"*Nein*," I said. "If I go, you have to stay here and mind the store. But I'm thinking of taking Ashleigh or Samantha along."

"Take them both. Those two brainiacs could be very helpful."

He finished off his whisky and rinsed his glass.

"Shipmate," he said. "You've got a lot on your plate."

"No shit. First thing I need to do is send *Cheetah* a 'Face Time' message. Then I'll put Ashleigh and Samantha on standby for a quick trip to *Deutschland*. Meantime, we'll see what additional info on Ramstein surfaces over night. Let's get outta here."

"I'll get the lights and lock up," Darps said.

It wasn't until I was halfway back to Chestertown that I remembered another couple of items on my full plate—the punk that "had the hots" for Elizabeth and Saturday's lunch with Khalil.

Chapter Eleven

When I went through the mud room and into the kitchen, Maria was putting a bowlful of red, green, and purple salad along with a couple of bottles of salad dressing on the kitchen table.

"Goody," she said. "You're home. Pour me a sherry and we'll chat with Elizabeth."

"About the sketch ball?" I asked.

"Yes. May as well get it out in the open sooner rather than later. *Elizabeth,*" she called.

I heard footsteps upstairs and then coming downstairs.

"Hi, Dad," she said with her always-winning smile.

"Hi, honey," I said.

Maybe I'm biased, but even wearing ratty old sweats and with a zit on her forehead, she looked sweet and as cute as a bug's ear.

"What's up?" she asked.

"Not much," Maria said. "But we need to have a little chat. Have a seat."

"Am I in trouble?" she asked, a little wide-eyed.

"No, sweetheart. You're not in trouble. Not in the least," I said.

She sat down on the far end of the sofa and looked at us warily.

"It concerns a boy. Who's quite a bit older than you. And has been calling and texting you. Jerrod Skinner," Maria said.

"Oh my God! Did Tala or Esmé tell you?"

"No," I answered. "Neither one. But, remember, it wasn't all that long ago when I was on the faculty and coaching staff at Augustine Washington

48

High. I still have spies there. And remember also, young lady, that in this house we try to avoid using the Lord's name in vain."

I felt a twinge of guilt at my hypocrisy, which I rationalized with the reflection that I usually didn't take the Lord's name in vain under this roof. I also figured there was no harm in dragging a red herring or two through this particular thicket to keep Tala and Esmé out of harm's way, as it were. And, it was true enough that neither girl had spilled the beans. At least, not to us. Esmé, the sly little weasel, had *leaked* the info to her mom, knowing it would get back to us. I could see a very successful career in politics and/ or journalism in her future.

"It's not a big deal, honey," Maria said. "But, he *is* sixteen. Kids that age sometimes try to play by different rules. We just wanted you to know that."

"'Playing by different rules' meaning trying to get in your pants," I said, earning myself a quick-shot warning glare from Maria.

"Well, there's nothing to worry about," Elizabeth said. "After a few days, Jerrod got to be very boring. He says the same things over and over. About how his teachers hate him. And you should hear what he calls his dad. He's such a *loser!*"

I knew why I had had an instant dislike for the little dipshit.

"Anyway, I don't talk to him any more. At all. I delete his voicemails and texts without listening to or reading them. He still calls, but the calls are getting farther and farther apart."

Well, I thought. *Once in a while, God does indeed smile upon us.*

"Needless to say, I hope you're not reading any of those texts in class," I said.

"No way, Dad. They take away the phones if you use them in class. And then they call you guys to come in and pick them up."

Maria glanced at her watch.

"Okay, honey. Sounds like everything is under control. Dinner in fifteen minutes," she said. She got up and carried her sherry into the kitchen.

That gave me enough time to throw together a special email that I'd only used once before. It was strictly for emergencies and—don't ask me how—goes straight to the man. *Cheetah.* There was no message. The "Subject" line told him I needed to see him ASAP.

From: allewellyn@bias.gov
To: keys@LISound.com
Subj: Face Time

I splashed a little more scotch in my glass and glanced through the day's snail mail. I had an answer to my email within five or six minutes, max.

From: keys@LISound.com
To: allewellyn@bias.gov
Subj: Face Time
5 miler at MCAF at 0845 2moro. No Hill Trail.
Keys

Translation. He was going to run five miles at the Marine Corps Air Facility at 8:45 a.m. tomorrow and was staying away from the infamous "Hill Trail" on which he, Darps, and I had nearly killed ourselves in the not-too-distant past. If I needed to see him, I was invited to join him.

I texted him back and told him I'd be there. I'd leave Darps back in Ripley Hall to handle whatever was breaking on the Ramstein bombing.

Then we sat down to dinner at the kitchen table. The tension over the sketch ball seemed to have atomized. Dinner was pork-cubed steaks with fettuccini and mushrooms in a *cacciatore* sauce. Elizabeth was a bit chatty about going to the Washington-Sheffield football game Friday night, which sparked a niggling doubt in my mind about the termination of the relationship with Sketch-ball Skinner. But I decided to give her the benefit of the doubt and let it go. For now, at least.

I told Maria and Elizabeth of my scheduled jog with the president tomorrow. No big deal to them. The presidential jogs were becoming commonplace. I resolved to check the Weather Channel before I hit the rack.

I did. Low tonight was predicted to be thirty-eight. High tomorrow sixty-two. I interpolated. Mid to upper forties at run time. Long sleeve tee, shorts, cotton gloves, and watch cap should do the job.

Chapter Twelve

I wore running togs when I left the house, but took time to swing by Ripley Hall on my way to Quantico. There were media reports that an obscure Islamist group had claimed credit for the bombing in Germany. Samantha was looking at various radical web sites, some in English, but most in Arabic.

"I never heard of most of these guys," she said. "A bunch of sites must have just popped up like mushrooms after a thunderstorm."

"Anything from Willi?" I asked.

"Not much. He's decided to stay away from Ramstein. Doesn't want the Germans looking at him too hard. Says the German newspapers are saying that police have ID'd the dead bomber as a Syrian who was on a student visa and who was residing in Hamburg. They haven't released a name, yet."

"How would you feel about a quick trip to Germany? With me? To run our eyeballs over the landscape? I'm going to invite Ashleigh as well."

"That would be great," she said.

One down, one to go.

My next stop was at Ashleigh's desk. She appeared to be surfing news sites in various languages. I leaned against her doorframe and she turned around.

"If I ask 'the powers that be' for an okay to put some *BIAS* boots on the ground here in the U.S. and in Canada, what are the legal ramifications?" I asked first.

"That's a huge question with an even bigger answer. And the answer depends," she said. She leaned back in her chair and stretched a bit. Modestly. "If those 'boots' are just reporting on, um, atmospherics—probably nothing. On the other hand, if we learn that some guy named Mustafa is going to put a bomb in the men's room at Union Station and

51

we then reported his name and intention to the D.C. Metropolitan Police Department, there could be some serious blowback. Presumably, the cops would arrest him. Presumably, they'd charge him. Then, one way or another, he gets a lawyer. And then the issue of probable cause comes up and God only knows where that goes. I'd say you'd have a serious dilemma on your hands at the very least."

"I was afraid you were going to say something like that," I said.

"If you want, I can do some hard research and be a lot more specific. If 'a,' then 'b.' That kind of thing. And Canada might be even tougher than here in CONUS," she added.

"Not yet," I said. "But it may come to that. You'll be the first to know. Now, I have another question."

"Okay."

"How would you like to travel to Germany—in a couple of days and for a couple of days. With me and maybe Samantha. To look around. Groom our intuition on the Arab presence in Germany, so to speak."

"That would be great. Super," she said.

My last stop was Darps's office. Judy and Sammy were there.

"I'm going up to the air facility to jog with *Cheetah*. Should be back around 10:30," I told them. They looked at me like I'd just told them that the sun was shining outside.

"See you in a couple of hours or so," I said.

I went outside, climbed into the truck, and headed over to I-95 and got on the northbound ramp.

Forty-five minutes later, a Marine MP directed me to a parking spot. I cut the engine and climbed out of the truck. I jogged a little, stretched out, and jogged a little more when I heard the choppers. Minutes later, a little knot of people with Kehoe in the center came through a gate in the fence and started jogging. Keys wore a Yankees ball cap, shades, and a black warm-up suit. He waved.

"Hey, Loose! C'mon and join the pack."

I did so, holding up my Secret Service ID so no one would shoot me.

"Lemme guess," he said. "You wanna talk about the Ramstein bombing and a possible connection between it and what we talked about Saturday. How am I doing?"

"Pretty damned well," I said as we ran past the Officer Candidate School "grinder"—the asphalt parade deck. Three platoons were practicing close-order drill with rifles. None of the Officer Candidates or the NCOs drilling them knew that their Commander-in-Chief was jogging by.

"On the Ramstein thing, we need a couple of more bods in Germany—at least temporarily."

"If it's only temporary, then redirect some in-house assets."

"That's what I'm planning to do. One of those assets is *moi*. Or *mich.*"

"That's right. You know German. But I'm not crazy about that idea. If the Germans lock your ass up, there's just one degree of separation between thee and me. And if someone makes *that* connection, the resulting shit-storm would be truly phenomenal. It would make Watergate look like a church social."

"Keys, I'm not planning on doing anything that would make the Germans even *think* of locking me up. *BIAS* operates in a passive mode. You know, ride the buses and trains, hang out in the bars and beer halls, and listen. We stay off the skyline. I'll be the same way. And it would be for three or four days, max."

"What about North Africa and the Middle East?"

"You're the guy who told me to nibble away at the problem and follow up on the 'hints.' The only hints we've gotten so far are from inside Germany."

"Okay. Go. Three days, max. And stay under the radar. Nothing even close to being illegal."

"Aye, aye, sir. And speaking of illegal..."

Our little clutch of runners was moving along a trail that snaked through hardwoods. President Kehoe shot me a wary look but didn't say anything.

"We need to do some looking in the States," I said.

"Jesus Christ."

"And Canada."

"Goddam. I have created a fucking monster," he said.

"I'm serious," I said.

"I'm sure I don't want to hear this," he said. "But duty compels. Talk to me."

"Look, Jim. I'm not talking about tapping anybody's phone or reading anybody's mail. Nor fingering anybody. Just going into Arab-Muslim enclaves in the States and Canada and seeing which way the wind is blowing. Coffee shops, maybe an occasional mosque. Very low profile."

"Yeah. And suppose you hear in one of those mosques or coffee shops that Omar Somebody is going to blow himself up in the Washington Monument. He gets his ass arrested and the *BIAS* cat is out of the bag."

"We'd keep the sourcing anonymous," I said.

"No. Absolutely not. No fucking way. If one of your guys fingers a couple of stateside Arabs—or even worse, Arab Americans—plotting whatever and some lawyer starts screaming about probable cause, I'm screwed. You're screwed. And the whole rationale for having a *BIAS* goes down the toilet. As does *BIAS*. Not to mention yours truly. Besides, the FBI as well as local law enforcement are trying to stay on top of the goings-on amongst the various Arab communities around the country. Likewise for Canada and the RCMP."

I felt like saying, "But we're better than they are," but refrained. Instead I said, "Okay. I understand. But, if you could find a way for Darps and/or me to see stuff that the FBI or the National Counter Terrorism Center are picking up that's in any way related to this particular threat—the threat to CONUS from Arabs/Islamists in Germany—that would be helpful. To say the least."

He nodded a couple of times as we ran, like a slightly lame horse.

"Let me look into that. I'm pretty sure we can work something out. Maybe with Mike and Luke and some of their D.C.-based counterparts. The Secret Service already gets a feed from the NCTC. And I know the RCMP is cooperating."

"I might make the same request again. About operating stateside. If whatever we find overseas points to something actually going on here in CONUS."

"And you'll get the same response. No. No fucking way."

We finished our run on the Engineer Road in a fairly leisurely manner. We walked towards the gate in the fence around the airfield. I heard a helo's engines start. We were both sweating.

"Remember—no poaching. Stay out in the cold," he said.

I knew what he meant.

"Out in the cold—you got it."

We shook hands and he headed for the gate to the chopper.

One out of two isn't bad, I thought. I'd go to Germany with Samantha and Ashleigh, and I wouldn't have to worry about the logistics of running 'listeners' around the U.S. and Canada. And all the fleas that accompanied that particular dog. But I still had the big problems. Finding out which terrorists were going to do what and also where and when. And what the hell "Revenge" and "Vengeance" were all about.

I stretched for three or four minutes before climbing into the truck and heading back to Chestertown.

Chapter Thirteen

I returned to Ripley Hall via a stop at fifteen-oh-six Prince Henry Street. Nobody was home but Cory. I took her for a walk around the block, took a quick shower and donned semi-civilized clothes. Since I'd already had my audience with Kehoe this morning, I figured I probably wouldn't be seeing anyone else in the big leagues for the rest of the day, so I went with business casual. Khakis and a lightweight plaid, long-sleeve shirt with a USNA windbreaker on top. I left a note for Maria and Elizabeth on the kitchen whiteboard, telling them that I'd walked Cory, gave the time, and walked back to work.

First things first. I gave Darps a debrief on my chat with Kehoe. Reluctant "yes" on a fast trip to Germany, emphatic "no" on CONUS operations.

"No surprises there," Darps said. "It's a testament to your salesmanship that you got an okay for the Germany foray, however reluctant. It's also a testament to your salesmanship that he didn't take you up in Marine One and throw your ass out the door after you mentioned *BIAS* running stateside ops. If some sort of *BIAS* operation here in the country went south and blew back, he'd be toast and so would we."

"That's pretty much what he said."

"When are you leaving for *Deutschland*?" he asked.

"Not sure," I said. "I'm thinking maybe Monday evening. But I need to talk to Ashleigh and Samantha before I nail that down. And Willi. And Kehoe told me three days maximum for Germany."

I glanced at my watch. Eleven-fifteen.

"Let me see if I can talk to Ashleigh and Samantha before lunch. I need to call Willi, too."

I talked to everyone and then to Judy about reservations. We would fly out Monday night to Hamburg, putting us there on Tuesday morning, stay through Thursday, and fly back to D.C. on Friday morning. Judy would get us three rooms at the Fairmont *Vier Jahrszeiten*. I decided to walk home for lunch.

It was twelve-ten when I left Ripley Hall and twelve-thirty when I got home. Once again, Cory was guarding the castle by her lonesome. It was a beautiful day and I walked her down by the river, letting her off the leash for a bit of stick retrieving. She sniffed around and raced around, which seemed to be her idea of heaven. When we got back home, it was still just the two of us. I fixed her some kibble and myself a salami sandwich and nuked a cup of coffee. Then I nibbled the sandwich while I did the crossword from the morning paper.

I was filling in the final squares when I heard a car in the driveway. I stood up and looked out. Maria's Jetta. She came in carrying a few grocery bags.

"Ciao, Bella," I said.

She put the grocery bags on the kitchen table and put her arms around my neck.

"You sly devil," she said.

I was quite a bit late getting back to the office after lunch, but nobody said anything.

On Saturday, I went for a seven-mile run—long and slow. While I was showering after the run, Maria popped her head into the steamy bathroom.

"Elizabeth and I are going shopping," she announced. "Have a nice lunch with Fat Harry's nephew."

Thirty minutes later, I walked into *Teacher Man*. Khalil was seated by a window table and appeared to be studying a menu.

"*Marhaba*," I said. "Hello."

He stood up and held out his hand.

"*Marhaba*, Alan. Thank you for coming."

We sat and ordered drinks. I had a Bass Ale, and he had iced tea. We chatted about his college experience—he had majored in economics and had gotten his master's in finance. He figured he might be able to teach high school mathematics and/or business. We talked about the plusses and minuses of the teaching profession. On the plus side were the kids, teaching children things that they needed to know, making a difference. On the minus side were the kids—many of whom were morons and determined to stay that way, the administrators, many of whom were morons in their own way, and, of course, the long hours and low pay.

"You'll never get rich being a teacher," I told him.

"Is that why you left the profession?" he asked.

"No, not at all. I left teaching because the President of the United States asked me to. And I'm sure as hell not getting rich now."

The waitress came back, and we both ordered chicken salad sandwiches.

"You don't paint a very attractive picture of teaching in a public school," Khalil said.

"Well, for what it's worth, I think it takes a certain type of personality to be a good teacher and to enjoy the work. And you can't have one without the other," I said. "It's certainly not the ideal job for everyone. And if someone tries teaching and hates it, he or she should bail out immediately. But if you like kids and want to contribute, teaching is a really good way to go. Every day is different, most days have some sort of excitement, and there just aren't all that many people who can teach algebra, geometry, and trig. Or chemistry or American history, for that matter. The psychic rewards are great even if the pay is way below where it should be. Hell, I'd still be doing it if Kehoe hadn't asked me to do something else."

"I thought I might give substitute teaching a try," he said. "That way, maybe I could see if teaching and I were a good fit."

"Don't expect too much from that," I cautioned. "High school kids can be absolute trolls—especially with subs. And, as a substitute, you're usually with them only for one period. If, for example, you had subbed for me last year, you'd have had two algebra one classes, two classes of geometry, and one calculus class. Then you'd also pick up my duty period, a study hall. All different. So, you really don't get to know a class very well.

"My school was on a traditional, seven-period schedule. Forty-five minutes per period. Sheffield High, just a few miles down the road, is on a so-called block schedule. Three two-hour instructional 'blocks.' Probably your best bet in subbing is seeing a few different schools and hearing what the regular teachers have to say about their kids and their principals. That way, too, you can make your own comparisons on how the different schools are run. That might tell you where you want to go and where you might want to avoid.

"And you should also know that there are classes and classes. A class of 'Standard English' is as different from a class of 'Honors English' as a McDonald's is from a Ruth's Chris Steakhouse. Some kids grow up in houses with lots of books; others grow up in houses with only big-screen TV sets. Zero books. They're different animals. Very different."

The waitress brought our sandwiches. We leaned into them in silence for a couple of minutes.

"How about security?" he asked. "I would imagine that, since Columbine, security has been increased or enhanced."

I thought for a couple of seconds.

"Well, yes and no," I said. "And it probably varies according to school districts. There are civilian security guards and a Sheriff's Department resource officer in the high schools here. The civilians are unarmed. The resource officers are armed police officers. They do keep an eye on things. And visitors have to get a pass and be escorted. But neither the kids nor the teachers are screened. So, if a couple of student goofballs wanted to bring weapons in and stage a Columbine II, I don't think it could or would be prevented."

"That's not very comforting," he said.

"No, it's not," I agreed. "But I never felt threatened at school. Except when the D.C. sniper was roaming through the area and taking pot shots at people. Killing several. The bastard shot a couple of people close to my school. They locked us down. The kids felt threatened then—big time. And that really pissed me off. Kids should feel safe in school. We owe them that. At the very least."

We finished our sandwiches and had coffee. I explained to him a bit of the mechanics of the hiring process in my old school district, some of the teacher certification guidelines, and the little I knew about the "atmosphere" in various area schools. He promised to keep me updated on his progress and paid for our lunch with an American Express card.

I spent the afternoon raking leaves and was bone-tired when I finished and went inside for cocktails at five-thirty.

Chapter Fourteen

Captain Diaz's artillery paper was crudely worded and contained numerous grammatical errors. But it made no difference. The form and substance of the paper were irrelevant. What was important was that the Cuban captain had entered into a clandestine, conspiratorial relationship with a representative of a foreign government. On top of that, the representative of the foreign country had *paid* the captain for his services. Major el-Shahawi had paid Captain Diaz the second installment in the arrangement when the latter delivered the paper two weeks early.

"There is an extra hundred dollars in the envelope since you completed the project ahead of time," el-Shahawi advised the captain. "It doesn't show up on the receipt that I need you to sign. The extra hundred is 'off the books' as they say. Just jot down your initials for the five-hundred dollar fee for the article."

The final link in the espionage chain was Captain Diaz's initials on the receipt.

They continued to meet for tennis matches and beer. After one match on a beautiful day, the Yemeni sipped beer and lowered his voice.

"I have another favor to ask, Antonio," he said. "This one is silly. Even more trivial than the last one. But there *is* a little more money involved."

Diaz raised his eyebrows.

"In your excellent artillery paper, you wrote that, after an artillery battery has a field firing exercise, unused propellant increments are burned immediately?"

"Yes. If the cannon is fired at less than the maximum charge, the leftover powder charges are saved and burned at the end of the day. They are useless. Hazardous to store. Unpredictable when exposed to humidity. So they can't be used later. We burn them at day's end. We spread them out on the ground so they're not concentrated. That way, they burn with a hot, fast flame, rather than exploding."

"I was wondering if you would make some unused powder charges available to me. For analysis. As I told you, our Army is like we're still stuck in World War I."

"Oh, I don't know, Faisal. That's different. It's ammunition."

"But, Antonio. It's ammunition you *burn*. 'Useless,' you said. It certainly won't be missed. You could just put a couple of powder bags in your pockets or a map case or something."

"It's still ammunition."

"But it's not like a rifle or a pistol. Or an entire artillery projectile, for that matter. It's leftovers. Leftovers that are burned at the end of the day. And I'm authorized to pay you one hundred dollars for every powder bag you provide. If you can get me ten, that's a thousand dollars. Twenty bags—two-thousand dollars."

"Let me think about it Faisal. We go to the field Wednesday. I'll see how things look and let you know."

"There's en envelope in my towel. It contains four hundred dollars. That's an advance for the first four powder bags. You can put the powder in a small grocery bag and leave it in Truchas Park. Under the bench by the pond."

Captain Diaz knew the park. It was a short walk from his apartment.

"But what if someone picks it up? A child?"

"Send me a text thirty minutes before you drop it. 'TP' is all you have to say. Thirty-one minutes after the text, it will be picked up."

The two exchanged their white towels. Again.

When Major el-Shahawi returned to his apartment, Laura was there. She was nibbling some cheese and crackers. There was a glass of sparkling water or tonic water on the table.

"Put that swill away. We'll have caviar. And champagne. Or vodka. After we take a shower."

"Why the celebration?" she asked, standing and starting to unbutton her blouse.

"A breakthrough," he said. "A real breakthrough."

He pulled his tennis jersey over his head.

Chapter Fifteen

Hamburg
November 11-12
Monday - Tuesday

We flew business class on Lufthansa. Ashleigh and Samantha had seats across the aisle from mine. We had a decent little meal of veal piccatta, orzo pasta, and a tiny salad after we got to cruising altitude out of Dulles. As soon as the attendants policed up the dinner detritus, the two *BIAS* women donned black sleep masks and curled up with Lufthansa pillows and blankets. I watched the original *Day of the Jackal* film and read for as long as I could. Then I sat there staring into the darkened cabin. I have some un-named phobia about sleeping in public view. I watched the GPS trace of our flight's track on the screen on the back of the seat in front of me in a kind of stupor. I was reasonably certain I didn't drool.

When we landed at Frankfurt, I was more or less wide awake but totally shot and felt like I was ninety years old. Ashleigh and Samantha were as perky as teenagers on their way to Disney World. The final leg of the journey was a quick flight from Frankfurt-am-Main to Hamburg's *Fuhlsbüttel* Airport where we landed in a steady, driving rain. It was 9:30 a.m., local time.

There was a *Vier Jahrszeiten* airport shuttle waiting for us and it zipped us through the rain to the hotel on the shores of the *Binnenalster*, the smaller of the two lakes formed in the city center by damming up the Alster River a long time ago. HanseStadt Hamburg—the architecture, the water, and the electrifying vivacity of the port city—fascinated the two women. They chattered away excitedly. I thought back to when I first came to Germany as a midshipman twenty years ago. That time, I went through the night on the plane en route without sleep but, immediately on arrival, embarked on a pub-crawl—or *Bierstube* crawl—that must have lasted fifteen hours or so. Not this time. We got lucky on our rooms—they were ready, even though we were early for check-in. I tipped the bellhop— his nametag said Ahmed, which could have been from almost anywhere in the Middle East. Then I took a quick shower, had a swift cognac from the minibar, and dove into the rack. I set my phone for one-thirty and fell asleep within seconds.

When the phone dinged, I awoke, totally. I had set the alarm tone for *sonar* and the sound boomed through my skull. For a second, I was completely disoriented. Then, during the next two or three seconds, I figured out where I was and remembered that I was scheduled to meet Ashleigh and Samantha for tea in the lounge at two. I turned off the fucking alarm and held a little mental debate with myself about standing them up and going back to sleep, which is what my body desperately wanted to do. Finally, I swung my legs out of the rack and sat up. Duty calls. It wouldn't do for me to drag these two women across the Atlantic Ocean and then sleep through a scheduled meeting with them. Plus, Kehoe had limited me to just three days. And already I was halfway through day one.

A glance out the window told me that the rain had stopped and that there were a few patches of blue sky scattered among the fast-moving clouds.

I let the shower water run on my head for a few minutes, shaved, and brushed my teeth. By the time I had clean clothes on and headed for the elevator, I was starting to feel human again. I met the two *Fräuleins* in the lounge downstairs in the hotel as planned. A fire burned merrily in a large fireplace and a piano player added to the cozy ambience. As I sat down, a man whose nametag identified him as a member of the hotel staff approached our table with an envelope on a tray.

"A message, Herr Llewellyn," he said, handing me the envelope.

"*Danke schőn*," I said.

"Well—aren't you going to open it?" Samantha asked.

"Of course, I am. But I thought we'd let them serve us, first," I said. A waiter had appeared as if by magic and poured tea. He reappeared with a platter of little sandwiches. I took a hearty swig—not a sip, if you please— of strong tea. It hit the spot. I opened the envelope. It was a note from Willi.

Alan,

Welcome to Germany! I'm sorry that I can't be with you in Hamburg to welcome Samantha, Ashleigh, and yourself in person today. I got a call from Berlin that I really have to follow up on. Let's plan on having a working lunch tomorrow (Wednesday). There's a little place within walking distance of the Vier Jahrszeiten and it's a little bit lower-profile than those fancy places in the hotel. How about I meet the three of you in the lobby at 12:15?

Hope to see you tomorrow,

Willi

There was a phone number under his signature. I passed the note around.

The three of us sipped tea and nibbled the tiny sandwiches.

"So what do we do today, Alan?" Samantha asked, putting down her teacup.

"My suggestion is that, for starters, we just look around and get the feel of the place. The last time I was here—a couple of decades ago—there were plenty of Turks. From what I've read, Hamburg's Asian and African populations have increased considerably. One of Hamburg's main claims to fame is its reputation as a wild-and-wooly seaport with all that goes with that. Sleazy bars, whorehouses, tattoo parlors, et cetera. It would be interesting to see if the strait-laced Islamists have been corrupted by the fleshpots of the decadent West."

"You want to go out and hang out in sleazy bars and whorehouses *now*?" Ashleigh asked.

I laughed.

"No, not at all," I said. "It's not even three o'clock in the afternoon. Although I gather that the sleaze is pretty much a twenty-four-seven operation. Since the rain has quit, we could wander around the city center and maybe even do some shopping. Then, we could repair to our rooms for a little rest and then re-connect for a civilized dinner around eight or so. One of these evenings, if you guys are up for it, we probably should hit one or two of the fleshpots. The ones that draw a lot of tourist traffic. So you two—or all three of us, for that matter—wouldn't stand out like the proverbial baboon's ass in some Baltic sailor hangout. The idea for now is to get a sense of the city. And the Arab presence here. And what's cooking with a possible terrorist plot against the U.S. If anything. That's about it. Then, when we get together for lunch with Willi tomorrow, we can compare notes and figure out where to go from there. And keep in mind, we're only here for three days. We may not pick up anything. Or nothing."

"Alan, you amaze me," Ashleigh said. "You just woke up from a nap and then threw together an entire intelligence operation plan on the fly between a few sips of tea."

Samantha looked like she was going to gag. Clearly, she was not nearly as impressed as Ashleigh. But I let myself bask in Ashleigh's praise for a microsecond nonetheless. Then I stood up.

"Let's meet in the lobby in fifteen minutes," I said. I signed the tab, adding a twenty percent tip.

Fifteen minutes later we did reconnect. We stepped outside, and the rain had indeed cooperated and departed. Skies were mostly blue with a few puffs of fast-moving clouds, courtesy of a brisk wind out of Scandinavia. Our first stop was a mall loaded with fashionable shops and anchored by a rather large department store. The place oozed big bucks. Or big euros. Ashleigh bought a leather pocket book and Samantha bought a cashmere sweater. The prices would water your eyes. I wondered if the government and I weren't overpaying them. Then I quashed that thought—they were worth every dime and then some.

There were a few bearded men of various ages in the mall. There were also a few women with *hijabs*—headscarves—and long raincoats. It was impossible to tell from their appearance whether they were Turks, Arabs, or Iranians. We got close enough to one pair of women so that Samantha, Ashleigh, and I could ascertain and agree that they were speaking Farsi. But that was about it. After wandering through the stores in the mall, we went back outside and sat down on a bench on the shore of the *Aussenalster*, the larger of the two downtown lakes. The ducks on the water were all facing south, away from where the wind was coming. An occasional ferry, packed with passengers, crisscrossed the *Aussenalster*.

"So what's your first impression of Hamburg?" I asked.

"A surprisingly large number of Muslim women," Samantha said, nodding at two women who were pushing strollers with tiny children heavily swaddled against the cold. Both women wore tan trench coats that came down to mid-calf. One woman had a dark, navy-blue headscarf; the other had a black scarf covering most of her hair.

"The women stand out a bit more than the men," I said. "But the men are here, too. Some German men have beards, and plenty of German men have dark hair. But I'm willing to bet that seventy percent of the young guys with dark hair and beards are non-German Muslims. And it seems to be a very diverse group. I'm guessing that we don't notice half of the Turks because a lot of them have been more or less assimilated. There's even a German national soccer team player—he holds a German passport—but his name is Mesut Ozil. Hardly sounds like Helmut Schmidt. But he's German. And a great midfielder, by the way. Then there are Iranians and Pakistanis. A sprinkling of Arabs."

I nodded toward a group of about six young guys with beards boarding a ferry.

"Like those guys," I said.

"But that doesn't mean anything," Ashleigh said. "So what?"

"You're right," I said. "Those guys can be—and probably are—as pure as the driven snow. All they tell us is that there is an Arab population in Hamburg. From what I've read, that's also the case in other parts of Germany. And that tells us that the likelihood of some Arab Muslim evildoers bent on causing a horror show in the good ole USA has also gone up. Which is what we said in our paper for the president."

"But," Samantha said. "What we said in our paper about the 'horror show in the USA' was based on more than demographics alone. If memory serves, it was a couple of nuggets of information about actual conversations over here that led you to include the now-infamous North American Addendum."

"And then, there's 'the Revenge of the Nerds'—or whoever," Ashleigh added.

"You are, as usual, absolutely correct," I admitted. "But the increases in the Muslim population of Germany do add fuel to the fire."

We got up from our bench and walked part way around the north end of the lake. There were more women wearing dark-colored headscarves and tan or gray trench coats. And more men with dark hair and beards. In two groups we passed, there were equal numbers of males and females, and they were speaking Turkish. They looked pretty western and pretty modern. In two more groups, there were only women. Wearing expensive-looking, fashionable suits and heels. Also speaking Turkish. Then we passed three bearded young males. Speaking Arabic. Egyptian Arabic,

Samantha said. My ear wasn't yet attuned to the degree where I could discern the various dialects and accents. Discerning a trend was impossible in a short afternoon.

We rode a ferry across the *Aussenalster,* returned to the hotel a little after dark and agreed to meet in the *Jahrszeiten* Grill at 7:30. I fought off the urge to take another nap and changed and went to the hotel fitness center instead. I had a pretty fair workout, doing the cross-country skiing routine on the elliptical trainer. Then I went back to my room and took another shower and got back into the clothes I'd worn earlier. I planned to send a small load of laundry out tomorrow.

Ashleigh and Samantha had a table and glasses of wine when I arrived downstairs. I ordered a beer.

"I'm going to call it a night early," I announced. "The jet lag and sleep-deprivation are kicking in again."

The two of them looked at me like I'd just told them I was constipated.

"Well, then," Samantha said. "Maybe we should just have dinner here."

"Works for me," I said.

I had *Aal und Hering*—eel and herring, pickled—and another beer. Both women had *Schnitzel* with noodles. We rehashed what we had seen during the afternoon and arranged to walk around some more after breakfast tomorrow. Still feeling like a wimp, I excused myself and went up to my room.

I was working my way through Patrick O'Brian's set of Jack Aubrey novels for a second time and had brought e-reader copies of *Master and Commander* and *Post Captain* and was enjoying the finish of *M&C* more than the first time. I wondered why the Naval Academy didn't have the mids read these things for a taste of naval history and traditions. I know that it was Royal Navy and not United States Navy, but a helluva lot of U.S. seafaring traditions and lingo came from our British forebears. Anyway, I finished *Master and Commander* with a satisfied sigh and decided to forego starting *Post Captain* till a later day—or night. I turned off the light and was asleep in less than a minute.

Chapter Sixteen

I had just taken my first sip of morning coffee when two splendid-looking women in jeans and sweaters suddenly appeared at my table.

"Mind if we join you, boss?" Samantha asked.

"I'd be delighted," I said, standing up. "And I'll be the envy of every man in the restaurant."

"Alan—you are so full of it," Samantha said, laughing. "The phrase 'Christmas goose' comes to mind."

We all sat down with a chuckle. Nothing like straight-talking Samantha to keep me honest.

"Sometimes, I'm guilty," I said. "But I was speaking God's truth a moment ago."

Ashleigh rolled her eyes, reminding me of Elizabeth. Then the two women ordered continental breakfasts from the waiter who had just magically appeared.

"So what's the plan today?" Samantha asked.

"It's not much of a plan," I said. "The main item is meeting Willi for lunch and hearing what he has to say. Right now, the weather looks okay. Cloudy but no rain. I was thinking of going to the *Reeperbahn* after breakfast. Just walking around and looking around. It might be a good thing to get my bearings during daylight before making a foray there after sundown."

"So we can go with you?" they both asked at once.

"Of course," I said. "Three pairs of eyes and all that. You might well see things that I miss."

Forty-five minutes later, we left the hotel. Ten minutes later, we were entering the sleazy side of Hamburg. At first it was bars and beer halls, many of which—but not all—were closed. Many of them sported photos of naked and nearly naked women and more than a few naked men. There were signs for "Sex Shows." The farther we walked, the raunchier the various establishments seemed to get. Finally, we turned a corner and encountered a solid six-foot green fence with white letters advising that no one under the age of eighteen was allowed to enter. There was also a conventional street sign on the corner that read *Herbertstrasse*.

"This must be the whorehouses," Ashleigh said.

"It is," I said. "At least the public whorehouses."

We entered. The fenced off section was a block long. There was another section of green fencing at the far end of the block. Along both sides of the *Herbertstrasse* were shop windows. About half of the windows featured women of various ethnicities, ages, shapes, and states of undress. One display across the street featured a large brass bed. A woman wearing a short satin robe sat in an easy chair beside the bed. She was smoking a cigarette and reading a magazine.

"When you said 'public whorehouses,' did you mean that they screw in the *window*?" Samantha asked in a whisper.

"Maybe we'll find out," I said.

A guy was knocking on the glass across the street. He was wearing a pea coat and looked like a merchant sailor, but it was difficult to tell. I would have guessed his ethnicity as Scandinavian or Slavic from his cheekbones and sandy hair, but I really had no idea. The woman on display put down her magazine and came to the window, carrying her cigarette. There was some sort of conversation and the guy went to a door alongside the display and went in. The woman crushed out her cigarette in a full ashtray and pulled curtains across the windows.

"Thank God," Samantha whispered.

We exited the *Herbertstrasse* at the end of the block.

"That's disgusting," Ashleigh snorted.

"They play by a whole different set of rules over here," I said.

"Let's go back to the lakes by the hotel and breathe some clean air," suggested Samantha.

It seemed like a good idea.

Twenty-five minutes later, we sat on the same benches we'd sat upon yesterday. The clouds were breaking up, and sunshine was breaking through.

"No obvious Arabs crawling through the fleshpots," Ashleigh said.

"You're right," I said. "But we were there at eleven o'clock in the morning. Let's see what the picture is like after the sun goes down. Meantime, let's take a break before we meet with Willi at 12:15. Wash up, check email, that sort of thing."

I stepped off the elevator in the lobby at 12:11, and Ashleigh and Samantha followed in the next elevator. Willi was waiting and greeted us warmly but quietly, as if he didn't want to draw attention to our little rendezvous. He looked more Italian than German. He wore sunglasses that looked expensive and a suede jacket that looked as if it cost even more than the shades. His jet-black hair was gelled and spiked. But his German was, as far as I could tell, letter perfect and accent free. He spoke with a doorman whose nametag read "Franz" about the weather and the tourists and both of them seemed to be speaking identical versions of the same language. Then he turned to us.

"There is a wonderful Vietnamese dive about three or four blocks away," he said, speaking English. "The weather's beautiful. Shall we walk?"

We did. And he was right. It had become a beautiful day with a clear blue sky. A few puffy clouds were reflected in the waters of the Binnenalster. Most of last summer's leaves were down, but a few loose ones skittered around in a breeze that was unseasonably warm. The restaurant was down a side street, was small, and seemed to be doing a rip-roaring business. We had to wait about twenty minutes for a tiny table. The clientele appeared to be about fifty-fifty German and Vietnamese. I think we were the only Americans. Nobody appeared to pay any attention to us.

"I recommend the *pho*," Willi said. "It's a noodle soup that I got hooked on during a trip to Hanoi. I also recommend the *Bánh mi xiu mai*. They're sandwiches on Vietnamese bread—which is very much like French bread and very good. Here, they make the sandwiches with pork, cilantro, thinly sliced carrot and cucumber, mayo, and a bit of fish sauce. Which is ubiquitous in Vietnamese cuisine."

"I'll give one a try," Ashleigh said.

"So will I," Samantha and I said together.

"For beverages, there's Coke and tea. There's also German and Vietnamese beer. *Ba Mui Ba.* Means 'Thirty-Three.' It's quite good."

"I never thought I'd see the day when I'd order Vietnamese beer in Germany," I said. "But what the hell."

We all ordered Thirty-Three, pho, and pork sandwiches.

The food was excellent and the beer was good—not up to the German standards—but good. The restaurant was still packed and we confined our lunch conversation to banalities. Willi insisted on picking up the tab for lunch. He paid and we left and found another pair of benches alongside the *Binnenalster*. The scattered leaves were still dancing around.

"Okay, here's all I have on the Ramstein bombing," Willi said. "The bomber was a Syrian with a student visa. One Rifat Ali Esaat. He lived here. In a Hamburg borough called Altona. Even though he had a student visa, he wasn't registered in any school and no school in Germany has a record of him. He lived in a good-sized suburban house with a bunch of Arabs who stayed out late and slept most of the day. They apparently didn't have jobs and didn't go to school. But they paid their rent on time. There were a few neighbors' complaints about them playing loud music late at night. The German Ministry of Interior is taking steps to deport all Rifat's non-German 'roommates'; although, they think they may have enough grounds to arrest a couple of them. There were two of them— Arabs—that hold German passports. The police will probably interview them and let them go. I'd imagine that CIA is absolutely salivating at the prospect of interrogating one or two of the non-Germans, but I doubt whether that will happen. The Germans don't like rendition. On the other hand, when a terrorist act—a suicide bombing, no less—takes place on German soil, their principles tend to, uh, shrivel a bit. So if they think the CIA can get more from these assholes than they—the Germans—can and will be willing to share 'the take,' they may be persuaded to turn the bastards over."

"Have you noticed anything that might point to an Arab scheme for a terrorist incident in the U.S.?" I asked.

"Nothing explicit," he said. "But I have to wonder if the Ramstein bombing could have been a rehearsal for something stateside."

The women and I exchanged looks

"The same idea occurred to us," I said.

He pulled a small notebook out of an inside pocket of the suede jacket and tore out a page.

"Here's Rifat's address, along with directions. You can catch the *U-Bahn* right near here and Rifat's place is just a couple blocks away from the Altona station. If you want to stroll by, it probably wouldn't hurt. Just make it brief. Someone will notice you and know you're Americans. No doubt. But not to worry. We can compare notes next Tuesday. I'll be back in Chestertown Monday afternoon and on campus the next morning."

"If you can get one of those Vietnamese sandwiches through customs for me, I'll be your friend for life," I said.

Willi laughed.

"A *Bánh mì*? I told you they were good. And I'll bet you can get them in Arlington, right on Wilson Boulevard."

"We were thinking about going to *Sankt Pauli* one of these nights before we leave and just looking around. Any thoughts?"

"Shouldn't be a problem. Stay together, stay sober, and stick to the well-lighted areas. It's nasty but pretty safe."

"What are we likely to see?" Ashleigh asked.

"Sleaze, mostly," Willi replied. "What you'd expect in a European seaport city. And that's all I have to say. It'll be good if we can sit down and compare notes after we get back. And I don't want to inject any personal bias ahead of time."

He stood up.

"Have to run. I'm catching a train back to Munich. I suggest keeping a low profile."

"Thanks for lunch, Willi. And the advice."

"*Bitte schön*," he said.

Less than a minute later he was out of sight.

Chapter Seventeen

Hamburg
November 13
Wednesday

The three of us sat in silence in the warm sunshine for a few minutes.

"It's about 7:45 back in Virginia," I said. "I should call Darps and see what's happening there. Probably should write up our observations here, meager as they are."

"I should wade through my email," Samantha said. "Then, there are a bunch of web sites that I've been tracking that I should look at."

"Ditto for me," Ashleigh said.

"Anyone wanna go for a run later?" I asked. "We could go around the smaller lake. A day like this in northern Germany in November should not be wasted."

"I agree and I'd like to run," Samantha said, glancing at her watch. "How 'bout we take care of work stuff for two hours and then run?"

"Second," said Ashleigh.

"Sounds good to me," I said and glanced at my watch. "How 'bout we meet in the lobby at four?"

We walked back to the hotel in the early afternoon sunshine.

I heard noises coming from my room as I approached the door with the key in hand and assumed it was the cleaning crew. But I opened the door just in time to see Ahmed—the bellhop who'd brought my bag up—drop my laptop case and pull out a switchblade which he flicked open with a menacing *snick*. I noticed right away that he was wearing latex gloves. He ducked into a crouch, stepped over the laptop, and came towards me, slowly and menacingly. I stepped quickly towards him—a move he obviously didn't expect, as he paused slightly, which was all I needed. I batted his knife hand away with my left hand and tattooed him with a right somewhere near the middle of his face and felt something crumple under the force of the blow, which I followed up with a left to the middle of his gut. He sat down heavily, dropping the knife and putting his hands up to his face. A narrow but substantial amount of blood streamed from his nose and mouth and down the front of his *Vier Jahrszeiten* Hotel uniform. I kicked the knife away, grabbed the bedside phone and jabbed the zero.

"Rufen die Polizei! Jetzt! Es gibt ein Dieb in meinen Zimmer!" I said.

Ahmed suddenly bolted to his feet and ran out the door leaving a little trail of blood droplets. By the time I got to the door, he had disappeared from the corridor. I turned back to my room. In addition to the blood spots on the carpet, Ahmed's switchblade lay where I'd kicked it after I hit him. I rubbed my knuckles. Both hands smarted but I felt fortunate that there was none of *my* blood on the floor or on the knife. Making sure I had my key card, I went back out into the hall and took the half-dozen or so steps toward the two elevators. I heard the door to my room slam shut behind me. It sounded like one or both elevators were in motion, but I couldn't be sure. Then the left elevator chimed and the doors opened. A man wearing steel-rimmed glasses and a tan suit got off.

"Herr Llewellyn?" he asked, holding out a leather folder with some sort of badge and ID.

"*Jawohl*," I said automatically. I thought I must have looked frazzled.

"My name is Stickel. Hotel Security. What's this about a thief in your room?"

"Come see," I said.

The knife, the laptop and some blood were still in the room where Ahmed and I had left them.

"Are you hurt?" he asked.

"No. But Ahmed is. The bellhop. He was going through my laptop case when I came back to the room. When he pulled the knife, I had to hit him. That's his knife—and his blood—on the floor. The laptop is mine."

"Let's go downstairs," he said, putting the little plastic *Nicht stören/ Do Not Disturb* sign in the door lock and closing the door carefully, using a handkerchief. "We'll call the police from my office."

On the way down, I remembered my promise to Kehoe about not attracting the attention of the German police. I hoped things wouldn't start to spin out of control.

The cop who arrived at the hotel in less than ten minutes could have been Herr Stickel's brother—or cousin. Same blonde-to-gray hair combed straight back, same steel-rimmed glasses, and same tan suit. The ties were different—Stickel's was a dark pink and the cop's was black with red-green-and-gold diagonal stripes. The shoes were different as well—the cop had toecap oxfords while Stickel wore tassel loafers.

"Zimmermann," the cop announced, offering his hand. I took it and he shook both of our hands vigorously.

"I understand someone broke into your room here at the hotel. Any thoughts?" he asked in perfect American English—if that's not an oxymoron.

He took a silver pencil and a small notebook from a suit jacket pocket.

"Yes," I said. "When I returned from lunch at about 1:45, a hotel employee named Ahmed was rummaging through my laptop bag. It had miscellaneous papers of no value—airline itinerary, old boarding passes, and a couple of magazines in addition to the computer. When I entered my room, he dropped the case and pulled out a knife. I had to hit him in self-defense, and I did. Twice. He dropped the knife and fell to the floor. I called the front desk and Ahmed got up and left. In a hurry. Then Herr Stickel was kind enough to come to the room and escort me down here and call the police. You, I guess."

"The only problem with that," interjected Herr Stickel, waving a computer list, "is that we have no one on the hotel staff named Ahmed."

"Well—something isn't right, then. The guy who brought my bags to my room yesterday was Ahmed. At least that's what his nametag said. And it was the same guy who was rooting around in my bag and pulled the knife today. And his nametag said 'Ahmed' again today. I'm sure of that."

Stickel turned to the police officer.

"Herr Llewellyn is correct. Something isn't right. The man in his room must be a hotel employee wearing a fraudulent nametag or someone who is not an employee but is disguised as one. And I think the latter unlikely. It would be too risky—someone on the staff would be bound to know the guy was a phony and report him."

Herr Zimmermann stood up and pocketed his notebook.

"Let's go up to Herr Llewellyn's room and look around," he said.

He chattered in German on a tiny cell phone as we walked to the elevators. While on the elevator, he pulled on a pair of latex gloves that he took from a plastic baggie in his brief case.

"Don't touch anything in the room until it's been cleared. And that won't take long. The police technicians will be here quite soon."

Both Herr Stickel and Herr Zimmermann jabbered on their cell phones non-stop. The police technicians arrived and immediately started farting around with fingerprint powder and snipping up little pieces of carpeting with what looked like nail scissors—both the bloodstained carpet and apparently random samples from around the room. They'd found fingerprints on my laptop bag—presumably mine as I don't usually wear gloves when handling my computer. Ahmed—or whatever the hell his name is—was more circumspect. The hotel management called—they had assigned me to another room. Zimmermann handed me my laptop case and I bagged the computer.

A bellhop showed up at the door with my new key. I gave him my old one and called Ashleigh and Samantha and told them I'd be delayed a few minutes. I still needed to talk to Darps. The women said they'd wait and we arranged to meet in the lobby for our afternoon run in half an hour. A few minutes later, Herr Stickel called me on the room phone and told me that the police were finished in my old room and a bellhop would bring my clothes and stuff to the new room. He'd let me know of any "developments" in the case. The thirty minutes were just about up, so I went down to the lobby. Ashleigh and Samantha were there waiting.

"Mother of God!" said Ashleigh when I told them what had been happening. "What in heaven's name is going on?"

"Damned if I know," I answered, stupidly. "But I do know this—there are guys, apparently Middle Eastern, and they're coming after us. Or at least trying to. That means that they must know that we're trying to come after them."

"But they're not all that sophisticated," Samantha said. "Getting caught going through your stuff in your room was pretty clumsy. Not very professional."

"But very brazen," said Ashleigh.

"Let's run," I said. "One of you set the pace. And keep it civilized. Please. I feel like I've run twenty miles already."

The two women were kind to their old boss. They kept the pace leisurely, which allowed us to talk while we got some exercise and savor the mild weather.

"Could you identify Ahmed's accent? Turkish? Iranian? Syrian?" Samantha asked.

"He didn't say anything today—just grunted when I hit him. If I had to guess from the few words we exchanged the other day, I'd say not Turkish and not Farsi—Arabic, probably, but I can't narrow it down further than that."

We chatted some more during the run. They quizzed me about Ahmed, Stickel, and Zimmermann. I got the impression that they felt that the Germans weren't really interested in finding out the scoop on Ahmed—or whatever the hell his name was.

"They probably just want him to disappear," Ashleigh said. "The hotel will fire him and won't write him a recommendation for a job, hoping that he disappears from the radar totally."

"If the hotel can figure out who the hell 'Ahmed' really is," Samantha said.

"I think they've got that figured out already," I said. "Herr Stickel said that he showed up on hotel surveillance video. He's a German national. But his parents are from Syria. His name—as far as they know—is Mustafa Şamlıan."

"The curious thing," Samantha said as we headed back to the hotel, "is how Ahmed—or Mustafa—knew that we—you—were someone who needed to be searched."

The daylight was fading when we arrived back at the hotel. We walked into the brightly lit lobby.

"I think we need to decide on what we're going to do and when," I said.

The two women looked at me.

"I would really like to go by Rifat's house. And grab a bite somewhere. So if we reconnoiter Rifat's digs in the burbs, then there probably won't be time to hit the fleshpots of *Sankt Pauli* tonight. There is still tomorrow, though."

"You mean if we go to Altona this evening, we should wait till tomorrow night to check out the sleaze?" Samantha asked.

"Exactly," I said. "And I doubt that walking past the late Rifat's old dwelling will tell us anything, but I'd feel like I'd blown it if we hadn't. Since we're here in Hamburg anyway."

We arranged to meet in the lobby at six.

Chapter Eighteen

The weather had started to return to its nasty November normalcy when we left the hotel. The sun had set and the night sky was starless, dark, and opaque. A chill, damp wind blew in from the Baltic. Our little expedition took longer than I'd estimated. The walk to the U-Bahn stop took longer, and we waited longer for a train than I had anticipated. Maybe it was just the chilly dampness. We got off the train and followed Willi's directions. Rifat-the-Bomber's dwelling epitomized the housing of prim-and-proper German bourgeoisie. It was just like its neighbors—red brick, two stories, on a tiny lot. Outdoors it was a little bit scruffier than the surrounding homes—the yard obviously hadn't seen much of a mower or a rake. I verified the house number with Willi's note. Although it was dark outside, there were no lights on in the house. We didn't loiter, and we didn't see anyone coming or going. We circled the block and headed back toward the U-Bahn station. Just before we got to the station, we started to pass a little dive in which I could see a vertical spit through a stack of what was probably sliced lamb turning slowly. Electric filaments glowed alongside the slowly turning cylinder of meat. A bald-headed guy with a fierce mustache was putting flatware wrapped in linen napkins on the dozen or so tables in the place. The restaurant was brightly lit and inviting. The sign over the window said *Abdullah's Kebabs*.

"Anyone interested in some *döner kebab*?" I asked.

"What's that?" Ashleigh asked.

I was about to explain, but Samantha beat me to it.

"Have you ever eaten gyros?" she asked, pronouncing it, *year-ohs*.

"You mean the Greek stuff? In pita?"

"Yeah," Samantha said. "The Greek places in the States usually use beef or pork or both. The Turks and Arabs use lamb. But it's fixed the same way. On a vertical spit with the cooking heat alongside."

She pointed through Abdullah's window.

"That one has electric heating elements. Back in the day—even today, actually, if you go to the boondocks—they used little trays of charcoal to roast the lamb on the sides. That way, the juices and fat from the meat don't cause flames to flare up."

"Sounds good to me. I'm game," Ashleigh said.

We went in, and Abdullah welcomed us effusively in German. The restaurant was warm and was a welcome change from the Baltic chill outside. Abdullah was amazed that Samantha and I spoke Turkish. Actually, Ashleigh also speaks it—slightly. But she learns quickly and is not afraid to try it.

A handsome lad, who looked to be about sixteen, was helping Abdullah with the place settings, and Abdullah introduced him proudly as his son, Attila. I heard an authoritative female voice coming from the back of the restaurant, and I assumed it belonged to Abdullah's wife and Attila's mom.

We started out with beer, *ekmek,* the Turkish fresh bread, crusty and delicious, and a light salad. That was followed by the entrée, thinly-sliced roasted lamb, topped with a light tomato salsa and drizzled melted butter, all served over pieces of fresh *pide,* which we Americans call "pita." There were a dollop of bulgur as well as fresh tomato slices and skinny green peppers on the side. It was an utterly scrumptious meal that brought home the realization that the top three *cuisines* in the world are French, Chinese—and Turkish.

Heading back to the *Vier Jahrszeiten* on the *U-Bahn,* we talked about the variety of beer we had sampled in the past couple of days and the utter banality of Rifat's residence. The beer varieties added up. Nothing else did.

Chapter Nineteen

In the morning, the sun was still gone and the chill Baltic fog had turned into an even chillier drizzle. I braved the weather and went for a morning run and probably used up half the hotel's supply of hot water for my post-run shower. I was just getting ready to go down for some breakfast when my phone buzzed. It was Willi.

"I may have picked up something," he said. "I think it can wait till Tuesday. There's something else I have to take care of today, and you guys are flying out tomorrow. But I'll pass along one word for you to gnaw on. Commonwealth."

I remembered he'd said he'd back at Ripley Hall on Tuesday. He was being pretty circumspect on the phone. I thought for a couple of seconds.

"Ours?" I asked.

"The same," he said. "I'll see you on Tuesday."

"One thing—one loose end you can help me with—is an incident here in the hotel."

I told him about Ahmed's visit to my room and my chat with Stickel and Zimmermann.

"They'll probably be glad when I'm gone from their city. As will I. But it wouldn't hurt to have somebody from the Consulate General close the loop with Stickel at the hotel. Maybe via him back to Herr Zimmermann of the Hamburg Police," I said.

"I'll take care of it. I know the RSO—the Regional Security Officer at the ConGen. He thinks I'm a professor on sabbatical. But, more importantly, he owes me a few favors. He'll make a call or two for me."

We rang off.

His reference must have meant the Commonwealth of Virginia. There are only four states that call themselves commonwealths—three besides ours—Massachusetts, Pennsylvania, and Kentucky.

When I went down to breakfast, the two *Fräuleins* were shoveling in forkfuls of what appeared to be pork chops and scrambled eggs. Continental breakfasts be damned this morning. They graciously allowed me to join them for breakfast. I ordered coffee and whatever they were having. We made small talk for a minute or two. The weather and the news.

Then, as we finished up, we discussed the plain appearance of Rifat's digs, and how a Syrian boy, living like an air-headed college kid in that red-brick house, could all of a sudden blow himself to bits, along with a bunch of other folks.

"Like I said yesterday on the *Reeperbahn*, they play by different rules here. Let's talk about today, tonight, and tomorrow."

Today, I needed to get on line, check and manage email, and organize my stuff for tomorrow's trip. I needed to close the loop with Darps, for starters. Surface the "Commonwealth" issue at a minimum. Our flight tomorrow wasn't till eleven, but we needed to be at *Fuhlsbüttel* by nine. That brought us to tonight.

"Let's try for dinner around 7:30," I suggested. "Afterwards, we can wander around and visit one or two dives. That should give us a decent feel for *Sankt Pauli* and the *Reeperbahn* at night. We may even get a sense of how the German-Arab winds are blowing. Plus, it should get us in at a somewhat decent hour."

That suited the *Fräuleins* fine. They wanted to do a bit more shopping and jog around the *Binnenalster* one last time.

Chapter Twenty

I met the ladies as scheduled at 7:30 p.m. in the hotel lobby. We decided to walk; although, it might not have been a wise decision. The night air held definite hints of the northern winter that was fast approaching. We went into a huge beer hall called *Der Blau Käse*—the Blue Cheese. A traditional German band blared and thumped out brassy tunes. We sat at a table, which we shared with three men and three women. They looked like young German professionals. They were drinking beer and speaking German. It sounded like office gossip, and they paid no attention to us. We ordered beer and then dinner—*Max und Moritz*—two kinds of sausages accompanied by some sort of pickled salad, containing beets, diced potatoes, and onions. All three of us washed the second half of the meal down with a second liter of beer. The Germans at our table seemed to be telling jokes, and I think they were on their fourth or fifth liter of beer since we joined them. The three of us *Amerikanerin* noshed, drank, and chatted. Mostly, Ashleigh and Samantha chatted and I listened. After visiting a lavatory where at least twenty men were urinating into a gutter between the floor and the back wall of the loo, I re-linked with my two companions. I didn't ask about the configuration of the ladies' loo. I didn't want to know.

"That seemed like a family kind of place," Ashleigh said as we stepped out into the cold fog.

"Actually, I did see a family in there. Complete with two kids. And they were speaking Turkish," Samantha added.

"But no Arabs," I said.

Both women agreed.

"Maybe the Arabs don't go to 'family kinds of places,'" Ashleigh said.

"Well, let's go to a dive, then," Samantha said.

"There are plenty to choose from," I said.

I wasn't really all that comfortable escorting Ashleigh and Samantha into some pesthole where they had "sex shows" and God knows what else. It was like contributing to the delinquency of two minors. They were both adults of course, but I was their boss and a lot older than they were. Plus, there was the issue of good old Roman Catholic guilt. I don't consider myself a prude, but the idea of leading two wholesome young women into a sleazy dump with naked dancers just didn't sit all that well with me. And probably not all that well with our Maker, either, I thought. My guardian angel seemed to be twisting my ear from her perch on my right shoulder.

We were passing a bar called *Pfifikus* that had a neon logo of a grinning and lipsticked fox with a huge tail and a top hat. I glanced at the photos hanging in the glass case outside the door. They didn't look *too* bad. A lot of boobs. The occasional pubic patch.

"Shall we try here?" I asked, my mouth dry in spite of the two liters of beer I'd quaffed with dinner.

"Sure," Samantha said.

The three of us filed in. The interior of the place stank of a feral mix of sweat, booze, and cigarette smoke. A blonde woman with thick, black eyebrows and wearing nothing but a "pair" of thong panties showed us to a table. They must have been between "skits" as the lights were up and the tiny stage down front was deserted. I ordered three cognacs for the three of us. The "waitress" returned with six shot glasses on a small tray just below her bare boobs. Her nipples were of the large-diameter variety.

"Two drink minimum," she said. Her accent sounded Russian.

She placed a pair of the glasses in front of each of us. Then she placed what appeared to be a cash register tape in front of me. *€ 150.00* was imprinted on the bottom. God help us! Two drinks for three of us and it came to almost two hundred dollars. I hauled out the plastic and our waitress jiggled off with it. I took a sip of cognac that had never been in France. I winced and looked at my two companions.

"A smattering of Arabs," Samantha whispered, leaning over the table. "Mostly men."

She flicked her head almost imperceptibly to her right.

I looked. At the table next to us were four guys, probably in the thirty to thirty-five age group. They were clean-shaven, wore what appeared to be cheap suits and slightly gray dress shirts with no ties. They were definitely speaking Arabic and there was a nearly empty bottle of what purported to be Johnny Walker scotch on the table. When Fräulein Boobs bounced into range, they requested another bottle of scotch. The guy who ordered spoke heavily accented German. I estimated that their bar tab must have been between twelve hundred and fifteen hundred dollars. Maybe more for the Johnny Walker. Before the tip.

The waitress returned with our tab, which I signed, cursing myself as I added in a twenty-euro tip.

Samantha nodded her beautiful head in the other direction. There were three guys at an adjacent table. And a young woman. An older guy had a scruffy partial beard and looked to be about fifty. The younger guys could have been between twenty and twenty-five and had a scraggly, unshaven look similar to that of their older companion, but without the gray. It was a look not all that unusual on NFL quarterbacks on game day. I often wondered if they shaved with clippers rather than razors. I also wondered who was imitating whom. The woman appeared to be young— early twenties. She had a navy blue headscarf and wore a gray raincoat. There was a bottle of *Stolichnaya* on the table in their midst. A shot glass and a taller glass of water stood in front of each of them. I thought the woman looked incongruous with her *hijab*, raincoat, and shot of Stoli in this sleaze pit. They were speaking Arabic.

"These sanctimonious Muslims are probably the type that wouldn't hesitate to masturbate in a mosque," Samantha murmured.

"Arghh," I said.

Suddenly, the lights dimmed and four men dressed in black took seats alongside the tiny stage and picked up musical instruments. A drummer started a slow, sinister beat on a snare. A spotlight flared, illuminating the tiny stage, and a woman stepped up into the light. She wore a short, kimono-style robe, and appeared to be perspiring mightily. She shuffled and clapped in time with the music that now included a keyboard, a trumpet, and a clarinet on top of the drums. Gradually, the robe came open and she finally shrugged out of it and dropped it at her feet, leaving her completely naked except for wedge-heeled sandals on her feet. As the robe hit the deck, the spotlight hit a curly-headed, athletic-looking young man prancing onto the stage, "clad" only in what appeared to be a black leather jockstrap that had a belt knotted at his waist. The belt had two tasseled ends, which flew around as he danced opposite his disrobed partner. The rhythm of the music accelerated and the woman dancer dropped to her knees. She grabbed one end of his knotted belt.

"That's enough for me," said Ashleigh, standing up.

"Me too," Samantha and I said together.

We headed for the door.

"Pretty sleazy," I said, weakly.

"Yeah, but those self-proclaimed, devout Arabs were there. Sucking up the sleaze. Including the woman. And I'm not the least bit surprised," Samantha said. "Some of those bastards are so damned hypocritical."

Outside, the salty, Baltic fog actually tasted good. We started walking, not knowing where the hell we were going. I kept my eyes peeled for a taxi to get us back to the *Vier Jahrszeiten*.

"I'm wondering if you heard what I heard back in that dump," Ashleigh said.

"Like what?" Samantha asked.

"A couple of morsels of table talk. From the old guy drinking Stoli with the younger guys and the woman."

"I think I know what you're talking about," Samantha responded. "'Virginia.'"

"Yeah. The old dude said it once and one of the younger guys mentioned it at least once," Ashleigh said.

"Do you think they were referring our Old Dominion?" I asked. "By the way, I thought I heard the older guy say it too. But I couldn't make out anything else."

"Well, I could," Samantha said. "One other thing that I think the old guy said. 'Revenge of the Muslim martyrs.' Twice."

"I heard him say 'shahid' a couple of times. Martyrs," Ashleigh agreed. "But I couldn't get the rest of it. Too much other noise."

"Look," Samantha said, pointing to her left.

Tätowierung! The sign said in blue neon. "Tattooing!"

"So?" I said. "Hamburg is a sailors' town. What's surprising about finding a tattoo parlor? There are probably dozens of them."

"I've wanted to get a tattoo since I was a sophomore in high school," Samantha responded.

I thought about Willi's advice to "stay sober," and I wondered if the three of us weren't a little sloshed from the two liters of German beer followed by two shots of faux, but still alcoholic cognac.

"I wonder what they cost?" mused Ashleigh.

"There's only one way to find out," Samantha answered and pushed open the door. Ashleigh followed her inside, and I had no choice but to accompany them.

There were two people inside—a guy who looked to be in his sixties and wore a Florida Marlins t-shirt and jeans and a woman who could have been the sister of our waitress at the Sleazy Fox raunchy nightclub. Except she had clothes on. Sort of. A purple tank top over yellow shorts and yellow sandals. She was listening to an iPod and seemed to be zoned out on the music. Or whatever. She could have been listening to an audio book version of *Ulysses* for all I knew. There was also a huge dog, a mostly black Alsatian, sleeping under a table in front of them.

I heard someone say "Fifty-five euros," and watched as the guy in the t-shirt and his girlfriend spread books open in front of Samantha and Ashleigh. Before I realized what was happening, Samantha had forked over fifty-five euros and was sitting down in a reclining chair and removing one of her shoes. The guy fooled around with what looked like tracing paper and carbon paper. Samantha turned sideways and the old guy wheeled a stool over and swabbed the outside of her ankle with what smelled like rubbing alcohol. Then, I guess he traced the image that she wanted turned into ink on the outside of her right ankle. Next, he picked up a gizmo that reminded me of a dentist's drill and started working on Samantha's ankle. The woman invited Ashleigh to have a seat in a second recliner, swabbed her ankle, did her thing with the tracing paper, and started in on her with another drill. Or whatever it was. Before long, I saw a tiny yellow rose starting to emerge from the geezer's ministrations on Samantha's ankle. There were a few droplets of blood—the real stuff—on her ankle that made me think of hepatitis. I stepped over to where the blonde was drilling on Ashleigh and saw what appeared to be a tiny cartoon Mad Hatter starting to appear. I went back to the table and started flipping through one of the pattern books. The Alsatian lifted his head and snarled.

"Shut up, Ernst," barked the old guy in the Marlins shirt.

Ernst? I thought. *A dog named "Ernst"?*

Ten minutes later, the old guy was taping a gauze pad on Samantha's rose. He turned to me and raised his eyebrows.

"*Du?*" he asked.

I asked him for a pencil and sketched a small N-star from my win against Army in the 800-meter run a long time ago.

"*Blau und gelb,*" I said. "Blue and yellow." I held my thumb and forefinger up about an inch and a half apart.

"*Sofort,*" he said. He farted around in a cabinet, surfaced with a couple of pieces of clear plastic with some sort of imagery and gestured me toward the chair recently vacated by Samantha. I forked over my fifty-five euros. He handed me a five back.

"*Nur fünfzig,*" he said. "*Einfach.*"

"Only fifty. Simple."

"You go, boss!" Samantha said with a giggle.

It didn't hurt all that much, but there was an unpleasant sensation of my skin being punctured rapidly and repeatedly. Ten minutes later, the geezer was taping a gauze pad to my ankle. As we headed for the door, I wondered what manner of wrath Maria would unload on me for this little escapade when I got home.

Chapter Twenty-One

Captain Diaz sent a text message on his phone. *TP.* He checked the time on the cell phone. 1411. He would place the small grocery bag in Truchas Park in exactly thirty minutes. At 1441. That meant he would leave his flat at 2:35. He had done the walk in person several times. Six minutes, give or take a few seconds. Every time. Today would be no different. This would be his sixth powder delivery. He wondered why he was sweating. He walked to the liquor cabinet and took out a glass and a bottle of dark rum. He poured generously and took a sip. He thought it helped. He looked at the time. 1413. *God damn it! The fucking time is standing still!*

Lourdes, his wife, walked into the parlor.

"Is today some holiday I don't know about? Rum in the afternoon?"

"Don't give me any *mierda*, Lourdes. I have enough shit to worry about without you giving me any more."

He walked across the room, looked out the window and tossed off half of the rum in his glass. He craved a cigarette but was reluctant to light one up with the propellant increments in the apartment. Intellectually, he knew that there was no danger unless he dropped a lighted cigarette directly into the grocery bag with the powder. He'd heard that the *Norte Americanos* believed in something they called "Murphy's Law": "If something can be fucked up, it will be." That was how he felt about smoking in his apartment when there was a bag of artillery propellant lying around. He glanced at his watch. Four more minutes. He finished off the rum and walked over to the sink where he rinsed out the glass.

"I'll be back in less than fifteen minutes," he said.

He picked up the grocery bag and left, feeling like a thief.

Chapter Twenty-Two

Chestertown
November 15
Friday

The flights back to Dulles were uneventful and on time. On the trip across the pond, we had three seats together.

"Um, I have to know," I said as we belted ourselves into our seats, "Is the reason you two are wearing slacks to minimize the visibility of the tattoo bandages?"

Both women giggled sheepishly.

"Well, neither of you faces the possibility of spousal wrath, at least. I can't say the same thing," I said.

"Eventually my mother will see it," Ashleigh said. "Maternal wrath is probably even rougher than spousal wrath."

"On a more serious note," Samantha whispered as the airplane started to taxi prior to takeoff. "Remember the guys and the woman who were drinking Stoli at the table next to us in the dive with the sex show? They mentioned 'Virginia' a couple of times?"

"Yes. Sure," I said. "We all heard that. But I certainly couldn't hear anything else."

"Any more thoughts about what they were talking about?" Samantha asked.

"I thought of a few possibilities," Ashleigh said. "One, of course, is our state. Two is a girl's name. Three is the University. And four is a code word. But that's as far as I got. Nowhere, basically."

"Willi is flying in on Monday," I said. "We'll meet with him first thing Tuesday morning and kick this thing around some. He called before we left and said something that suggested he might have something to add to the mix."

Once again, when we got to Dulles, I enjoyed the friendliness and camaraderie with which the U.S. immigration and customs officials greeted their returning fellow citizens. It was one of the things, I thought, that made being an American so special. At least at Dulles. I'd arrived at Atlanta from overseas a few months ago and thought the Immigration dipshit there was doing a lousy Vladimir Putin imitation.

Being the sympathetic and kindly boss that I was, I told the two women to take the rest of the weekend off.

I looked over the heads of the folks waiting for arrivals and immediately spotted Maria's jet-black locks. I noticed a big grin on her face. Good, I thought, she's as happy to see me as I am to see her. At least, almost as happy. Elizabeth was with her, and she had a big grin on her face as well. *It doesn't get any better than this*, I thought.

The ride home was relatively uneventful. Traffic was horrible, as usual. Both women were very talkative on the way home. I decided to delay any announcement about my new tattoo till a more propitious time. Ditto for descriptions of strolling among the whorehouses on the *Herbertstrasse*.

When we turned off I-95 to head into Chestertown, it started to snow. By the time we pulled into the driveway at fifteen-oh-six Prince Henry Street, the snow was coming down with some authority but wasn't sticking. I grabbed some kindling and a couple of split logs on the way in. It didn't take me long to get a fire going and close the glass doors on the fireplace. Elizabeth snapped a leash on Cory's collar and headed back into the falling snow.

"Ready for a sherry?" I asked Maria.

"Yes indeedy," she said. "I haven't had a glass of sherry since before you left for Germany. We haven't had a fire either, for that matter."

"Chinese takeout okay?" I asked. "Being it's Friday, and all. Unless you have a caterer scheduled to bring us a prime rib dinner."

"Chinese is fine," she said.

I poured our drinks and called in an order for the Chinese. Crab Rangoon, steamed dumplings, and Mongolian beef. I wondered if it were possible to order Crab Rangoon in Yongan. Like ordering Peking Duck in Beijing.

Elizabeth and Cory came back from their walk sporting a fairly serious dusting of snow.

"It's starting to stick," Elizabeth announced. She wiped off the hound with the doggie towel. I walked the four blocks to China Wok, picked up our order and walked back home in the snow. Elizabeth was right. The snow was definitely starting to stick.

Before going to bed, I peeled off the Hamburg tattoo artist's taped-on gauze pad in the bathroom. My N-star looked reasonably healthy. I daubed a little antibiotic ointment on the ink and covered it with a large Band-Aid. Later, in bed, I was beginning to enjoy my homecoming with Maria when she suddenly said, "What's the matter with your ankle?"

She slid her gorgeous foot up and down across the Band-Aid a couple of times.

"Um," I said.

"Did you cut yourself?" she asked.

"Well, yes and no," I said, lamely.

"What does that mean?" she asked.

"I got a small tattoo," I said.

"*What?*" she snarled.

"Shhh," I responded.

That just made her madder.

"I can't believe this," she growled.

Then I told her the whole story. About being out with Ashleigh and Samantha and having a couple liters of beer. And then going to the Perverted Fox and having *faux* cognac. And then stopping at the tattoo parlor. And all three of us getting small tattoos.

"Jesus Christ!" she hissed. She never swears. "You're supposed to be smart. You hired those girls because they're supposed to be smart. And then the three of you, like a trio of drooling high school morons, get tattooed in some pesthole in Hamburg-freaking Germany. Did you think of blood-borne pathogens? Mother of God! This is the twenty-first century. You're forty years old and a father—not a high-school airhead on spring break."

To say that this little one-way conversation dashed cold water on the homecoming celebration would be an understatement of truly stupendous proportions.

Chapter Twenty-Three

Saturday was miserable—November weather in Virginia at its worst. Cold, slimy rain had washed all traces of last night's snow away. The temperatures hovered barely above freezing under dark gray skies. I needed a run after the long flight yesterday, so I bundled up, forced myself out the door and took off. Maria had said nothing this morning about last night's little chat about my new ankle art. Needless to say, I sure as hell didn't raise the issue. The cold rain smacked my face, but after a while, I ceased to notice. Mother Nature heated up the old bod, the muscles loosened up, and pretty soon, I was gliding along and feeling pretty decent, rain or no rain. When I finished up forty-five minutes later, my running clothes were sodden but I felt alive and well with nary a thought of the new tattoo.

Maria and Elizabeth had gone out. The kitchen white board said "Library, Giant, Back by 11:30." I jumped into the shower and let it run hot. For a long time. When I got out, I debated about shaving. The "shave, you bum" side won, so I scraped off the whiskers. Looking seedy today would probably not help my case. I slipped into a pair of jeans and a sweatshirt as well as socks and shoes. As I reached the bottom of the stairs, Cory raised her head from the rug in front of the cold fireplace and gave a little "woof." That's when I heard Maria's Jetta in the driveway.

It was 11:45—lunchtime. I was thinking that soup would be good and a fire would be even better. I wondered if the ladies had picked up any delicacies at Giant. They trundled supermarket bags into the kitchen and plunked them down on the countertop. I noticed that Elizabeth now was almost as tall as her mother

"You're in luck," Maria said, removing her gloves. "That is if you haven't already eaten lunch."

"Nope," I said. "Are you guys gonna take me out to lunch?"

"Even better. We picked up homemade soup and deli sandwiches at Giant. Tomato-and-basil soup," she said, taking a quart-sized container from a bag. "And then, there's the prosciutto-and-mozzarella sandwiches."

"And we even got you a kosher pickle," Elizabeth added. "Not to mention the home-baked chocolate chip cookies."

Needless to say, lunch hit the spot. But I was thankful that I'd run a hard six miles in the rain. Running does great things in dealing with guilt. As well as managing big lunches.

As we were nibbling the cookies, Maria turned to me.

"So—was the trip useful?" she asked. Nothing about the tat, Allah be praised.

We hadn't really gotten into detail about the trip yesterday at all. Elizabeth's report card from All Saints was straight As. Maria had made good progress on her book exploring the exploits of the many New Yorkers in the Union Army.

"I don't know," I said. "We saw a fair amount of sleaze. Hamburg is noted for that. We also saw a fair number of Arabs there. That was no surprise, either. We learned that the suicide bomber that blew up the nightclub outside the base at Ramstein lived in Hamburg. Or a Hamburg suburb. He was a Syrian on a student visa. But not enrolled in any school. We even went by his house."

I paused for another nibble of cookie and a sip of coffee.

I heard the tune of Elizabeth's phone signaling that a text had arrived. She was finished with lunch. Actually, we all were.

"May I please be excused?" she asked.

"Sure, sweetie," I said.

"There's another thing that's bothersome," I said to Maria. "On our second day there, I caught some clown in my room. He was going through my laptop case and pulled a knife on me when I interrupted him."

"Let me guess," Maria said. She lowered her voice. "You kicked his ass."

I nodded. "Right. Self-defense. But there's more. He was a Middle Easterner and was disguised as a hotel employee. And he had a bogus name tag."

"Did you go to the police?"

"Indirectly," I said. "I called hotel security and they called the cops. We had a long chat. Willi is following up with the consulate and the German police. I want to minimize my involvement with the *Polizei*. Kehoe is absolutely paranoid that someone official—like the police—will make the connection between him and me. Blowback from that could be a total disaster. And," I paused.

"And what?" Maria asked. She sensed, correctly, that there was something else.

"Both Samantha and Ashleigh heard the name, 'Virginia,' dropped in a conversations in Hamburg. Arab conversations. In Arabic. For that matter, I heard it too."

"It's a popular name," Maria said.

"Not among Arabs," I said.

"So what's your point?" Maria asked.

"I wonder if they were talking about the Commonwealth. Our fair state. The Old Dominion. As opposed to some chick named Virginia."

"Who knows?" she said.

"I don't," I said.

Chapter Twenty-Four

I went into work a little early. An in-basket full of bureaucratic drivel awaited me. I prioritized it all as quickly as I could and then started on a little tour of Ripley Hall. First stop: Judy. The GIC. Pronounced "Gick." Goddess-in-Charge. Somehow she sees all and knows all.

"How was *Deutschland*?" she asked.

"Interesting," I said. "But hardly enlightening. I have to sit down with the two Valkyries who went with me and try and sort everything out. Willi is flying in today and will come in tomorrow. Maybe we'll be able to make some sense out of things."

"Valkyries?" she said. "Weren't they the maidens who decided who was to die?"

"I spoke in jest. Germany and all. Beautiful women. And if you tell them that I referred to them as Valkyries, I'm dead meat."

"Your secret is safe with me, Alan," she said with something between a grin and a smirk.

I spent the morning jumping through my ass with the prioritized paperwork and getting very little of substance accomplished. I was trying to sort through all the bullshit when the secure line from the White House buzzed like a swarm of hornets. It was from "*Chipmunk*," the vice president. Syd Girtler. Needless to say, I had to answer it. I did.

"Good morning, sir," I said.

Some female functionary told me to hold for the vice president. I did.

"Hey Alan," he said, when he came on the line. "Should we really take this out-of-left-field terrorist threat seriously?"

"Sir?" I asked, stupidly.

"You know what I mean, Alan," he continued in his jovial, charm-the-pants-off-anyone tone of voice. "There's a highly-classified, tightlycompartmented piece of paper floating around the West Wing that says Islamists in Europe are plotting a second nine-eleven. I've got to think that the idea came from *BIAS*."

The phone line was supposed to be totally secure, but my phone paranoia kicked in nevertheless.

"Well, Mr. Vice President, you're right. That may be an oversimplification. But we did give the President a paper suggesting such a possibility. As far as I know, President Kehoe is taking it seriously. And I don't know of any other views floating around the White House suggesting the same thing."

"Yeah, I know. And that's what's got me concerned. No collateral from anyone else."

Suddenly my threat alarm buzzed or rang or whatever mental alarms do. I took a deep breath.

"No doubt you're comfortable making that call, Mr. Vice President. But the boss man hired me to give him alternative viewpoints. I just call them the way we see them."

"Well I'm telling you that the way you see them, in this case, is questionable," he said. The politician's jocular charm had given way to an earnest seriousness. I had to wonder what in hell the Vice President of the United States of America was trying to do by injecting himself into the intelligence production process. Even a backdoor, low-rent process like ours.

"Well sir, I have to agree with you that we are out on a limb. But, if I'm not mistaken, that's what the boss is paying us for. Going out on limbs."

"Well, you have to be careful with that. If you go too far out on limbs in this town, the fecal matter can hit the fan."

"Yes sir. I understand. But the president wants the plain, unvarnished truth out of *BIAS,* and he doesn't want the *BIAS* views widely shared. To say the least. If leaks can be avoided, it should keep the fecal matter away from the fan."

The veep chuckled. It wasn't a happy chuckle.

"Those leaks are what worry me, Alan."

"Now that you mention them sir, they're starting to worry me too."

"Be careful, Alan," he said.

There was a click, followed by a dial tone. I didn't know what to make of the conversation. *Chipmunk* did not sound at all hostile. But there were definite undertones of warning in the conversation.

It was time for a Wilderness session with Darps. Brainstorming was in order. Secure brainstorming.

Is that conversation on tape?" I asked Judy from her office door.

"Actually, it's on a flash drive. But I'm sure it's all there," she said.

Shortly after some guy from the White House Communications Agency installed that special phone, Darps contacted some "old friend" and had him come in and rig the phone and computers so that every conversation was automatically recorded.

"Darps and I are heading for the boondocks," I said.

"Gotcha."

I found Darps in short order. He looked up from a stack of papers. I pointed towards the west. He understood immediately and gave me a thumbs-up. I pointed my thumb at my chest and then made steering-wheel motions with my hands. He gave me another thumbs-up and we were out of there. I drove my beat-up Explorer toward the Wilderness.

After we got through the battery of traffic and traffic lights on Route Three and out into "the country," I said, "We may have a fucking problem."

"I guessed as much," Darps said. "What gives?"

"*Chipmunk*," I said.

"Hmm," he said. "What's Smirking Syd's problem now?"

We were nearing the approach to our destination. I flipped the turn signal on and slowed down. Darps seemed to understand my reticence. I pulled the Explorer in behind the little dump that we use as a safe house, thinking that it was high time that we got a new place. If this house wasn't compromised already, odds were that it soon would be.

Darps jumped out and unlocked the door into the kitchen, and I followed him in. It was freezing. He went to the thermostat and pushed a couple of buttons. There was a low rumble and air started moving. Cold air, but I could feel it starting to warm up. Slowly.

Darps went to the pantry and broke out a canister of coffee and a paper filter.

"Coffee?" he asked.

"As long as it's hot," I said.

He put together about a third of a pot of coffee and plugged it in. It started moaning and dripping immediately. He got two mugs from the dish cupboard and set them down on the counter by the coffee maker.

"So what's up with *Chipmunk*?" he asked.

"He's got some sort of wild hair up his ass," I said. "He thinks that the idea of a terrorist threat to the U.S. coming out of Europe is very squirrelly. Because it's a view held only by *BIAS*—and no one else in the Intelligence Community. No collateral, he says. And, he says, he's worried about leaks. And that has me worried about leaks."

The air was getting warmer. As was the kitchen. The coffee maker has one of those automatic shut-off gizmos that lets you pour while the coffee is still brewing. The dripping liquid was emitting a nice aroma. Darps poured each of us a half-cup and replaced the carafe. It started dripping again. We sipped from our mugs.

"We may or may not have a problem," Darps said.

"Whadda you mean 'we may or may not have a problem'?" I said. "Either way you slice this one, we have a problem."

"Let me re-phrase that," Darps said. "We either have a small problem or a *big* problem."

"I hate to repeat myself, but whadda you mean?"

"Okay, if we have a little problem, it's probably along lines like these. *Chipmunk* is feeling his political oats. His monumental ego is at work. He thinks he needs to insert his great self into a major but highly classified national security issue. And he thinks he's an intelligence analyst. 'No collateral' indeed. My aching ass. And he thinks the best way to get on the skyline with *Cheetah* is to throw up a few little roadblocks. Who's going to say he's wrong? Not us. And nobody else is in the loop. He gets to demonstrate his national security wisdom and awareness to Kehoe. After a while he quiets down, pulls the roadblocks down. *Cheetah* does what he wants. Life goes on. Girtler's gravitas is demonstrated. Albeit to a tiny but elite audience."

"And that's a *little* problem?" I sputtered.

"Hell yes," Darps replied. "It's a minor-league, politician-ego issue. The proverbial tempest in the teapot. And if that's all it is, it'll disappear very soon. And it won't affect us at *BIAS* or the country one whit."

"Suppose he blows the whistle on *BIAS*? Says we're out of touch. Wrong. Dumb. Irrelevant. All of the above. Brings us down."

"I know he says and does some dumb things, but he's not that dumb," Darps responded. "He knows that *BIAS* is Kehoe's project. He knows that bringing us down would more than likely take Kehoe down as well but he also knows that Kehoe would take Girtler down with him and probably cut his balls off in the process. With a rusty fish knife." Darps took a sip of coffee and didn't say anything else.

"What's the 'big' problem you alluded to?" I asked.

He turned on the old TV. ESPN was on. They were discussing Heisman chances. He amped up the volume.

"The big problem is exactly what *Chipmunk* told you," he said. "Leaks."

"This is Washington, D.C.," I said. "Leaks are a fact of life. Everybody at *BIAS* needs to be goddamn careful about security. But, if we start fretting and stressing about leaks, we'll never get any sleep and all end up in the nuthouse."

"You're right," he said. "But what bothers me is that he opted to raise the issue of leaks. Today."

"Meaning what?"

Darps topped off our mugs and turned the coffee machine off.

"Maybe he knows of a leak or a potential leak. Not from us," he said. "Somewhere else. At his end of the interstate."

"Well Jesus Christ," I said. "If he does, then he's gotta do something to cut it off at the pass."

"You know that. I know that. But does *Chipmunk* know that? And even if he does know, I suppose he could opt to not do anything."

I finished my coffee and rinsed out my cup in the sink.

"Let's hope it's just an issue with his ego," I said.

Suddenly, a name popped into my mind. Suzanne Racey. Channel Thirteen News anchorwoman. And, according to some rumor mongers, the anonymous writer of a column titled *Morsels and Motes* that ran on Sundays in the Washington *Mirror*.

"Do you have any idea whether Suzanne Racey is still prowling around the White House or the Capitol?" I asked.

Darps looked startled.

"No," he said. "Why do you ask?"

"Just a thought," I said. "It may be unfair, but when we start talking about leaks, good old 'Racey Suzanne' leaps to mind."

Darps raised his eyebrows.

"Your logic is on solid ground," he said. "But I have no idea where she spends her off-air time. She's still on the air, by the way. I watched her last evening. Six o'clock news. Said she'd back on at 11:00. By which time I'd hit the rack. Her old beaux seem to be out of the picture."

Darps was right on that score. One of her old beaux was six feet under the sod of the Congressional Cemetery, while the other was back in New York working on his political career.

"Let's have Luke and Mike check with their buddies on the White House detail and see if Suzanne has been lurking around number sixteen hundred," I said.

We stopped at Fat Harry's for lunch on the way back to the office and each of us had a steak bomb sandwich and a draft. I asked Hafez how Khalil was doing.

"Good, good!" he said. "He substitute teaches almost every day, now. And, after Christmas holidays, he will start as a full-time math teacher at Augustine Washington High School. Some teacher is leaving to have a baby and will stay on leave for the rest of the year. And the principal likes Khalil. So he hired him. Khalil's very excited. And he often asks about you."

"Give him my best regards, please," I said.

"I will, Alan. I will," Hafez assured me.

Chapter Twenty-Five

Captain Diaz's serve had improved, Major el-Shahawi observed. So had his stamina. The captain had won the first set on his own, six-four. He was ahead five games to one in the second. But it didn't matter. Diaz had delivered seventy-five powder bags over the past several weeks. Perfect for three vests. The emissaries from Germany were due in Cuba in the middle of next week. It was time to put some distance between him and his agent. Let him go to sleep, for a while. Perhaps, in a year or so, someone other than el-Shahawi would awaken Agent *Krait*, whose appetite for *Yanqui* dollars would no doubt have grown considerably by that time.

"Your game has certainly improved, Antonio," el-Shahawi said. "You whipped me in both sets. I think that's a first."

"Perhaps it's your age, Faisal," Diaz said with a laugh. "You may be getting old."

"Perhaps," he answered. "At any rate, I think I'll have a gin and tonic instead of beer today."

"I'll have a *Presidente*, as usual," the captain said.

The bartender brought their drinks. The two men clinked glasses and drank.

"I'm afraid this will be our last tennis match for a while," el-Shahawi said. "I have to do some traveling."

"That's a shame," Diaz said. "I really enjoy beating you. Finally."

He took a generous sip of the *Presidente*.

"I take it that means you don't require any more propellant," he said.

"That's true. We have plenty. Seventy-five bags. Thanks to you. I'm advised that the testing and analyses are going well. And by the way, the towel envelope contains not only nine hundred dollars for the last group of nine charges, there's a five hundred dollar bonus as well."

"Well I thank you for that. So I guess that we won't be seeing much of each other for a while?"

"For a while. I'll probably see you once in a while at one of these diplomatic circle jerks. But who knows? The world is a strange place and strange things happen. But for now, you would probably be well-advised to forget all about Faisal el-Shahawi."

"I think I understand, Major," Diaz said.

He reached for the far towel and stood up and reached for the major's hand.

"Adios," he said.

"Buenas noches," el-Shahawi thought. "Ciao," he said instead.

Chapter Twenty-Six

Chestertown
November 26
Tuesday

This morning, I went in to work at 7:25. Judy was unlocking the place as I arrived. Mike and Darps arrived by the time she had disabled the alarm system.

"Anyone hear from Willi?" I asked.

"He called in yesterday evening after he landed. He'll be here soon," Judy said, glancing at her watch.

She makes it a practice of checking *BIAS* voicemail before she comes in, avoiding early-morning ambushes.

"We've got something from the big house coming in on an HMX-One chopper in forty-five minutes," Mike said, glancing at *his* watch. "There's a 'parcel pickup' email from last night."

Mike stays well on top of *BIAS* email via his iPhone.

"I'll run up to the air facility and pick it up," he said.

The day was starting to get big. In a hurry.

I raced through my email. Judy told me that Willi was indeed inbound as we spoke and would be there by 8:00. I looked at the clock. 7:51. I looked at the sign-in/sign-out board on the computer. Samantha and Ashleigh were both on board. I swung by their side-by-side offices.

"Top of the morning, ladies. Hope your weekends went well," I said.

"I slept most of the time, Ashleigh said. "I think I'm completely over my jet lag."

"Any grief about the new ink?" Samantha asked, a mischievous smile on her face.

I rolled my eyes and drew a forefinger across my throat.

"Let's not go there. I'm trying not to think about it," I responded. "As planned, a sit-down in 'Paycheck' at 8:00," I added.

Both women started gathering notebooks, iPhones, and coffee cups.

Willi arrived on time, hung up his expensive-looking leather jacket, and accepted a mug of coffee from Darps. The two beautiful women came in, followed by Sammy. Who was followed by Luke. Everybody found a seat in short order.

"Okay," I said. "For the record, Ashleigh, Samantha, and I returned from a quick trip to Germany Friday. Willi has been over in Germany and Austria for three weeks and returned Stateside yesterday. The reason for the increased attention on Germany was the combination of the part of our estimate about a terrorist attack on the U.S. from Europe, and particularly Germany, and the actual suicide attack outside the U.S. base complex at Ramstein last week."

I nodded at Judy who started a PowerPoint presentation, which came up on the Smart board in front of the room. We showed them an agenda that had me leading off, followed by Samantha and Ashleigh. I had saved Willi for last. We plunged right in. I gave my little wrap-up, Samantha and Ashleigh did the same, and Willi brought up the rear with a fairly thorough rundown on Rifat and the Ramstein bombing. I called for a break at 9:30. People staggered off in the direction of the rest rooms. I'd already decided to hold off with the "Virginia" and "Revenge of the Muslim Martyrs" issues till after the break.

Mike picked then to show up at my office door with one of the special briefcases we used to send classified material back and forth between the White House and Ripley Hall.

"Here's what the Marines hauled in on the HMX-One chopper," he said.

"Let's see what we've got," I said as he handed me the briefcase.

I entered the code and popped the hasps.

There was a purple-and-white checkered folder with a variety of classification markings on it. There was a small piece of paper with the Kehoe family crest on it clipped to the folder. Today's date was scrawled in ink, followed by a penned note:

Loose:

What's your reaction to the attached? Use "Meatball" as the

subject in whatever communications you use and it will

get to me right away. Welcome back!

Keys

The folder contained a white envelope. The envelope held a flash drive. I removed it from the envelope and popped it into a USB port on my computer. The drive contained two documents: *DHSDoc1* and *DHSDoc2*. I opened the first one. It was dynamite, but I didn't realize how explosive it was—at first.

It was indeed a Department of Homeland Security document. The addressee line as well as the date were redacted in black marker. The text was clear.

> Received advice from GOG[1] that Mehmet al-Husni, a German national of Egyptian origin, plans to depart Germany. He has reservations on a Condor flight from Frankfurt to Havana this week. Husni, a known Islamist ringleader, is believed to be the director of the recent suicide bombing in Kaiserslautern. However, German police have no tangible evidence of his involvement.

A pretty clear mug shot of Husni was part of *DHSDoc1*. He looked vaguely familiar. The usual grizzled five-to-seven days' worth of beard growth that these clowns seemed to want to cultivate. But behind the scraggily, half-assed bearded look, there was something else. Something that I couldn't put my finger on.

I took the flash drive out of the computer and went back to the meeting in Paycheck.

"We have something from up the road," I announced to everybody, handing Judy the flash drive. "And it's related to what we're discussing."

She plugged it into her computer.

"Let's start with Document One," I said. "I haven't even looked at the second one yet."

---

1   Government of Germany

Judy clicked the mouse on *DHSDoc*1 and it jumped to the Smart board.

"Jesus Christ!" hissed Willi. "Husni was one of Rifat's roomies in the Altona house outside Hamburg. He's about fifty years old. All those other rats were in their mid-twenties to early thirties. The Germans—not unreasonably—think he was the mother hen. That he ran the show for the Ramstein bombing. But they have no proof. And he has a German passport, so we can't touch him."

"But they can," I replied.

"But they won't," Willi said. "Not unless they have hard-core evidence. That will stand up in court. He's a German citizen from an Arab country. That makes him almost untouchable."

Judy scrolled down with the mouse, bringing up the headshot.

"That's him," Willi said. "A German police official showed me that exact photo."

"My God! *We* saw him," Ashleigh said. "In person. In that skuzzy bar. *Pfifikus,* or whatever the heck it was called. 'The Sleazy Fox.' He was the guy that was drinking *Stoli* with the two young guys and the young woman in the raincoat. He also was the guy that mumbled 'Virginia.'"

Then I remembered where I'd seen the face. *Bar Pfifikus.* The place with the waitress with the wide-diameter nipples.

"What?" Willi whispered. "He actually said *'Virginia'*?"

"Yes," Ashleigh said. "He did. So what?"

"Because a German source of mine said that the word 'Virginia' has shown up several times in German *SIGINT* chatter. Arabic-language chatter."

"Dare I say this as an interloper?" Sammy began. "I haven't been to Germany and really haven't been working this problem, but it seems to me that available evidence suggests that this turd Husni (a) ran a rehearsal suicide bombing in Kaiserslautern, and (b) is heading this way, via Cuba, and, finally, (c) is planning a culminating activity for our fair Commonwealth. Or am I jumping to conclusions?"

"You may be jumping, Sammy," I said, "but I don't think your conclusions are unreasonable. Excuse me for a minute. Keep talking," I said and I left the room.

I went back to my office and my computer and started banging out a short email.

From: allewellyn@bias.gov

To: keys@lisound.com

Subj: Face time for meatball wedges.

There was no message. I sent it with the subject line only. I had an answer in just under five minutes.

From: keys@lisound.com

To: allewellyn@bias.gov

Subj: Meatball

Loose:

Tomorrow. Prince William Forest Park. 0800. 6 miles. Slow and easy.

CU,

Keys

Okay. I was going to run with the man at 8:00 a.m. tomorrow, and it would be six miles in Prince William Forest Park. A beautiful place to run. Thank God the leader of the free world promised that the six miles would be slow. That park has some very sporty hills. If push came to shove, I could probably bust his balls, but that wouldn't do much for our relationship.

When I returned to "my" meeting, everything was out of control. Sidebar discussions were raging all over the place.

"Are the Germans going to stay on top of Husni in Cuba?" Sammy asked. "We sure as hell can't."

"I have no idea. Probably not. They probably don't have the assets," Willi said.

"Let's open the other DHS document," I said to Judy. The noise in the room stopped.

It was similar to the first one in that it was an official Department of Homeland Security document and was heavily redacted with black smears at the front end. The legible part read:

GOG advises that computer seized at the Hamburg
home of Kaiserslautern suicide bomber Rifat Ali Esaat
contained "numerous" Google Earth maps of "several"
Virginia and Maryland locations.

"That's pretty damned vague," Sammy said, echoing my thoughts
perfectly.

"Yes and no," I said. "The 'Virginia' part isn't vague at all. The 'where
in Virginia' part is what's vague."

"That's what I meant," Sammy said.

It was rare indeed that I got an advantage in a discussion with Sammy.

Chapter Twenty-Seven

The thermometer outside our living-room window showed a temperature of twenty-two degrees when I glanced at it before heading out to Prince William Forest Park. The interior of my Explorer felt even colder, but that was probably an illusion. And it warmed up quickly as soon as I hit I-95. The road into the park was blocked with a couple of Park Service vehicles. A uniformed Secret Service officer inspected my badge. A Park Ranger told me where to park—in a small parking lot about a half-mile down the road. My watch read 7:50. Kehoe would be there in ten minutes, plus or minus a couple of seconds. His chopper had probably already landed somewhere on the base at Quantico. I'd learned that he was punctual to a fault. Sure enough, nine minutes and thirty seconds later, a small convoy of black SUVs pulled into the parking lot. My high-school running mate wore a purple Holy Cross hoody, a black ski jock, dark shades, and black running tights as he emerged from one of the armor-plated gas-guzzlers.

"Hey Alan," he said. "Let's make the first mile the warm-up. Then we can slow down a bit for the next five."

"Sounds good. I'd like to finish the six miles without having a Park Service Ranger having to pick up my carcass off the road two or three miles out," I said.

We started running.

Three Secret Service guys jumped in front of us and three more fell in behind. They were all in running gear and didn't look like they'd have any trouble staying with us. But I missed the Marine Corps escorts we had on base.

"Okay—you first," he said. "You sent the face-time meatball message. What's up?"

"You already know what's up," I said. "You sent me the DHS papers."

"Right. I know that. But there must be more. Do you guys have a reaction already?"

"We do. And there is more," I said. "The guy flying in to Cuba. Al-Husni. We actually saw him in Germany. In person. In a very sketchy bar in Hamburg. And the word, 'Virginia,' tumbled from his mouth. Not once but twice. All three of us heard it—two of our analysts and I."

"Shit. I'm not liking what I'm hearing. There was an NCTC blurb that said that the Arabs in Hamburg had Virginia and Maryland maps on their computer."

"Not only that," I said. "My guy on the ground in Germany said that some of his German sources are saying that German SIGINT has been picking up 'Virginia' and 'Maryland' in their Arabic chatter."

"What does that really mean?" he asked.

"It means a bunch of things," I said. "For starters, it means that the Germans probably don't have enough cleared Arabic speakers to translate everything they collect. I'm guessing that we're in the same boat, by the way. So they—the Germans—probably concentrate on high-level communications. Translating embassy-to-ministry stuff. And traffic between or among high-value targets. They don't have enough eyeballs and brains to translate the lower-level, everyday stuff. So they just track the volume of the riffraff traffic and screen it for key words that are recognizable—like 'Berlin' and 'München' and 'Virginia' and 'Maryland.' As well as other, readily recognizable hot-button words or phrases such as 'explosives,' 'martyrdom,' 'death to infidels,' and like. Then they send up reports saying that the 'chatter' is up or down—meaning traffic volume—and it contains the following key words. Like 'Virginia' and 'Maryland.' And that's what Willi's source told him. And on top of all that, one of the smart *BIAS* women picked up the phrase, 'Revenge of the Muslim Martyrs,' in a Hamburg bar."

"So what's your bottom line?" he asked.

"For starters, it probably wouldn't hurt to float that phrase—'Revenge of the Muslim Martyrs'—into the Intel Community as a key word or phrase. That could help with relevant communications traffic."

We hit the bottom of a long hill, ran across a bridge over a gin-clear creek and started up the hill on the other side. I was warm except for my face. My nose was streaming. I used the cotton gloves to clear my upper lip.

"The rest of the bottom line comes in two parts," I said. "First of all, we need to worry about something possibly in the D.C. metro area. Maryland

and Virginia. Although that's far from a lock at present. Second of all, I would like some sort of emergency money for *BIAS* to run operations on the ground. Here. In the U.S.A. and in Canada. Like six people—minimum."

"I'm going to give you the same answer as I did the last time we had this conversation," he said. "Not only 'no,' but 'hell no!' There's no way that I can authorize that. It'd have to involve Congress—both committees— and the *BIAS* cat would be out of the bag in a New York minute. Then you'd be back teaching high school algebra, and I'd probably be in the Fort Leavenworth Federal Prison. No way!"

Teaching high school algebra was beginning to take on a definite appeal at this point. On the other hand, I'm sure the idea of a cell at Leavenworth was not.

We had finally gotten to some more or less level ground where the running was more relaxed.

"I think I get the fucking message," I said without the usual decorousness that adorned my speech with the president.

"That's what I pay you for," he said. "What else?"

"Here's where it gets fuzzy," I said. "I—we—have no idea about this guy al-Husni. The guy who's going to Cuba. While he's been in Germany, the Germans knew where he was and what he was doing or with whom he was doing it. And who his friends were. More or less. And they shared that info with us. More or less. But now the bastard's going into a black hole in Cuba. We'll have no idea what he's doing or with whom he's doing it. Sammy thinks he's coming to the States. 'Gut-think.' But Sammy's gut-think is the best there is—after Maria's, that is. And he also thinks that al-Husni is the Papa Bear of a plot to blow stuff up in the D.C. metro area. As in the District, Maryland, and Virginia."

The sun had grown warmer. I pulled the watch cap off my head. The president and I continued to plod along the beautiful road.

"Jesus Christ," he said. "I can jack up the Coast Guard and ICE in south Florida. In case this guy tries to come into the country through the Keys. There's no guarantee that we'd catch him, but we'd at least have a chance. If he wants to come through Mexico, I don't think we even have a chance. Maybe we do, but it's minuscule. We'd have to get lucky. Very lucky."

"Is there any way we can track him while he's in Cuba?" I asked.

"I'm not sure," the president said. "I don't think so. Unless he starts using a sat phone. Or even a cell phone. Which he probably won't. These assholes are smarter than that. But I'll give it a shot."

We finished the run—fairly hard—spent. All six miles. It was like we needed to burn off some stress. I was out of fuel and I think Kehoe was, too.

"You can eat up a storm tomorrow," he said. "After that run. Happy Thanksgiving."

"You can too, Keys," I said. "Is Frannie slaving away in the kitchen?"

"She may be. She's out at Camp David. She said she was going to make a pie and a bunch of brownies."

"My whole family is glad that you pardoned the turkey," I said.

"I'm glad you're glad. And your family. But the Kehoe family *is* eating turkey tomorrow. With all the trimmings."

He grinned as we shook hands.

"Happy Thanksgiving. Enjoy the bird, giblets and all."

Chapter Twenty-eight

I'm absolutely paranoid about telephones. I waited till my SUV was clear of the base at Quantico on I-95—there are some weird things that happen to cell phone transmissions there—and called Darps's mobile.

"Yo," he answered.

"Grab Judy and the two of you set up a meeting," I said. "Like in twenty minutes. I should be there by then. The Germany crowd. Ashleigh and Samantha and Willi. Invite Sammy, too. And either Mike or Luke or both. It'll be a brainstormer, so it might last a while."

It went without saying that Darps would be there as well. My alter ego.

"Roger," he said. "See you in twenty." We hung up.

I got there in just under twenty minutes. All invitees were in the Paycheck conference room. Normally, I don't run meetings wearing sweaty running clothes, and normally I don't schedule them for times like the morning before a big holiday, but we were way outside of normal.

I didn't say anything about having just run ten clicks with *Cheetah*, but I'm pretty sure they all had that part of it figured out.

"It's all starting to come together," I said, to lead things off. "And it looks like Sammy's gut-think may well be right on target. The guy we saw in Germany, al-Husni is, (a) the probable ringleader of the Ramstein bombing, (b) is going to Cuba, and (c) was mumbling about 'Virginia' and 'revenge of the Muslim martyrs' within earshot of Ashleigh and Samantha when we were there. Then there's what Willi heard in Germany about German-intercepts and Arabic chatter. More Virginia. And Maryland. And then, there's the NCTC stuff on the Arabs' computers in Hamburg. Google Earth maps of Virginia and Maryland."

I paused and sipped coffee.

"And if all that isn't bad enough, *Cheetah* basically told me to go screw myself when I surfaced the idea of putting *BIAS* boots on the ground in CONUS. Except, if anything, he was more emphatic than that."

"Wow," Sammy said.

"He also wasn't very confident about the Feds' picking up al-Husni's trail, either while he's in Cuba or, if and when, he tries to come into the States," I added.

"Well, shit," Darps said, sounding disgusted. "It sounds like we're hosed in, let me count the ways.

"First of all, we don't know specific locations in Virginia and/or Maryland that Husni and his buddies are eyeballing as possible targets. We don't know who his boys are. Much less where they are. We don't know where the hell Husni is, except that he has a reservation for Cuba this week. We don't know when the reservation is for. He could be on the way here, for that matter. And we don't know that. We don't know whether the Cubans know what's going on. We don't know what the Arab-Germans or German-Arabs are plotting—a bomb in a mall or ricin in the D.C. Metro, or something else. And we don't know when they're planning to do whatever they're planning to do. Talk about a clean fucking slate."

"Okay." I said. "We're hosed all around. But we need to start to figure out a way to break out. As in identifying some realistic goals. And throwing in a little priority."

"Ahem," coughed Sammy. "It looks like we need to know specific locations, for starters. The surfacing of the words 'Virginia' and 'Maryland' doesn't tell us squat. Virginia is a big state. Maryland is not, but, like Virginia, it's a target-rich environment. And the targets are spread out. There's Annapolis. There's Camp David. There's Norfolk. There's Arlington. We need specificity."

I scrawled, *"Location, location location!"* on the Smart board in red.

Ashleigh jumped in with her silky-soft voice. "Is there any way the Germans can give us a *list* of the places they got from the Hamburg bombers' computers. The *Google Earth* stuff that they were looking at in Virginia and Maryland?"

"I can try my sources," Willi said. "I'll have to go back to Germany to do that, though. Email and cell phones won't work on something that sensitive. Maybe going back through DHS and/or NCTC would be faster."

I scrawled some more. *"Willi & Germans??"*

"Okay, Willi. We have to do that. Sorry. Don't cancel any Thanksgiving Day plans. But head back to Germany sometime over the weekend. And see what you can do to run those locations down on Monday."

I turned to Mike and Luke.

"Is there any way you guys could get DHS or NCTC to refine the Google Earth locations they found on the bombers' computers in Germany?" I asked.

They looked at each other.

"We can give it a shot," Luke said.

"But my guess is that you'll have to go back to *Cheetah* to get that kind of info," Mike said. "If it's even available at all. Maybe DHS didn't even get it from the Germans."

"Give it a shot. Let me know. If you strike out, I'll go back to the boss man himself. Meantime Willi will be trying in Germany. Unless you guys can get us some hard data before he leaves."

I went back to the Smart board and wrote, *"DHS/NCTC? Luke/Mike? Cheetah?"*

"Ahem," Sammy said again. We all turned toward him. "We know that al-Husni is bound for Cuba and maybe is already there," he said. "We think that he may be bound for the good ole USA. But we don't know who his friends are. Much less where they are. If he's the mastermind of a bombing operation—which he probably is—who's the trigger man? Or men? Or women? And where is he? Or they?"

A moment of silence followed Sammy's question.

"Willi," I said, feeling like I was being unfair to lay so much on him. "When you're back in Deutschland, can you see if you can get the IDs of any German-Arabs that traveled with Husni and/or get an ID on some contact that he might have in Cuba or here in the good ole USA?"

Willi shook his head.

"I'm not even sure that I can float those kinds of questions without getting my ass thrown out of the country," he said.

"Well, keep your ears open," I said, weakly.

I looked at my watch. It was pushing noon.

"Okay," I said. "I'm on the clock but the rest of you are off. Don't turn your phones off and have a nice Thanksgiving with your families or whatevers. We're back in here Friday starting at 0800."

I'd originally planned on following Federal guidelines and giving everybody Friday off. But it just wasn't in the cards this year.

Before he left, Darps reminded me of our date tomorrow morning for a high school football game in the Shenandoah Valley. His nephew would be starting at quarterback.

After everyone had gone, I walked over to Alfredo's and bought an Italian cold-cut sandwich and a cream soda and took them back to the office. I had to unlock the place and deactivate the alarms when I got back. I guessed that Willi was either making his reservations for Germany from home or had already made them. I savored the silence in the empty office, munched on the sandwich, and scribbled random thoughts on an engineering pad. One series of thoughts was a random walk of events: al-Husni leaves Germany—al-Husni arrives in Cuba—alone or accompanied—al-Husni leaves Cuba—alone or with comrades—al-Husni arrives in USA or Mexico. I swore to myself. We just flat didn't have enough information. I doubted if hanging around Ripley Hall would change that. Maybe talking with Maria would reveal some useful insights. I locked up, set the alarms, and walked home.

Chapter Twenty-Nine

There is a little town called Cladwell's Gap in the foothills of the Blue Ridge Mountains west of Chestertown. A Catholic boys boarding school is located there, named the Mission of Mary Academy. My classmate and shipmate, Darps, has a nephew who attends Mission of Mary. The nephew and his family are from Juneau, Alaska. Which makes it tough and a rare thing for the immediate family to cheer him on at football games in Virginia. Darps invited Maria, Elizabeth, and me to join him and his wife, Annie, to attend a "Turkey Bowl" football game on Thanksgiving morning between Mission of Mary and their cross-town rivals, Cladwell High School. Their nephew, the quarterback, was a junior named Will Plunkett.

Darps and I had arranged to meet in the parking lot of Mission of Mary at 9:30, thirty minutes before kickoff, which we did. The morning was crisp, bright, and cold in Cladwell's Gap. In the parking lot, we could hear a marching band from inside the stadium. They were playing *The Bells of Saint Mary's*. No doubt it was the home team band performing. Darps, the sly devil, had brought a thermos of Bloody Marys.

"For the honor of the home team *and* in deference to Elizabeth's tender age, I also brought along *Virgin* Marys," he said, handing each of us a plastic tumbler.

"Just the healthy juice with a few benign spices—no vile, vicious vodka," he said, pouring Mr. T's bloody Mary mix directly into Elizabeth's glass.

"For the rest of us sinners, however," he said, leaving the sentence unfinished. He poured from the thermos and filled our cups with reddish liquid that I could almost see through. Finally, he took out a sandwich bag from which he extracted lime wedges, which he dropped into our drinks. I took a small sip of mine.

"Arghh," I said. "Did you think you were mixing vodka martinis and the Mr. T was the vermouth?"

117

"Something like that," he said. "Cheers."

It was a satisfying—if not a very exciting—game. The Mission of Mary Grizzlies thrashed the Cladwell Cougars pretty thoroughly. I think the final score was thirty-five to seven. Darps's and Annie's nephew, Will, threw two TD passes, ran for another touchdown, and chatted with us after the game. When the young man called Darps, "Uncle Darpley," it amused me mightily. Elizabeth had her picture taken with the handsome quarterback who had grass stains on his white-and-blue uniform and his arm around her shoulders. Her grin may have raised the outdoor temperature in Cladwell's Gap a few degrees.

As we were walking to the cars, my phone trembled. I glanced at the caller ID and thumbed it on.

"Hi, Luke."

"Hi. Got something. Where are you?"

"Leaving a high school football game in Cladwell's Gap. Should be home in about an hour."

"How 'bout I meet you at your house in an hour? That wouldn't screw up your dinner plans or anything?" he asked.

"No. Not a problem. How about yours?"

"No. It'll only take a couple of minutes."

"Okay. See you in an hour."

Well! I thought. *I wonder what the hell that is all about.*

I wondered all the way back to Chestertown.

Chapter Thirty

I half expected to see Luke sitting on our front stoop as I turned into our driveway, but then I reflected that Luke would never make his presence obvious like that.

Our kitchen stove has a timer, and we had set it to start roasting the turkey an hour before we were planning to be home, so one of the world's greatest aromas was wafting through the air of our old, white colonial on Prince Henry Street. I hadn't finished savoring the smell of roasting turkey when the doorbell rang.

It was Luke, wearing a Baltimore Ravens jacket.

"Wanna go for a walk?" he asked.

"Sure," I said. "But you're welcome to come in for a Thanksgiving drink."

"Thanks. Let's walk. I need to make this quick. Nothing against your hospitality, but a woman, kid, and dinner await me. And maybe out in the open air is safer than indoors."

I got his drift. I still had my jacket on from Cladwell's Gap.

"I'll be back in ten or fifteen minutes," I called into the house and then left with Luke. We headed north on Prince Henry.

"NCTC says they have nothing on the Google Earth locations on the Hamburg computers, other than 'Maryland' and 'Virginia.' That's the bad news," he said.

"Then, there's some *good* news?" I asked.

"I think so," he said.

"Tell me," I said.

"A guy in DHS told me that the Italians have a red-hot source in Cuba. And this source told them—the Italians—that al-Husni landed in Havana yesterday evening. There were three people with him. Two younger dudes.

119

And a chick. He went from the airport to some place on the northern shore called *Palizada*. It's basically a ghost town. The three other people—from Germany—went there as well. Then, all four of them disappeared. That's according to the Italians and their source, about whom we know nothing. That's all, folks."

We turned left on Phillip Street. Chestertown's streets were pretty deserted. Folks were inside watching crappy NFL games or starting to pig out. I thought for a couple of seconds.

"Okay," I said. "We know more than we did yesterday. Al-Husni arrived in Cuba. There may be two guys and a woman with him. That's a big step, I guess. At this point, we're not sure where the bastards are. Possibilities would seem to be Cuba, on their way here, or here in the States already. And we need to hope that the boss man's orders to the Coast Guard and Immigration and Customs Enforcement will result in them being picked up, if and when they come this way. Unfortunately, the man himself said that the odds on that happening were pretty long."

We walked in silence. The Chestertown air was growing colder, due no doubt to a fresh breeze out of the northeast.

"Let's hope Willi picks up something in Germany about the Google Earth maps on the dirt bags' computers," I said.

Luke stopped.

"Amen," he said. I recognized his car parked next to us.

"Anything else?" he asked.

"No. But thanks for this. And happy Thanksgiving to you and the family. See you tomorrow," I said.

We shook hands and I walked home. I wondered about the other two guys and the chick that appeared to be accompanying al-Husni.

At home, our Thanksgiving dinner was fabulous.

Chapter Thirty-One

Major el-Shahawi wore casual civilian clothes when he went to Havana's Jose Marti International Airport. Khaki slacks, a black polo shirt, and a Florida Marlins' black ball cap. Dark glasses. He took the bus. He went only to see, to look. To confirm the Egyptian's arrival and transfer. And perhaps those of his associates. Communications had been spotty, given the delicate nature of Yemen's alliance with the United States and the El Qaeda direction of the operation.

The Condor Airlines flight from Frankfurt was on time. He watched as passengers cleared Immigration and Passport Control. He spotted the man from Germany. He was surprised at how old the man looked. But it was definitely he. Mehmet al-Husni. Code-named *Saladdin.* The Egyptian. He watched as *el viejo* went to the bank of cabs. Three other people approached the taxis. They appeared to be two men and a woman. All much younger than al-Husni. The old man got into one cab, and the three younger people got into the next car in the queue. They left more or less in tandem. El-Shahawi recalled a classified cable that listed three Arabs—two males and a female—who would accompany Saladdin. He left the terminal and took a bus back to his flat. When he let himself in, Laura was there. She had a soap opera on the TV and sipped from a glass of white wine. El-Shahawi closed and locked the door.

"I have to leave. For the countryside. *Palizada,*" He said.

"When?" she asked.

"In the morning. Early morning."

"Well, then, we still have some time. When will you return?"

"In about a week," he said.

"Let us put our time to good use," she said, standing up. "Do you have any champagne?"

"No. But there's cognac. Martell."

"Even better," she said. She unbuttoned her top. He reached for two glasses and the Martell.

"What will you be doing in *Palizada*? she asked.

She unfastened her bra and let it drop to the floor.

"Turning a plan into action—across the water from *Palizada,* " he said as he pulled his shirt over his head.

"Don't forget the cognac," she said.

It was 4:30 when the alarm on el-Shahawi's mobile phone shrieked. His hangover was epic fierce. His eyes burned. His mouth was dry. His torso was slimed with cold sweat. His head throbbed. In the bed beside him, Laura, snored gently. He felt like slapping her on her naked ass, but feared what would happen if and when she awoke. He cursed silently in Arabic and climbed stiffly out of the musky bed.

A taxi was scheduled to pick him up at five, while it was still dark. He dressed in the same clothes he'd worn to the airport yesterday. He checked two small duffels and a shiny backpack, which he'd already packed. One duffel contained changes of clothes and extra money in Cuban pesos and U.S. dollars. The second held more clothes and a Russian 9-mm Makarov pistol with two magazines of ammunition. The shiny backpack contained grocery bags of artillery propellant supplied by Captain Antonio Diaz. There were also three American fly-fishing vests, a reel of detonation cord, and several string-activated blasting caps. And several glass-and-steel chemical fuzes. Finally, there were two fat rolls of silver-gray duct tape.

El-Shahawi was thirsty. He took a bottle of water from the tiny fridge and sucked it down. He thought dimly of last night. *I guess being with a real woman has its price,* he thought. He silently vowed to go easier on the cognac the next time. He took the duffels and the backpack and went downstairs and out the door to meet the cab, his head still aching mercilessly.

Amazingly, the cab was already there, its motor running.

"Palizada," he said as he climbed into the back of the taxi.

The driver nodded and they left.

A little over an hour later, daylight had begun to wash over the terrain. The taxi stopped in front of a small building that appeared to be deserted. El-Shahawi gave the driver one hundred U.S. dollars and got out of the cab. He was sure that his superiors had already paid the man, but the driver pocketed the notes, saying only *"Gracias, Señor,"* before sputtering off.

The sun wasn't quite up yet but it was growing lighter. The Yemeni removed the Makarov from the bag and made sure that there was a round in the chamber. He tucked the weapon into the waistband of his trousers at the small of his back. He went up to the front door of the building, carrying the two duffels and the backpack. Suddenly, three people appeared from around corners of the building. They wielded AK-47 assault rifles.

"Put your hands on your head!" one of them snapped.

"Fuck your mother!" el Shahawi snarled in Arabic. "Don't you swine give me any shit or I'll blow us all to bits. I have enough explosive here to level everything within fifty meters. Including us! You'll burn in hell, which is where you belong anyway. Put those fucking weapons down!"

Even though he'd been warned, el Shahawi had trouble grappling with the truth. One of these swine was a female.

The thugs glanced at one another, but did not lower the weapons. El-Shahawi reached swiftly behind his back, pulled out the Makarov and shot the middle gunmen in the groin. The man screamed. His weapon clattered to the sidewalk, and he fell to the ground, clutching his crotch. Blood streamed between his fingers and streamed across the dirt. El-Shahawi brandished the handgun at the other two. The latter raised their hands, comically holding the AK-47s in the air in their right hands.

"Drop the weapons, you shit-eating dogs," el-Shahawi snapped.

The man and the woman complied, and the assault rifles dropped to the ground. The man with the bloody crotch continued to moan.

"Get on your knees and put your hands on your heads or I'll shoot your crotch off, too, you pigs," he ordered.

The two obeyed.

"Okay, it's time for you two animals to cooperate. Who the hell are you? I don't have much patience and you know already that I won't hesitate to use this," he said, brandishing the handgun.

"W-we came from Germany. With Saladdin. Mehmet Baba. For security. His security. And for the mission in America. We are executing the mission in America," the kneeling man stammered, speaking Syrian-accented Arabic. The bleeding man moaned.

Major el-Shahawi could scarcely believe his ears.

"Fools! Imbeciles! I am el-Yemeni, Husni's handler in Cuba!" el-Shahawi said, using his code name.

"Where is al-Husni?" he demanded.

"Inside," the woman whispered.

"Is he so old that he sleeps through gunfire?"

"No, he does not," said a voice from inside the house. "But he does have a loaded assault rifle and it is aimed at your chest."

"Allah be praised! He lives! Let's have a fucking gun battle right here and now. Then the Cubans will swoop down on us, capture whoever is still alive, torture us, and this fiasco of an operation will be totally blown. If it's not already."

"I am sorry. These people are young. Not experienced. Except for Ayşa. She is a veteran. Besides, you were twenty minutes early."

"Did living amongst all those Germans for so many years make you so anal-fixated that you get suspicious and nervous when a contact in Cuba arrives a little early? Allah, Allah!"

Al-Husni emerged from the building. He still held the Kalashnikov, but its muzzle was pointed at the ground.

"It appears that we are faced with a decision," el-Shahawi said. "Do we continue with this fucking operation or not?"

"Praise Allah! Of course we continue. Why would we not?" Husni asked.

"Because of these morons on the ground here," el-Shahawi answered, gesturing with the handgun toward the kneeling man and woman. "Veterans or not. They are major complications."

They all heard the engine of an approaching vehicle.

"The decision time is upon us," el-Shahawi said. "Our transport is here."

Chapter Thirty-Two

An ancient green Ford pickup wheezed to a stop. Tariq, the sergeant from el-Shahawi's office at the Yemeni Embassy, was at the wheel. He turned off the motor and climbed out of the truck. He wore Levis, a black and white Yankees t-shirt and Nike running shoes. He raised his eyebrows in curiosity.

"Tariq, we have a small disaster on our hands that we need to clean up. Pick up the Kalashnikovs, clear and lock them, and put them in the cab," el-Shahawi commanded.

He gestured with the pistol toward the kneeling man and woman.

"You two. Stand up. Put your bleeding whore-son comrade in the bed of the truck and then get in with him."

El-Shahawi turned to the older man.

"Mehmet Baba, kindly clear and lock your weapon and get in the truck. We're going forward with the operation. Tariq, we will go to the camp as planned."

It was crowded in the cab of the pickup with three men, three assault rifles, two duffels, and a backpack. Tariq guided the truck along a bumpy, dirt road through thick jungle. The sorry condition of the road and the heat made the ride even more uncomfortable. The wounded man in back moaned and whined for about fifteen minutes and then was silent. One of the other passengers in back wailed. Major el-Shahawi couldn't tell whether it was the male or the female. He cursed quietly and frequently. Thirty minutes later, Tariq brought the pickup to a halt. A narrow path led off the road and between the trees. In the distance, down the path, they could see the blue waters of the Atlantic.

"Tariq, help the morons in back get their wounded comrade to the camp. Drag him, carry him, roll him—I don't give a shit."

The man and woman sitting in back were weeping.

"Yusuf has become a *shahid*, a martyr. He's dead," the woman said.

"So much the better," el-Shahawi said. "No doubt he is feasting on the fruits of Paradise and our task just became easier."

The man el-Shahawi had shot had turned gray. His lips were blue and his eyes were half-open. His upper incisors protruded. The blood around his crotch had dried and turned nearly black. It was obvious that he wasn't breathing. It was obvious that he was dead.

"What will we do with him?" his male companion asked with another sob.

"*He* is in Paradise. You two swine will help Tariq carry *this* to the sea," he said. "Then we'll let Allah and the sea take care of things. What are your names?"

"Ayşa," said the woman. She pronounced it Eye-shuh.

"Farouk," said the man.

Thirty meters inland of the high-water mark on the sandy beach was a military-style tent with a camouflage pattern, surrounded by coconut palm trees. Tariq had outfitted it over a period of several weeks with canned goods, bottled water, two lanterns, and a small camp stove. There were four folding cots in the tent. Each one had a folded blanket on top.

"Wrap the corpse in a blanket. Put the Kalashnikovs in there with it to weigh it down. Then use the duct tape to close it up tightly. When it is ready, take it into the sea."

He glanced at the ocean. The surf was low, wavelets of between one and two feet, breaking on the wet sand.

"The tide is almost dead low. Take the corpse beyond the waves. That way, with the Kalashnikovs weighing it down, it will stay on the bottom and out of sight. Unless the fish take it away."

The younger man continued to weep. The woman was silent. Al-Husni remained silent but occasionally appeared to be praying. He fingered worry beads.

Tariq unfolded one of the blankets and spread it on the ground next to the corpse. El-Shahawi groped in the backpack and produced one of the big rolls of tape.

"Use the minimum you need to bind the blanket. We need the tape for the vests," he said, handing the roll of tape to Tariq. "The fish and crabs will have the blanket open within minutes anyway," he added.

"Now, Mehmet Baba, you and I need to build some martyrs' vests," el-Shahawi said to the older man. "The vests of *true* martyrs, not like this worthless piece of shit who put our mission at such grave risk."

He unzipped the shiny backpack that he'd brought and took out the artillery propellant in the plastic grocery bags.

Tariq supervised as Farouk and Ayşa lifted the blanket-wrapped corpse and carried it to the high water mark. Silently, they put their burden down on the wet sand and removed their shoes. Then they picked the body up and waded into the low surf. When they were waist deep, Tariq said, "It's enough. Let it go."

"Would you like some Coca-Cola, Mehmet Baba?" el-Shahawi asked the older man. "If not, we'll have to pour it out on the ground."

El-Shahawi took a red can from one of several six-packs that were stacked on the tent floor. He popped the top and took a swig. His hangover was still raging deep within his skull and the Coke tasted good, even though it was warm. He belched and took another swig.

"Help yourself. I assume you'll need only two vests since that pig is now sleeping with the fishes. We need four of the large cans and six of the small ones for the each vest."

"I need three vests. Three targets. The other *shahid* is in America," the old man said, taking a can of Coke. "But he probably does not remember. He received his martyr indoctrination seven or eight years ago. He is our backup."

El-Shahawi offered Coke to Tariq and the young Arabs when they approached the tent.

"Drink it up or pour it out," he said. "We need the empty cans."

El-Shahawi and al-Husni put the vests together. They packed artillery propellant in the empty soda cans, which they had rinsed and dried. They used el- Shahawi's Swiss Army knife to punch holes through the sides of the aluminum cans. They threaded detonating cord through the cans of explosive. They then used the duct tape to attach a thick coat of nails and small screws to all of the explosive-filled cans. Under el-Shahawi's supervision, they used more duct tape to bind the cans of explosive together and then packed the cans into the pockets of the fishing vests.

"Here are two fuzes for each vest," el-Shahawi said to al-Husni. "When clipped to the detonating cord and activated, they will cause the det cord to explode after a three-second delay. Which will cause the propellant to explode immediately. The second fuze is a spare in case the first one fails. The vests should be fail-safe."

"I understand that, of course," Husni said. "But I'm not familiar with these pellets. I'm more accustomed to *plastique*. Like C-Four."

"These 'pellets' will send a fifty-kilogram artillery projectile thirty kilometers down range. Packed in a vest with a coating of shrapnel, they'll do massive damage. A roomful of two or three hundred American teenagers having lunch. A crowd of a hundred fifty waiting tourists at the world-famous Washington Monument. A courtyard packed with five hundred tourists and over two thousand midshipmen. And the shrapnel is lethal. These vests will be more than adequate. Perhaps a few of the people in the target zones will survive, but most will die a painful death. Do you have contact with the *shahid* in America?"

"Not since arriving here. He is in Virginia. I'll contact him at the proper time."

"Be careful of your communications. They should be minimal to non-existent. Abu-Sayyed will send me a coded text when you arrive in Florida. What about them?" he asked, nodding toward the young man and woman. "Are they reliable? The woman? As martyrs?"

"They are very devout."

"Well and good. But they all but shit themselves at the first bit of gunfire this morning. As soldiers, they're as useless as tits on a male goat. I'll be glad to see the last of them here in Cuba. *Inshallah,* they won't fuck up again in America."

"They will not. But we need two martyrs plus the other *shahid* for the mission to succeed. Ayşa, the woman is extremely devout and will draw less attention approaching one of the targets. Farouk, the young man, is a bit of a question mark. I'm not sure he has the spine of a martyr. But they are ready. So am I. The third *shahid*, the one in America, is reported to be devout and courageous. I hope so. We should go soon."

"When you say that Farouk may not have 'the spine of a martyr,' together with what I've seen of their cowardice, it gives me pause."

He made a decision.

"Tariq," he called.

"Yes sir, major."

"Will that truck make it to Havana and back today?"

"Yes sir," he answered. "It may need a little babying, but it will make it back and forth. In about four hours."

"Okay. That's it. Take the truck back to Havana. Go to Laura's flat—I don't care what time it is. If she's not there, call her at work. Take my mobile. Tell her to give you a dozen Xanax tablets. These swine need something to settle their fucking nerves. Especially that slime dog Farouk. And Laura has the Xanax. She will give you the pills. Then get your ass and the pills back here as fast as you can."

Tariq saluted and jogged toward the truck.

"When do we leave for Florida?" al-Husni asked.

"Pretty soon. It's eleven hundred now. Your boat will pick you up here on the beach at twenty-one thirty. After dark. It should have you at Marathon in the Florida Keys by zero four hundred. A vehicle will meet you there. Perhaps you should try and get some sleep."

"Perhaps after some lunch," al-Husni said.

El-Shahawi handed him a backpack.

"This bag is waterproof. It is nylon coated with polyurethane. From L. L. Bean. They are quite famous for high-quality sporting equipment. It will keep the vests dry during your transit."

Conversation on the beach ceased. Gradually, all four people wandered into the open tent and rummaged around in the canned food. El-Shahawi selected a can of tuna and some salted crackers. He took a plastic flask out of one of his duffels. The vodka was warm and that added to the burning sensation in the back of his throat as he swallowed. He took another swig before eating the tuna and crackers. Then he took another pull from the flask to rid his mouth of the salty dryness.

"Farouk," he called. "Put all the garbage in a trash bag and bury it in the sand, well away from the tent. Allah knows what sort of creature will come out of the jungle in search of it."

One by one they finished snacking and flopped on the cots. They were all sweating but dozed off nonetheless.

El-Shahawi woke to the sound of the wheezing pickup. He sat up. His watch said 5:35.

"I got the pills, major," Tariq announced as he dismounted from the truck. "Plus I had a chicken sandwich and a beer while you were eating this rubbish."

He grinned broadly.

"You miserable bastard," el-Shahawi replied.

Tariq laughed and held out an envelope.

"Xanax," he said.

El-Shahawi wondered if Tariq had fucked Laura while he was getting the pills. He wouldn't put it past either of them.

Farouk, Ayşa, and al-Husni climbed stiffly out of the cots. Al-Husni wandered into the woods. Ayşa and Farouk began rummaging around in the canned food box. The sun had lost much of its intensity as it lowered in the western sky. El-Shahawi took another pull from the plastic flask.

Al-Husni emerged from the woods, zipping his fly.

"Mehmet Baba," el-Shahawi called out. "I have something that will help with your mission."

He gestured toward the water's edge. The two men walked toward the lapping waves. The others paid the two older men no heed. El-Shahawi took the envelope from a pocket.

"These are pills," he said softly. "An anxiety medication. I think you should let your *shahids* have access to them a couple of hours before they try to execute their missions."

"They are trained to face down anxiety against all odds," al-Husni said. "Allah will assist them."

"I know, I know," el-Shahawi retorted. "But this is the twenty-first century. A little aid from medical science could put further guarantees on the success of your operation. Take them. Use them. There are enough pills here that, should one or more of the *shahids* become dangerously anxious before carrying out the operation, this will calm them down. Add to their focus."

He handed the older man the envelope.

"Put this in the waterproof rucksack with the vests for the transit so they'll stay dry," he said.

The four men smoked in silence as night fell. Ayşa lay down on one of the cots and appeared to sleep.

The boat's approach was silent and dark. From beyond the gentle surf a light winked on for about one second and then off. Then it winked on and off briefly three times in quick succession. The letter *B* in Morse code. El-

Shahawi and the smuggler had arranged the signal when they had closed the deal for the boat trip. He answered, using a flashlight, sending the same signal.

It took less than ten minutes for the boat to approach to within fifty meters of the beach where it stopped and idled. Tariq slid an old rowboat with shipped oars across the sand and into the water. He waded a few steps through the gentle wavelets breaking on the dark beach.

"This way, Mehmet Baba," he called, softly. "Climb in. Brace yourself on my shoulder. Sit there."

Husni and his younger companions waded through the shallow plashing surf and climbed into the rowboat, al-Husni and Farouk taking the seat in the stern. The young man held the L.L. Bean backpack containing the loaded vests in his lap. Ayşa sat in the narrow seat in the bow. Tariq climbed in after them, almost tipping the rowboat over in the process. He took his place on the middle seat and used an oar to push them into deeper water. He glanced over his shoulder, focused on the silhouette of the larger vessel offshore and began to row. A few minutes later, he brought the rowboat alongside.

"Here are your passengers," he said, in English. "Here's your first half of the payment," he said, handing up a plastic food storage bag holding twelve thousand, five hundred dollars in U.S. currency. "We'll deliver the second half in Havana as we planned after we learn that these martyrs have made it safely to Florida."

A man in the larger boat reached out to help the three passengers aboard and take the money package. As soon as they were aboard, the hum of the boat's jets rose in pitch. Seconds later, it was gone. Tariq rowed the old boat ashore.

Chapter Thirty-Three

Friday was—what can I say—the day after Thanksgiving. The troops came in to Ripley Hall, as instructed. We worked, or tried to. Everybody whaled through email and various websites and blogs, and I called a heads-together meeting at 10:30. The Smart board was blank. I put up the words, "Al-Husni confirmed in Cuba."

"Does that mean he's just disappeared there?" Ashleigh asked.

"Not quite," I said. I scrawled, *"Palizada???"* on the Smart board. "He may very well be here."

Darps pulled up a map of Cuba and pointed the mouse arrow at *Palizada* on the northern coast.

We brainstormed some—shot the shit is more like it—and then I sent everybody home.

"Keep your phones turned on and handy. We'll meet again in here tomorrow morning. I'll try and make it quick unless we've got some new info or guidance." Nobody let the door hit them in the ass on the way out.

I took a detour north to Fat Harry's on my way home. I thought a dietary change of pace was in order. So I'd called in an order for a pepperoni-and-mushroom pizza. I rounded out the order with an antipasto platter.

I greeted Fat Harry with my usual, *"Es selaamu aleikum!"* and he responded in kind: *"Waa aleikum es salaam!"* But his heart didn't seem to be in it.

"Twenty-five, ninety-five, Alan," he said. I gave him a ten and a twenty and said, "We're good."

"How's Khalil doing?" I asked, hoping to draw him out of his dark thoughts to a more pleasant topic.

He frowned and shook his head.

"I don't know," he said. "He has a girlfriend; a beautiful American girl. He has a full-time teacher contract for after the Christmas holidays. He does the high school substitute thing almost every day. But there's something wrong. One day, he comes in here and is all smiles, joking, everything is great. Then two days later, he walks in and everything is dark and gloomy."

I wondered if Fat Harry meant "Gloom and doom."

"But then again," he continued, "He walks in two days later, eats a steak bomb and is as happy as the fat cat that ate the canary. I'm suspecting that there are tensions with the girlfriend."

"Stranger things than that happen with girlfriends," I offered. "As people say, 'issues' develop. Who knows? *Inshallah*, Khalil and the girlfriend can work through them and he will stop having the mood swings."

Hafez has been married for around forty years. Happily, as far as I know.

"*Inshallah*," he mumbled. "God willing."

I took our antipasto and pizza and turned to leave.

"Hang in there, Hafez," I said. "And give my best regards to Khalil when you see him."

I glanced at Hafez before heading for the door. He nodded and said "Mashhkur." "Thanks." But he didn't look very happy.

Chapter Thirty-Four

I went into Ripley Hall early—got there about 7:10 and opened up. I was disappointed at the fact that there was no new, relevant email. I loaded three of Judy's catered coffee canisters with water and little foil packages of coffee and turned them on. Then I went back to my computer. Now there *was* a new email. From Mike. Arrived a minute ago. He said he was diverting to the Marine Corps Air Facility for a pickup on his way in. I assumed that meant that an HMX-One helo was bringing something down from the White House. My assumption was confirmed by another inbound email.

From: keys@lisound.com

To: allewellyn@bias.gov

Subj: South Florida.

Radar-equipped drone picked up an unidentified small craft heading into Marathon in the Keys around 0345 this morning and back out almost immediately. At this point, nobody knows if it was drugs or human smuggling or just guys on a fishing trip. The analysts say its immediate departure at that time of night makes it suspicious. The boat got out of Dodge quickly and lost itself among coastal small craft before anyone could make an ID. Could be our evildoers from Germany coming in from Cuba.

Keys

Shortly after the email from Kehoe arrived, Mike came in from Quantico with one of the secure briefcases. Inside, there was a scrawled note from the man himself.

Loose,

I have a bad feeling about this fucking small craft that went into Marathon this a.m. Pure 'gut-think,' as you call it. If I'm right, we've lost the turd. Nobody knows if anyone got off the boat in Marathon, much less where he or she or they might be headed. Put your smart heads together and see what you guys can figure out. I've already talked to the NCTC, who is talking to state and local cops. Drones are up but aren't seeing anything. But I'm thinking we may have lost a serious terrorist and that he/she won't reappear until he/she flings the shit into the fan and a bunch of our fellow Americans die. Pop this message into the shredder as soon as you've read it.

Keys

About the time I finished reading the unsettling presidential note, Darps showed up in my office door, coffee mug in hand.

"C'mon in, shipmate," I said. "We need to do some serious brainstorming. Quickly."

I turned my laptop so he could see it.

"Let's start with the email. Then take a look at this," I said, holding up the Kehoe note.

"Holy Christ," he whispered. "The bastard is ashore in CONUS. Al-Husni. The bomber *überführer.*"

"Willi's still in Germany," I said. "But let's get Ashleigh, Samantha, and Sammy together in, say, fifteen minutes and kick this hairball around some."

Twelve minutes later, everyone was gathered in the Paycheck conference room. Judy had *Cheetah*'s email on a computer and had scanned his handwritten note. She showed them both on the Smart board.

"Okay. The time of arrival of the mysterious boat in Marathon was 0345 this morning," Sammy said. "Assumptions are dangerous, but let's assume two things. The boat's passenger or passengers didn't go south and west toward Key West, and they didn't stay in Marathon. Ergo they went north. If he's heading north, he's probably on I-95 and should cross into Georgia sometime early this afternoon. Unless they stopped and holed up somewhere along the way."

"Christ, Sammy," Darps interjected. "You're right, but there's a shitload of 'ifs' buried in those assumptions. We don't know if he's in a VW Bug or a Lincoln Continental. We don't know if he's going 60 miles per hour or 90 miles per hour. We don't know if he stopped and holed up for a snooze. We don't know if he isn't turning west on I-10 and heading for someplace in Alabama or Mississippi. And we don't even know if it's al-Husni."

Sammy remained his calm, unflappable self.

"I know we all hate assumptions, and nobody hates them more than I do. But we have to make the working assumption that it *is* al-Husni. It could be a feint to throw us off the scent, but I doubt that. It could be some fishermen heading home. But the indications are that al-Husni's interested in Maryland and/or Virginia. And he seems to be coming this way. So, I think we have to assume that it's him and he's coming north," Sammy said. "My guess is that whoever is transporting him will stick close to the posted speed limits. If he goes too slow, that'll attract attention. If he goes too fast, he may get a ticket. You can bet he doesn't want to be stopped by a cop if he's involved in a terrorist operation, especially if he happens to have bombs or bomb-making stuff with him."

"What about his traveling companion? Or companions, plural?" Darps asked.

"Right now, we really don't know a damned thing. There could be two guys and a woman with him. But we just don't know," I said.

I did some calculations in my head.

"If he is in fact heading north, he could cross the North Carolina-Virginia border by around 1900 this evening," I said. "That's worst case. If they don't stop except for gas and pit stops."

"I'm guessing that they *will* stop for a meal or two and some sleep," Ashleigh interjected. "Al-Husni isn't an eighteen-year-old kid. If this guy is our man, he must have crossed from Cuba into Florida overnight. A ninety-mile, open-ocean trip in a small boat isn't exactly conducive to a good night's rest. He no doubt wants to be clear-headed in directing whatever operation he's got planned. I think he's probably stopped to get some sleep. And probably some food, as well."

"If we assume that, then where would he might stop and crash?" I asked.

"*South of the Border*?" Samantha asked.

She is quick. *South of the Border* is a notorious tourist fleece machine just south of the North Carolina-South Carolina border astride I-95. Hotel, campground, mini, and tacky carnival-style rides and raunchy, greasy restaurants. Big crowds of turistas.

"Talk to me," I said to Samantha.

"Well, if Ashleigh is right and they—Husni and whoever—wanted to stop for food and sleep, *South of the Border* seems right. It's about right on the timelines; they would hit there around 4:00 or 4:30 this afternoon. There are tons of tourists and travelers, so they wouldn't stand out. Even an Egyptian-Arab-German could get himself lost there. Husni and his buddies will blend right in. If they stop at a mom and pop motel in the boondocks, they'll stand out, big-time. But not at *South of the Border*."

I went to my email. Immediately.

From: allewellyn@bias.gov

To: keys@lisound.com

Subj: SOB

Keys,

In accordance with your burn note, can you have FBI or someone eyeball the big South of the Border motel-and-restaurant complex on I-95 in South Carolina to see if somebody resembling our man visits the place? Tonight? My guys think he may stop and spend the night there. And he probably has company.

Loose

I got a return email in less than fifteen minutes. *Cheetah* said he'd get somebody on *SOB* right away.

"He's gonna have somebody check it out," I told my meeting colleagues. "Do we have anything from Willi on locations?"

"Willi just sent us an email. Encoded. PGP. Decoded, it had five words. 'Annapolis. Baltimore. Mall. Arlington. Suburbs.' And that was all," Judy said. She put the five words up on the screen.

"Those must be the targets. ID'd by the Germans. 'Annapolis' probably means the Naval Academy," I said. "Although it could be the state Capitol or the Annapolis Mall, I guess. Baltimore is probably M&T Bank Stadium in Camden Yards or the Inner Harbor. I'm guessing that 'Mall' means the National Mall, between the Capitol and the Lincoln Memorial. With the Washington Monument in the middle and the White House sitting right on the edge. Jesus Christ. Pardon me while I send yet another email."

From: allewellyn@bias.gov

To: keys@lisound.com

Subj: Target

Quote, Mall, unquote was in the Hamburg bomber's computer maps. Right outside your windows. He could be here by sometime early tomorrow—assuming that he got off the boat in Marathon this a.m. There's a shitload of territory in MD and VA covered by those maps as well. Our VERY rough guess is that he won't get here till sometime around midday tomorrow. If he even comes here. You might think about taking Franny to Camp David.

More later,

Loose

I sent the email to the White House and returned to the Smart board.

"'Arlington' probably means Crystal City or Roslyn," I said. "'Suburbs' isn't any fucking use at all."

Judy glared at me. She doesn't appreciate F-bombs being dropped around Ripley Hall when she can hear them.

"Sorry, Judy," I said, contritely. "Is Willi on his way back?"

"Don't know, but I doubt it," she said. "If he were, he'd have probably said so. I'll ask him."

She started typing.

"'Suburbs?' D.C. suburbs? Baltimore 'burbs? Or both?" Darps asked rhetorically.

"Either or," said Samantha. "Inside the Beltways or outside is another big question."

"Which Beltway?" Ashleigh asked. "Capital or Baltimore?"

"Here's another email from Willi," Judy said. "Uncoded. He says that this was the best he could do. He understands the vagueness of the response. But if he probes any more, he (a) won't get anything more and (b) probably will be thrown out of the country. He also says that he's flying tomorrow and should be here at Ripley Hall at around 1400. Two o'clock. Tomorrow."

"We have to respect that. *BIAS* has to stay under the radar. And we've got to trust our guys in the field. If Willi says he can't probe any more, we don't ask him to probe anymore," I said

"He can't get here any too soon," Sammy said. "Right now, the target area is over two-thousand square miles in two states. We've got to whittle that down—a lot."

"From the emails we've received, I'm not sure Willi's presence here will help with that," I said. "That last one seemed to say that he's already given it his best shot. But let's keep our fingers crossed."

I looked around the room.

"Any thoughts?" I asked.

Dead silence.

"Keep thinking," I said and turned and left the room.

Chapter Thirty-Five

Havana
December 1
Sunday

Major El-Shahawi climbed stiffly out of the pickup. He closed the door and slapped his hand on the roof. His phone trembled in his pocket at the same moment. He pulled it out and opened it. It was a text.

A dash followed by three periods appeared on the screen. *Dash-dot-dot-dot.* Morse for the letter B. *Bravo.* Saladdin, the Egyptian, was ashore. In Florida. He glanced at the top of his phone screen. It was just after 4:00 a.m.

"Okay, Tariq. The old bastard and his two losers are ashore in Florida. Inshallah, they won't fuck up anything else. Get rid of the camping gear as we planned. Then get some sleep." He slapped his hand gently on the roof of the pickup again.

"See you tomorrow, Major," said Tariq, slipping the pickup into gear. The truck rattled away down the street.

El-Shahawi let himself into his apartment and turned on the bathroom light. He then immediately turned on the shower. The water pressure was weak, but the water was warm. He stripped out of his filthy clothes and stepped under the flaccid stream. Struggling with fatigue, he shampooed his hair and soaped down his body. It took several minutes for the water to rinse his hair and his body and he almost fell asleep under the weakly running warm shower. Finally, he climbed out, toweled himself semi dry, and collapsed onto the bed, naked. He was asleep instantly.

Twenty minutes later, a key snapped into the lock of his front door. He didn't hear anything. He didn't see Laura as she stepped into his bedroom.

He didn't see her as she stripped off her clothes and, naked, slid into bed with him. El-Shahawi continued to snore quietly. He didn't hear Laura when she began to snore as well.

It was ten-thirty and the morning sun lit up the apartment when Major el-Shahawi finally opened his eyes and stretched. Laura had been drifting in and out of sleep for an hour. She sat up, hugging the sheet to her breasts. She smiled at el-Shahawi.

"*Buon giorno,*" she said.

"*Allah, Allah,*" he said. "Look at the time. It's going on eleven o'clock. I've got to get to the embassy."

He climbed out of the bed and stood up.

"If you go to the embassy in that condition, people will talk," Laura said with a smirk.

"Then come with me to the shower and see what you can do to relieve my 'condition,'" he said.

"Take your shower," she said. "Then come beck to bed. We'll see about curing your condition in bed."

"That'll work," he said, stepping into the bathroom. "But I might need a second shower."

He took another lukewarm, drizzly shower. He was still damp when he tumbled back into the bed. His 'condition' had intensified.

"Well, well," said Laura. "Maybe you should have lunch here and go to the embassy after that."

Chapter Thirty-Six

The alarm went off at 4:00. I jumped into a pair of jeans and a flannel shirt, made myself a peanut butter and jelly sandwich, and rolled out the door, munching the sandwich. Cory gazed at me with feigned horror as I left the house without her.

"Relax, baby. Your girlfriend will be down to walk you in an hour and a half or so."

Unlocking the door of a darkened Ripley Hall at 4:25, I shut down the alarm system, turned on some lights, and went in and started a vat of coffee. Then I went to my computer, booted up, ate the rest of my sandwich, and went to my email.

Nothing! Zip! Zilch! Nada! I couldn't believe it. This al-Husni terrorist bastard was heading north on the U.S. east coast and nobody was saying anything. Not a goddam thing from the NCTC. At least not to *BIAS*.

I poured myself a cup of coffee and sent a terse email to Kehoe.

From: allewellyn@bias.gov

To: keys@lisound.com

Subj: SOB

Anything doing w/ SOB last night?

Loose

As I sipped hot coffee at my desk, I heard a thud at the door. That should be the *Washington Post*. Since the papers still hadn't been delivered when I left my darkened house, I was news-impoverished. I flicked the remote to turn on the TV and got up and retrieved the paper. Neither the newspaper nor the TV news satisfied my lust for hard information. There wasn't a fucking morsel. A terrorist mastermind bomber was running up the east coast towards the nation's capital and I was in an information black hole. And there wasn't a damned thing I could do about it.

After glancing at the paper, I heard a ping from my computer. A new email had arrived. From the boss man. He was up early.

From: keys@lisound.com

To: allewellyn@bias.gov

Subj: SOB

FBI has just determined that a guest matching the description of our buddy spent the night at Pedro's Carolina Inn, located in the SOB complex in SC. UNSUB was accompanied by two younger, quote, Mediterranean-looking, unquote, men and a young woman—also Mediterranean in appearance They had registered as driving a 2002 Green VW Jetta with Florida plates J54-1WS. The names they signed in with were Joseph Minnelli, Alex Gomez, Michael Garcia, and Giovanna Amato. They paid with a credit card in the name of Joseph Minnelli. They left sometime around 0430. The NCTC is running down the tag and the credit card as we speak.

Keys

It was about 5:50 when Darps showed up. He poked his bearded face into my office.

"Ahoy," he said. "I just heard something. Could be important."

"Speak to me," I said.

"Outside," he said, gesturing toward the pre-dawn darkness.

We stepped out into the cold.

"Cell phone call. From Dillon, South Carolina to Stafford, Virginia. Short, one-way-message. *Quote: Ahn roo. Unquote.* Probably means *en route.* Time zero four-thirty this a.m."

"Jesus H. Christ!" I hissed. "I hesitate to ask, but where the fuck did you get *that* from?"

"Squash team buddy, Ray Smiley. A year ahead of us at Navy. Sixteenth Company. Working in a different world, now. You can guess where."

I vaguely remembered an upper-class mid named, Smiley. Tall, skinny, redheaded with a healthy dose of acne. God knows what he looks like now.

"So how the hell does he know you're interested in cell phone traffic from South Carolina to Virginia?"

"I told him," he said. "Anyhow, he risked his ass, hat and overcoat—not to mention his career—to get me the info. Drove right to our house after getting off watch. Scared the shit out of me when he rang the doorbell at a few minutes before five o'clock. Wasn't an ideal start for Annie's day, either. She's still freaking out."

"Jesus Christ," I said again. "I'm about to start bleeding out through my eyeballs. Kehoe will crucify me for stateside collecting if he gets wind of this. Zero four thirty, Dillon, South Carolina. Let's assume the call was from al-Husni or one of his minions. And let's start timing him out."

"Let's not forget that the phone call went to Stafford, Virginia, either," Darps said. "And besides, we didn't collect that morsel. Ray Smiley did. Or his agency did."

We went back inside.

"That's probably worse than if we *did* collect it. More of us get to go to jail. For longer terms. Conspiracy. But forget that. Stafford's in 'the suburbs,'" I said. "That could be the target. Just to our north. This stuff is radioactive. I have no idea how we can use it without us getting locked up and shut down."

"Maybe we only use it in house," Darps said.

"As of now, not even in house. You know. I know. That's it. We may have to make a run out west to brainstorm."

I was thinking of the Wilderness safe house. With its rumbling heater.

Darps glanced at his watch.

"The son of a bitch could be there by zero-nine-thirty," he said. "'There' being Stafford."

We wandered into my office. I looked at a clock. A few minutes before six. Then I heard rattling at the door, followed by female voices. Darps poked his head out the office door.

"Judy, Samantha, and Ashleigh, all at once," he said. "They're heading this way."

"Good," I said.

I stepped out into the little hallway.

"Good morning, ladies," I said. "It's good to see you. Grab some coffee or whatever and let's sit down in Paycheck and swap ideas around some."

They were all wearing jeans and sweaters or sweatshirts. Under winter jackets. In less than a minute, everyone was assembled.

I slid my laptop over to Judy. Kehoe's email was still on the screen. I pointed at the Smart board. Seconds later the email was up on the board

I waited till everyone read the email.

"What do you think?" I asked, rhetorically.

"He could well be on the way. But we don't know to where," Ashleigh said, half to herself. "D.C.?"

I thought of Smiley's phone intercept, but didn't say anything.

"I think we have to make that assumption," I said. "At least for now. It's all we have. NCTC isn't producing squat. Other than they found that a guy resembling our man spent the night at South of the Border. Good catch on that, Samantha. Other than that, our assumptions are the only things on which we can hang our hats."

The chatter started again. Sammy wandered into the conference room and took off his coat. I was always glad to have his intellectual horsepower in play when we were dealing with a seemingly intractable problem. And this one was indeed intractable. It appeared that al-Husni had stayed at South of the Border last night, had left there, possibly in a VW Jetta with a Florida license plate, early this morning.

"So he's coming this way. But even if he drives in and parks across the street, we have no idea what he's got in mind," Samantha said.

"Except maybe blowing something up," Sammy mumbled, echoing my thoughts exactly.

My laptop dinged. There was a new email from the man:

From: keys@lisound.com

To: allewellyn@bias.gov

Subj: New Stuff

There was a hit on a cell phone call from Dillon, SC. Near where SOB is. To Stafford, VA. It was very brief and nobody's sure what it says, but it was made around 0430. What do you guys think?

I thought that it was pretty cool for *BIAS* to get good hot intelligence before the President of the United States. But I left that thought unvoiced. We shot the shit in the small conference room for a few minutes, and then I told Judy to send the man an email. It emerged on the smart board as she poked it up.

From: allewellyn@bias.gov

To: keys@lisound.com

Subj: Call

Keys,

We think it may be our guy and he may be on the way to Stafford. No idea whether Stafford is target or a staging area for an attack elsewhere in the vicinity. But we have to assume that he's inbound along with a couple of buddies.

Loose

Okay. Now we're corroborating intel that he gets from the big boys. We could let that cat part way out of the bag, I thought. I turned to Darps.

"Tell them what you heard, shipmate," I said. "And no questions about sources," I added, for everybody's benefit.

"I also heard that there was a phone call from Dillon around 4:30 this morning. To a cell phone in Stafford, Virginia. Message was very short. Sounded like 'en route.'"

That prompted an outburst of chatter. Finally, Ashleigh cut it off. She folded her hands on the table in front of her, her glasses perched on her pert nose.

"I don't know," she said. "It looks like al-Husni is coming here. But the waters are still pretty muddy."

I started to put together another email for Kehoe. I let it show up on the Smart board as I tapped away on the laptop.

From: allewellyn@bias.gov

To: keys@lisound.com

Subj: Possible Destination

This guy may well be headed for Stafford, VA. It's in the 'burbs. We have no tracking assets. Any way you can get FBI and/or North Carolina/Virginia State Police to track that 2002 VW? And get the word to us?

Loose

I clicked on *Send* and glanced at my watch. Six twenty. Still early. But al-Husni could be in Stafford inside of three hours.

"I don't know if we're going to get any help with this or not," I told the group. "Go back to your desks and computers. If you have any flashes of insight or inspiration, let me or Darps know immediately. I'm thinking of a clumsy, ham-handed effort that we can make and that has an abysmally low payoff probability, but it's the best I can do so far. Let's reconvene at 7:15 and hope that we have more useful information then."

Chairs pushed back. Bods left the office. Except those of Darps and Sammy.

"We're dealing with a lot of unknowns," Sammy said.

"No shit," Darps added. "He could well be headed this way. But we don't have a clue what his target is."

"We don't know who his trigger man is," Sammy said. "Or men. In Germany, al-Husni was the *Marionettenmeister.* The puppet master. He arranged everything. But some poor son of a bitch put on the vest or the belt, went into the nightclub, and blew himself up. Al-Husni is probably pulling the puppet strings here. *He's* not going to blow himself up. There's a quote, martyr, unquote, who's going to blow himself up. Or a few of them. It could be either his Mediterranean-looking traveling companions or someone already here. In the States. Or here in Virginia."

"Stafford, Virginia," I said. It was just as much a question as a supposition. "And it definitely could be 'martyrs.' Plural. As in 'Revenge of the Muslim Martyrs.'"

Chapter Thirty-Seven

At 7:10 a.m., we had nothing. No message from *Cheetah* about FBI or state police activity on the northbound Jetta. We reconvened in Paycheck. Judy had run out to Einstein Brothers for a bag of bacon-and-egg bagels. They disappeared swiftly. I told everybody that I had decided on a short *BIAS* road watch. I had already run back to 1506 Prince Henry Street and retrieved my only two pairs of binoculars from the house. One pair of seven by fifties, one pair of ten by thirty-fives.

"Here's what we're going to do. I may go to jail for it, but I think we're out of options," I said. "Ashleigh, take your phone and this pair of binoculars, jump in your car, and get on I-95 south. Go to the Thornburg rest stop. Cross over to the northbound side of the interchange. You'll have to get off 95 and come back north. But I want you to be able to see license tags on northbound cars. And Florida cars only have tags on the back. Park facing the highway. Look for the green Jetta with Florida tags. With four people in it. But any green Jetta with Florida tags is fair game. Call it in. Darps will relieve you at 9:30.

"Sammy, you take these glasses and do the same thing from the McDonald's parking lot on Route One in Thornburg."

I handed him my other pair of binoculars.

"Look for the northbound green Jetta with Florida tags. Samantha will relieve you at 9:30 as well."

I stopped to think for a second and then continued.

"If we don't have a tally-ho by 11:30, we'll call off the search. *BIAS* doesn't have the assets for a large-scale highway search for longer and wider than that. Plus, the President of the United States may throw my ass in jail once he hears about us scoping out I-95. But we'll give it a try in the short run and keep our fingers crossed."

The first watch-standers left, looking none too happy. Their reliefs didn't look very happy either. They all were action analyzers. Watching and waiting quietly wasn't their cup of tea. I knew that they'd prefer punching keys and actively searching for clues rather than sitting passively watching cars roll by on a Virginia highway. I don't think they were crazy about the idea of jumping off the reservation, either. I made a mental note to visit each of the watchers sometime in the middle of their tours of duty. I didn't hold out a hell of a lot of hope that we'd nail the 2002 Jetta, much less Al-Husni. A blink of an eye, a change of cars, a side trip to U.S. Route 301 to continue the northward trek, or whatever, could knock us off the rails and result in a big, fat zero. But I felt that we had to give it a shot. It seemed like whatever machinery Kehoe put into action took a long time to do anything and wasn't all that effective.

It was a few minutes after 8:15 when I rolled into the northbound I-95 rest stop at Thornburg. Ashleigh was a little agitated. She was standing outside her car, holding her mobile in one hand and the binoculars in the other.

"I think the Jetta just blew past," she said, excitedly. "I couldn't make out the tag number, but the car was dark green. And it definitely was a Jetta. The license plate looked like it had an orange in the middle. Like a lot of the Florida tags. The car was in the middle lane. It looked like there were four people in it. Three guys and a gal."

I counted on my fingers. Al-Husni-one. Unknown driver-two. Male companion-three. Female companion-four. It added up.

"Okay," I said. "That probably means they're here. Al-Husni and his buddies."

Stafford was about five miles north of where we stood. But it's a huge county. I called Sammy.

"I think they just passed us northbound on 95," I told him. "Let's head back to the ranch."

Then I called back to Ripley Hall and told Judy to shut down the second half of the watch and that we'd all be back inside of fifteen minutes. We'd caucus again. I punched up an email on my phone.

From: allewellyn@bias.gov

To: keys@lisound.com

Subj: Green Jetta

There was a green Jetta on I-95 north a few minutes ago. It

had a driver plus 3 pax. We think their destination is Stafford, VA. Didn't make the tag; so we're not sure, but the timeline fits w/the 0430 departure time from SOB. This clown could be our guy with a couple of his altar boys as well.

Loose

"Okay, Ash. Let's go back to Rip. We need to analyze some more."

She headed onto the ramp with me not far behind.

Chapter Thirty-Eight

B ack at the ranch, we reconvened. It wasn't very constructive.

There was a White House email that didn't help very much. Not surprisingly, the man was pissed. To say the least.

> From: keys@lisound.com
>
> To: allewellyn@bias.gov
>
> Subj: Poaching
>
> How the f**k are you getting that stuff? 'No fishing allowed' means 'No fishing allowed.' I could have sworn I was clear on that!
>
> Do you really think he could be our guy?
>
> Keys

I decided to ignore it for now, but I had Judy put it up on the Smart board.

"It appears that I'm on Kehoe's current shit list. More importantly, it also appears that al-Husni is here in the D.C. metro area," I said. "But we don't know that for sure. For all we know, he could be in Atlanta or New Orleans. Or still in Cuba. But the flabby indicators we do have suggest that he's here. Perhaps even in Stafford. But we don't have the investigative assets—much less the authority—to nail that down. The little surveillance episode we just ran in which we may have caught sight of him was no doubt illegal and contrary to direct orders from the President of the United States to me. And you can see that it pissed him off. Mightily. I'll take the heat on that if it goes to court. Meantime, I think it was worth it and the right thing for us to do. I think we've convinced ourselves that Al-Husni is here. The dark side is that there's nothing we can do about it other than watch and wait and see if he pops his head up. If any of you have a creative thought on this mess, follow it up and let me know. But I'm not putting any of us out on the streets anymore. I have to tell myself—and you—that our job is to second-guess the big boys—not out-guess them before the fact. But I have the feeling that we're chasing a dangerous rat here and that the big boys are several miles behind us."

Sammy slapped the table gently.

"I don't think we can go into a 'coast' mode on this, boss," he said. "There's an Islamofascist asshole in the D.C. metro area determined to do major harm. I think we've got to try and stop him."

"My thought is that you don't need to tell *Cheetah* every little detail about what the hell we're doing," Darps added.

"I agree. With both of you. But we need more information. Said asshole came zooming in here and disappeared, for all intents and purposes. We— BIAS—don't have the assets to *find* him, let alone catch him and stop him."

"Massive listening. Massive monitoring. Everything and anything we can get our hands—or our ears—on. That's what we can legally do," Darps said.

"I'm not so sure all *that* stuff is legal," Ashleigh said.

"But that's exactly what we're going to do," I said. "It's close enough. Keep it in-house, keep it more or less passive, and don't leave Ripley Hall on any operational stuff without a conference. With me."

My guys and gals were smart and, more importantly, extremely creative. I hadn't said, "No hacking." Nor had I said, "No listening."

"In-house, more or less passive," was the guidance. The troops were smart enough to not leave fingerprints around. If Kehoe didn't have me locked up for what I'd already done, I'd probably still be around and on the loose for Christmas with my family. In just over three weeks. As long as nobody went public. That probably called for a silent Hail Mary.

About 3:15, Samantha popped into my office. She looked over her shoulder and looked back at me.

"I got a phone hit," she said. "'Heavenly vengeance' was part of the conversation. I couldn't get the rest except for one word: 'Saladdin.'"

"Jesus," I said. "From whom to whom? Or where to where?"

"Both local. Cell phones. One in Stafford, the other right here in beautiful downtown Chestertown."

"Jesus Christ," I said. I stood up.

"Let's put that on the Smart board," I said, heading for the Paycheck conference room.

The info stream slowed and fizzled entirely as the afternoon rolled on. At 4:15, I told Darps and Judy to shut things down. I walked home in the cold and the almost-dark.

Chapter Thirty-Nine

Next morning, I awoke at a little after 5:00. It was completely dark. I could hear some sort of precipitation outside. If I could hear it, it wasn't snow. But it sounded more percussive than rain. I got up and peeked through the blinds. The tree limbs and the power lines were agleam with ice. Freezing rain and sleet.

By the time I had that figured out, I was wide awake and had started thinking about al-Husni hiding in Stafford. Or Chestertown. Or maybe somewhere else in the D.C. metro area. More sleep was out of the question. We had a terrorist rooting around in our backyard. I shrugged and stretched into some Navy sweats, pulled on a pair of slipper socks, and sneaked downstairs in the dark. Cory was wide-awake, tail a-wag. I let her out the front door for a quick whiz while I fetched the bagged papers from the stoop. She doesn't seem to give a rat's ass about sleet— she leapt out the door into the front yard. After sniffing around and then taking care of business, she pressed her nose on the glass of the storm door. I was confident that her nose on the glass was because of her interest in breakfast rather than her dislike of sleet. I started the coffee and let her in, after which I wiped her down with an old towel reserved for that task. She followed me around, toenails clicking, till I gave her breakfast.

I checked my email on the phones. A couple of administrative bullshit messages that could well wait till later, but nothing substantive. I wondered about the classified network that I had access to via Ripley Hall computers, but not on the iPhones.

I turned on the TV. There were a number of schools closed due to the weather—including All Saints' Academy. I slipped a note to that effect under Elizabeth's door.

A few weeks ago, I'd made a policy decision. If the Marine Corps Base at Quantico closed due to bad weather, *BIAS* would also close. If the Marines stayed open, we'd do likewise. That way, we kept the *BIAS* name off the skyline. Today it appeared that Quantico was open, so we were too.

The coffeemaker had become quiet—meaning the coffee was done. I poured a mug full and peered out the front door again. I could see in the street light that it was still sleeting. Blobs of almost-snow were falling through the lamplight. It was still dark. I figured I could, with rubber overshoes, walk to Ripley Hall in fifteen or twenty minutes or so. There, I could access the classified net and see if anything was cooking thereon. I popped half a bagel into the toaster oven and started it ticking. The clock atop the microwave read 5:25. I could have a half-bagel mini-breakfast, throw some clothes on, and get in to Ripley Hall by 6:00 or so. I could check email and voicemail, and, by that time, the troops would start showing up. I slathered salmon spread on my bagel half and munched.

My old rubber galoshes were good on the ice. I made it in to Ripley Hall in twenty minutes, putting me at the front door at 6:05. It was still dark. I unlocked, disabled the alarm, and turned on some lights. I hung up my sleet-spattered coat and booted up my computer.

It was as if all my Washington-area colleagues had decided, in concert, to ignore me. I knew that that was a paranoid thought, but I was amazed at the total lack of email, much less information. But one message did catch my eye. It was from Judy. And it had come in yesterday.

From: jpaladino@bias.gov

To: allewellyn@bias.gov

Cc: Dtaylor@bias.gov

Subj: Our friend

I stopped by our favorite pizzeria last night for Saturday night supper. Your buddy seemed to be very down in the dumps and not his usual, cheery self. I can't believe pizza sales are down in a college town, but something has got the guy lower than I've ever seen him.

We can kick it around tomorrow if you like.

Judy

Hmm, I thought. *Hafez Bey must have been really down for Judy to have noticed. Maybe I'll pick up a steak bomb sandwich for lunch and see what's cooking.* I cleaned up my email inbox and grazed my way through a few news sites as I slurped through a cup of coffee.

I was halfway through the coffee when my left pocket cell strummed. I pulled it out. It was Luke.

"Good morning," I said.

"Hi, boss," Luke said. "Have you seen yesterday's *Mirror*? *Morsels and Motes*?"

"Oh, Jesus," I said. "I can tell that I'm not going to like this already. But no, I have not."

"You're right, Alan. It's not good. But it's not as bad as it could have been."

I didn't know what to make of that.

"Umm," I said.

"I'm bringing my copy in," Luke said. "I should be there in ten minutes or so."

He had carried the paper under his parka to protect it from the sleet while he walked to Ripley from his car. There were droplets of melting sleet and snow on his head and shoulders.

"Page seventeen," he said, handing me the dry paper.

I turned to page seventeen. The first two "morsels" were about the possible entry of a northeastern governor into the Democratic Primary brouhaha and a rumored "romantic connection" between a senior aide to a Virginia Congressman and a "high-level" State Department official. The usual horseshit. Then came item number three.

Spooky New Intel Agency???

M&M sources have picked up rumors that some government (???!!) has created a new intelligence collection and analysis apparatus in the Washington area. Supposedly it has surfaced a new terrorist threat against the United States that the "other" intel producers have not. More later.

Jesus! Smirking Syd's phone call about leaks coming home to roost. I had no idea how to cover tracks on this one. Other than total stonewalling. But I had to wonder who the son of a bitch was who had leaked some pretty sensitive—and not all that inaccurate—stuff about *BIAS* to Racey

Suzanne or whoever wrote the damned thing. I took the paper and went upstairs to Darps's office.

"Morning, shipmate. Check out yesterday's *Morsels and Motes*," I said, handing him the paper.

He read in silence for a few seconds and then erupted.

"Jesus H. Christ on a bicycle!" he snorted. "You gotta wonder. This coming on the heels of Smirking Syd's fortune telling a couple of weeks ago."

My phone chimed for a text. I pulled it out of my pants pocket. It was from Kehoe. Uh oh.

Loose. HMX helo will pick you up at the fifty-yard line of the JM High School football field in exactly three-zero minutes. That's 8:40. We need to shoot the shit. I'll have you back at JM by 10:30 latest. Please confirm. Keys.

"He's sending a chopper for me. Pickup on the Jayem football field. I wonder how they got clearance for that."

"School's cancelled today. Plus, he's President of the United States," Darps pointed out.

"I wonder if he read yesterday's *Mirror*," I said, getting to my feet. "On the other hand, he may be coming after me because of the bit of highway watching we pulled on Saturday."

"You should probably text him back," Darps said.

"Yeah. I'll do that. Then I need to get on the stick and get my ass over to James Monroe."

I texted Kehoe back as I walked out the door to Darps's office.

Keys, C U soon

Then I went downstairs and put on my jacket. I couldn't get the damned *M&M* blurb out of my mind. And I couldn't get Smirkin' Syd Girtler out of my mind, either.

Chapter Forty

The chopper landed on the JayEm fifty-yard line right on schedule. The sleet had quit, but the rotor wash kicked up a fair amount of icy water from the sodden field. I scurried over to the hatch and climbed in with the assistance of a Marine corporal who looked to be about eighteen years old. I probably looked like a refugee from a geezer village to him. We took off and headed north, following I-95, with its packed northbound lanes. Less than twenty minutes later, we were landing on the south lawn of the White House. I got a good look at the National Christmas Tree just before we touched down.

I got lucky. First Lady Francine Kehoe, Secret Service code name, *Chatelaine*, had come out to meet me with Sham, the First Dog. Back in high school in Clancyville, New York, Franny and I had dated a couple of times. Nothing serious, but it was always good to see her. She was every bit as good-looking now as she was back in the day. Today, she wore a red parka and black pants tucked into black boots. Caramel-colored hair falling almost to the shoulder framed green eyes in a pretty, pixie-like face. Sham was a golden retriever who wasn't the least bit bothered by the cold, damp day.

"Hi Franny," I said. "Seeing you is like the sun coming out on a gloomy day."

She laughed.

"You're shameless," she said and gave me a chaste little smooch at the corner of my mouth. There are worse ways to arrive in the Nation's Capital than to be smooched by a pretty First Lady.

"Jim is on the phone with the Israeli Prime Minister. He sent Sham and me out to meet you."

"Thank the Lord for telephones," I said and gave Sham a little scritch behind the ears as we headed toward the big house.

A Marine in dress blues held the door for us, and, seconds later, we were at the Oval Office door. Kehoe was still on the phone and waving his free arm. I turned around to leave to give him privacy and Franny pushed me in the chest.

"Go on in," she said.

Kehoe dropped his arm.

"Yes sir, Mr. Prime Minister. We definitely see eye-to eye on that. *Shalom.*"

He hung up the phone and turned around.

"C'mon in, Alan," he said. "Merry Christmas! Take off your coat and have a seat. Coffee?"

It didn't seem like I was getting fired or having my ass chewed, but with civilians, one never knows. Especially political civilians. A steward showed up with a cup of coffee as if by magic and took my coat.

"Nice seeing you, Alan," Franny said, unbuttoning the red parka.

"My pleasure, Franny," I said. "It's been too long."

Franny left with a little wave as she shucked out of the parka.

"I agree," she said.

Sham stayed. Under the desk.

Kehoe and I sat.

"Let's talk probabilities, Alan," Kehoe said. "And I don't even want to know how you know about the green Jetta on I-95 in northern Virginia yesterday morning."

"Well, I'll tell you about it anyway. We knew about it in large part because *you* told me about it in an email you sent us yesterday. The one about the FBI and the Jetta leaving Dillon, South Carolina, at oh-dark-thirty. Which I received at *BIAS* a mere twenty-four hours after we asked you to have the Fibbies check out South of the Border. And by the way, have you seen yesterday morning's *Mirror?*"

I figured it would be a good move to put the ball in his court. For a couple of seconds, at least.

He didn't really take the bait. But he did respond.

"I'm going to kill that fucking paper. That bitch Suzanne Racey will be lucky to get a job selling lottery tickets at a truck stop in Oklahoma.

I've cut all access to anyone even remotely connected with that rag. And Syd is leaving on a two-week fact-finding tour of Sub-Saharan Africa. That ridiculous story should die a quick death. You and I will stonewall. 'Ridiculous! No comment! Not sure what other governments are doing. End of story.' That's all, folks."

Well. It was good to know where he stood.

"Okay, back to the green Jetta," I said. "The one you told me about. A few hours after I got your email, figuring time was of the essence, I put watchers on I-95 and Route One just south of Chestertown," I said. "One of them spotted a green Jetta with Florida tags heading north about zero-nine thirty. We put two and two together."

"It's those damned 'watchers' of yours that could blow up in our faces. They bring to mind the notorious 'plumbers' of Watergate fame. I can see the headline now. 'Spies Surveilling Virginia Traffic Report Directly to White House.' Sweet Jesus! So please don't put out any more 'watchers' inside U.S. territory. And tell your people to keep the lid on."

"Yes sir," I said. As ass-chewings go, this one wasn't really all that bad. I've had much worse over the years.

"Not to mention the problem of the *Morsels & Motes* piece," I said.

"Forget that. It's dead. Let's talk probabilities. What's your estimate of the probability that the 9:30 a.m. Jetta was carrying our Arab/German bomber?" he asked.

I thought for a few seconds. The man didn't like me collecting intelligence on U.S. turf, but wasn't above using said intel.

"Point two-five. Twenty-five percent," I said, totally winging it.

"You said there were four people in the Jetta," he said. "Four."

"Yeah. I'm guessing it was al-Husni and the three goons that came with him from Germany."

"There's only one thing wrong with that guess. The Italian source in Cuba is now saying that an Arab military attaché shot and killed an 'Arab visitor.' That could have been—probably was—one of those goons before they left Cuba."

"Holy shit. That would mean it's al-Husni and two goons. They probably linked up with the driver of the Jetta somewhere in the Keys."

"And, what do you think the probability is that he—al-Husni—is here in the D.C. metro area?" he asked.

"Probably about the same. Twenty-five percent. Maybe twenty," I said. I was *really* winging it now.

"So, if I remember my math classes correctly, the probability of al-Husni (a) having come into Northern Virginia—including Chestertown—and (b) *staying* here, is the product of those two probabilities—point two-five times point two zero. Point zero-five. Five percent. Five chances out of a hundred."

"Yes," I said. "We are winging it here, but yes. If we need a number—and I think we do—point zero five is pretty good. Five percent."

He stood up and walked to the famous Oval Office windows.

"Shit!" he said. "It's the needle in the proverbial haystack. On top of all that, I'm getting nothing—almost zippo—from the rest of the Intel Community. Some of them think I've gone off the deep end worrying about a non-existent threat. The only hard stuff available to me are a few NSA reports with a few key words and chatter. Plus a few bits and pieces the CIA got from the Germans and Italians. These American interagency working groups don't believe Arabs coming from Germany are getting ready to blow stuff up. But they don't have the balls to go on record and say those reports to that effect are all bullshit.

"So, I guess here's where I tell the Department of Homeland Security to make sure that every swinging dick that we have at our disposal in the Washington-Baltimore area—including Chestertown and Stafford County, Virginia—goes on the lookout for the green Jetta, Florida license number J54-1WS. And every swinging dick goes on the lookout for a fifty-something-old dude who speaks Arabic and German and looks like a bum. And once such a dude is identified, he is detained immediately. DHS has his pictures."

He picked up a phone.

"Get Frank Hopewell, Jim Knapper, Bob Gibbons, and Gabby Daniele in here in ninety minutes for an emergency meeting. Pull 'em out of wherever," he snapped into the handset.

I recognized the names. Hopewell is DHS, Knapper is the DCI, Gibbons is SecDef, and Daniele is Attorney General. Kehoe put the phone down and glanced at his wristwatch. The door of the Oval Office snapped open. An admin assistant pointed at her wristwatch.

"Time for a ridiculous photo op. With some American Legion group from Alaska," Kehoe said, rolling his eyes.

He started for the door and I followed.

"It better be a quickie. The big dogs will be here in less than an hour and a half," he added, half to himself.

He stopped in mid-stride and turned back to me.

"One last thing. If these guys are planning to blow something up, do we have a timeline? Hours, days, weeks?" Kehoe asked.

"Don't know. My gut says days. Maybe I can give you a better answer a little later today," I said. "But there's something else."

"What's that?" he asked.

"The female," I said.

"What are you talking about? Racey?"

"No," I said. "There may have been three people accompanying al-Husni from Germany to Cuba. Two guys and a female. If that Arab attaché offed one of the guys in Cuba, then the bomb team now consists of al-Husni plus two martyrs. One of which may be a female," I said.

"Damn," he said. "That'd be a switch."

"Not totally," I said. "Seems that the number of Islamist female suicide bombers is on the rise. Still small. But growing."

I followed him through the open door.

The same steward held my coat for me. When I got outside, the chopper's engines were running up. It was still cold and damp. Twenty minutes later, they dropped me on the James Madison fifty-yard line.

Chapter Forty-One

Chestertown
December 2
Monday

Istepped off the James Madison football field and onto their rubberized running track at 10:15 a.m. and called *BIAS*. The HMX chopper had taken off with a roar and was just about out of sight to the northeast. Judy answered on the second ring.

"Happy Monday. The National Christmas tree looks great," I told her. "Can you start rounding up the Arab/German team for a meeting soon?"

"They're all here. Champing at the bit. We're waiting for you."

"I'll be there in five or ten minutes, as soon as I can get there. I'm walking. From Jayem. Is Darps there?"

"Yes, he is. He seems agitated."

"I'm not surprised. Tell him I'll be there anon."

We rang off.

I started walking and called Maria.

"I'm back in C-Town," I told her. "Heading for the office as we speak."

"Will you be home for lunch?"

"I should be," I said. "If that changes, I'll call."

"Fair enough," she said.

The sleet started to fall again as I headed for campus.

I walked into Ripley Hall at 10:25. Judy fairly jumped out of her office and I heard galloping footsteps coming down the stairs that I recognized as belonging to Darps. I noticed that someone had put up a miniature Christmas tree on a table in the hall. There was Christmas music mixed with Chanukah music coming from the little Bose stereo system that Samantha had brought in.

"What did *Cheetah* want?" Darps asked. "Chew your ass?"

"A little of that, but more, 'When, when, when? When will al-Husni strike?' And then, 'Where, where, where?' In his mind, the 'when' is more important than the 'where' right now. If something blows in half an hour, knowing the 'where' right now is pretty fucking unimportant. But if something is going to blow up in a week, then the 'where' becomes very important. But 'when' is the five-hundred pound gorilla in the room as we speak. And he's still not getting much in the way of collateral from the big boys. Some, but very little."

"Makes sense," Darps said. "But what about that fucking *Morsels and Motes* piece? Surely he'd heard about it."

"Yeah. I think he's dealt with it. He says *Sunday Mirror* and Racey are dead meat. And that *Chipmunk* is safely out of town for a while," I said. "Shall we cluster in Paycheck conference room in five minutes?"

"I think Judy has got that already scheduled," Darps replied.

Darps and Judy spread out into Ripley Hall to round up the troops. Three minutes later we were all in the small conference room.

I played back my meeting with *Cheetah*, omitting any reference to *Chatelaine* and the neat little smooch on the corner of my mouth.

Sammy was drumming his fingers on a closed laptop sitting on his knees. When I finished, he said, "I've found something that might give us some insight into 'when,'" he said.

"Speak," I said.

"There's a professor at the Hebrew University of Jerusalem who has published an unclassified study titled, *Suicide Bombing Tactics and Techniques.* He's a guy named Leon Fleischmann. Originally from Argentina. PhD from Indiana University. He was able to examine after-action reports written by police and IDF investigators of over one-hundred-fifty suicide bombings in Israel, Gaza, and the so-called occupied territories. There are some striking commonalities," he said.

"Keep going, Sammy," I said.

He opened up his Mac Book Pro and tickled keys.

"The big commonality is the relationship between the *shahid*—the martyr—and his mentor. Even though, in both *intifadas*, there was a huge abundance of 'volunteers' for martyrdom—folks willing to blow themselves to bits as long as they could kill a bunch of Jews in the process—there was a fairly lengthy time interval during which the mentor—the *hodja*—would indoctrinate the *shahid.* Ostensibly to preclude last-minute second thoughts."

"What kind of timelines are we talking about, Sammy?" I asked.

"Usually two to four weeks," Sammy replied. "The mentor would indoctrinate the martyr on the bennies of martyrdom—the seventy-two, self-renewing virgins, the land of milk and honey, et cetera—as well as the *guarantee* of the bennies. There were classroom lectures and discussion groups. According to Fleischmann, the 'practical application' part of this indoctrination process was very intense, including having the martyr-candidate spend a night in a coffin. In the fucking ground. Not as in buried with the lid closed. But still, in an open grave."

Judy glared at Sammy and glanced at me. Neither of us said anything.

"The next morning, the *hodja* would inform the martyr that his remains would never be housed in a coffin because his body would be blown to bits, but that his *life* would continue with Allah and the fruits of paradise, including all the virgins.

"According to Fleischmann, there was also some pretty intense psychological training, preparing the *shahid* for second thoughts and hesitation and how to deal with that. Bottom line, if al-Husni arrived in the D.C. metro area yesterday, his martyr—if he's local—probably isn't ready to go boom. They'll probably need a couple of weeks to wind him or her up."

"But our guy is coming in from Germany. With friends. They're not Palestinians in Israel or Gaza," I said.

"Yeah. Meaning he may have his *shahid* with him. He could have started his indoctrination a couple of weeks or even months ago in Germany," Darps added.

"You're both right, of course," Sammy said. "But we're stretching and groping here. Maybe the Egyptian-Arab-German puppet master has read the same training manual that his Palestinian pals have read. And maybe his martyr or martyrs have been here in the states. Plus, we have the simultaneity and multiple target issues."

"So, I can tell *Cheetah* that al-Husni, wherever he is, probably isn't going to wind up his martyrs and turn him and/or her loose for a week or two?"

"Yeah. Kind of. If he pins you down. Emphasis on the 'probably.' Is there a way to water down 'probably'? It's a best guess. A desperate one at that. And even best guesses can be wrong," Sammy said. "You should tell him that, too."

"I guess we can play pull-out-of-our-ass probability games with this," I said.

I went to my laptop and my email.

From: allewllyn@bias.gov

To: keys@lisound.com

Subj: Timelines

BIAS's best guess now is that the big event is two to three weeks away, due to psycho prep times for at least one of the bad guys. It's not random, but it is still a guess. Probability point six. That leaves a 40 percent probability that he will strike within the next two weeks or after three weeks. I think we need to direct our energy toward figuring out "where" as soon as we can and drill down from there. And finding our guy, needless to say. That's what I'm going to do unless you tell me otherwise.

Loose

I passed the laptop to Judy and nodded toward the Smart board. In a few seconds, the message was up. Several heads nodded. Then mine nodded toward Judy. She clicked on <SEND> and the message was on its way. To the White House.

"Okay," I said. "Thanks to everyone for coming in on a nasty Monday morning. Check road conditions and decide if you're going to stay or need to get home before the roads get really bad. I'll stay here for a while and see what *Cheetah* sends back. It could well be nothing. You guys can stay here and plough the ground or get out of Dodge. Keep your phones on. We'll be back here first thing in the a.m. Unless I call you. Check the media. If Quantico is open, so are we. See you tomorrow."

Pretty much everyone left the conference room except for Judy, Darps, and Sammy. And *moi*. Some headed for the outside door. Others went back to their desks. It was still sleeting outside.

"Okay, tell me about Fat Harry," I said, turning to Judy.

"I will," she said. "I've been buying pizza at Fat Harry's at a rate of about a pizza per month since I moved to Chestertown. And that was seven years ago. And I've gotten to know the guy pretty well. He's always pleasant to me, cheerful, and funny. And every once in a while, he includes a little present with my pizza. Like a couple of poppers or a few garlic knots. When I went in last night, he looked and acted like he'd lost his last friend. Glassy-eyed, maybe. Dazed even. But mostly sad. It just struck me as odd—that's all."

"I'll try and make it a point to stop there within the next day or two," I said. "Maybe he got some bad news from home."

Judy got up and retrieved her raincoat. She glanced at the clock.

"I'm whupped. Even though it's Monday," she said to me. "If it's not a problem, I'm going to take a long lunch at home. Maybe a cup of tomato soup with a grilled cheese sandwich. And your recommended short nap. But I'll be back later this afternoon. Around 3:00 or 3:30."

"I'm going home to have lunch with Maria," I said. "But I'll be back in an hour or so."

"I just want to see how *Cheetah* reacts to your email," Darps said after Judy left.

"*Yo, tambien,*" Sammy said.

I looked at my watch.

"I'll wait thirty minutes for an answer," I said. "Then I'm outta here and homeward bound. Christmas is coming and I'm tired. And *Cheetah* can reach out and touch me wherever and whenever he wants. But, since the three of us are here, let's use that thirty minutes to take a rough-cut look at where this motherfucker is and where he might be aiming."

"Allow me?" asked Sammy.

"Please," I said. "Go for it."

He stepped to the smart board and drew five circles. He labeled them, *Annapolis, Baltimore, Mall, Arlington, Burbs.*

"Those were the locations off the terrorists' computer in Germany," he said. He drew a sixth circle and labeled it, *Elsewhere.*

"At this point, I don't think we should think that the five places are all-inclusive. Now, let's play with probabilities," he said with a thin smile.

I liked his approach.

"Let's add another circle. About half the size of the 'burbs' circle and superimposed right on top of it," I said. "Label it, *Stafford*," I added.

Darps nodded vigorously.

"Yeah. We can't forget that phone call," he said.

"Let's start with *elsewhere*," I said. "For starters, stick in a point-one. Ten percent."

Sammy wielded the marker.

"Do you really think it's that low?" Darps asked.

"I'm not sure what I think. Let's get some other numbers up, and we can massage them if need be. Let's try point-three for the *burbs*, including Stafford," I said.

"Then, if we go with one-tenth each for Annapolis and Baltimore, that leaves forty percent for both the National Mall and Arlington. Point-two for each. That adds up to one. One hundred percent."

We all stared at the board for a few seconds.

"The numbers are pretty squishy," I said. "We pretty much pulled them out of our asses."

"Actually, you pretty much pulled them out of your ass," Darps said.

"They're certainly not chiseled in stone," I said. "We have to start somewhere."

"And we do have that cell phone call from South Carolina to Stafford," Sammy said. "Plus, I think that the National Mall and Arlington are higher-value and more spectacular targets than Baltimore and Annapolis. Hence higher probabilities. So we've got that covered too."

"Okay," I said. "Go on, have lunch. I'll send Kehoe some hard data in the afternoon through our Secret Service channel. And I'll tell him that we'll advise him whenever we adjust the numbers as we get more and better info."

I stood up and the others followed suit.

"Do we need to lock up for lunch or will be one of you guys be here?' I asked.

"We've got it covered, boss," Darps said.

"Let's hope Professor Fleischmann is right and we're right and nothing's going to blow any time soon," Sammy said.

"No shit," I said. "But that's out of our hands, now."

It was still sleeting when I walked home but it felt like the temperature was getting colder. About half way there, my iPhone chimed. The right-pocket one. Keys. A text. I stopped under a bus stop shelter and thumbed it up.

> VA State Police spotted the green Jetta @ MM 41 on I95. That's SOUTH of Richmond. Heading SOUTH. Driver only—no pax. VA will hand him off to NC. Thought u should know.

I pocketed the phone. South. The sleet had changed to all snow while I read the text in the bus stop. It definitely felt colder. I headed for home.

Chapter Forty-Two

By the time I got to the house, the snow had gotten serious. I glanced at the thermometer outside the mudroom in back and it read thirty-two exactly. I let myself in and shed my parka. There was a hint of a yummy smell in the air, and it intensified as I walked into the kitchen and saw a pile of Christmas cookies on a platter. I reached out and touched the top cookie on the pile. It was warm but edible. It had some sort of red grit on top but it was a chocolate chip-Macadamia nut combo, which I devoured with relish. Once again, I heard classical Christmas music. I stepped into the family room and the girls were there, looking very content. Maria had her laptop on her knees and her Tina Fey glasses on her nose. Elizabeth, Tala, and Esmè were working on something with pens, markers, and loose-leaf pages. All three of them were snickering, as if they were delighted at having a snow day. Cory looked up and thumped her tail. Then she got to her feet. She was ready to go out.

"Hi, everybody," I said.

"Hi, Love," Maria said, removing her glasses. I gave her a kiss on her lovely forehead.

"Hi, Dad," Elizabeth said, with her great grin. "Hi, Mr. Llewellyn," said Mutt and Jeff.

Cory shoved her nose into my kneecap.

"Guess the hound and I will take a walk in the snow," I said, thinking that the kneecap was an infinitely better cold-nose target than the crotch.

"Is it snowing?" Elizabeth asked.

"It is now," I said.

"I think I could use a walk, too," Maria said, moving the laptop to a table.

A couple of minutes later, after telling the teenagers not to burn down our house, the three of us were walking along Prince Henry Street. The

170

thermometer on the front stoop read thirty-one and the snow was starting to stick. I thought about how much I loved the uncompromising absoluteness of nature's laws.

"How's it going with the New Yorkers in the Civil War?" I asked.

"Very well," she said. "I'm not sure that a lot of Southerners will be happy to learn that one of the reasons they lost the Civil War was that the north had twice as many horses than the south had. It kind of busts up some popular myths. You know, about gallant Confederate cavalrymen kicking the asses of crude Federal city slickers. Some of those Confederate cavalrymen had their asses kicked by Northern cavalrymen. New Yorkers."

"Ouch," I said. "That could be a tough sell in these parts."

"Oh, I know."

The walk in the snow was delightful but cold. Cory didn't mind the cold or the snow at all. On the contrary, she gamboled through the bit of snow that was on the ground, occasionally pausing long enough to poke her nose into the white stuff and toss a little clump into the air.

Getting home and kindling a fire was delightful as well. Cory flopped in front of the fire and worried at the little ice balls between her hairy toes.

The girls stood up, collecting papers and writing implements.

"That play should win all kinds of awards," Esmè said as she shrugged into a camel's hair parka. She was still snickering.

"What play?" I had to ask.

"The one we just wrote," Tala said. "It's a modern-day, *A Christmas Carol*. Featuring some of our closest friends."

"It also features English accents," Elizabeth said. "Right out of *Harry Potter*."

Now it was my turn to roll my eyes.

We had chicken salad sandwiches for lunch. Maria put green onions and carrot shavings in her chicken salad. She also puts in a few drops of balsamic vinegar. Her chicken salad is uncommonly good.

After lunch, I looked out the window and it was still snowing. I figured a walk back to Rip through the snow followed by a cup of Judy's coffee would suppress my tendency—particularly in cold, snowy weather—to grow drowsy after a nice lunch. I put galoshes back on, bundled up with hat, trench coat with zip-in liner, and gloves and set off.

The fresh snow muffled the little ambient noise of the Chestertown streets. During my twenty-minute walk, two not-so-random thoughts managed to squirm their way into my consciousness. Simultaneity was one. Four versus one was the other. Simultaneity went back to nine-eleven when the attacks were clearly orchestrated to occur together. The hijackers arranged their ticket purchases to make the four deadly jetliner impacts as close together as possible. The four versus one idea was something different. But related. On September eleventh, there were four hijackers. That thought led me to the VW on I-95. Four people in the northbound Jetta and one guy in the southbound car two days later. Three people left behind. Was there somebody else? A fourth terrorist here in the D.C. metro area?

When I got back to Rip, I sat down at the computer and checked out various websites. I wasn't sure what I was looking for. Possible targets. Simultaneous happenings, maybe. Stuff that was scheduled for the same date and time.

I looked at pro sports teams and found no patterns. Went to the *Washington Post* and looked for simultaneous events. The Marine Corps Band was giving its Christmas concert at Wolf Trap Farm Park in just over a week. Big crowd of people, bunch of high-school music groups. World-famous Marine Corps Band—the President's Own. Tempting target but nothing simultaneous. Because of the "Maryland" tag on the German/Arab computer, I went to the U.S. Naval Academy's website and checked their calendar. Christmas leave was due to commence after noon meal formation on Thursday, December 19th. And "noon" meal formation would be early that day. 10:30. I visited several D.C. area colleges websites and there didn't seem to be any rhyme or reason to their dismissals for the holiday break. Pretty much depended on individual students' semester exams. Georgetown had a basketball game, but it was in Honolulu. Maryland also had a basketball game scheduled. But it was in Palo Alto. Then, I went to several local school districts' websites. Their "Winter Breaks" were scheduled to start on different dates and times. They were all close. But Augustine Washington High School was scheduled to start vacation on December 19th. Finally, at fifteen past four, I jotted down a couple of quick notes, which I'd add to the Smart board later. I spent the rest of the afternoon off on various tangents. When I left, I wondered if I hadn't just wasted a bunch of time on a random walk through cyberspace.

I grilled lamb chops in the cold back yard and, to compensate for the cold, allowed myself a finger and a half of cognac in a tooth glass, which I brought out into the yard along with the chops.

"And here I thought you were taking that brandy out to use for cooking the lamb," Maria said. "Silly me."

I raised my eyebrows for a half-second, but was otherwise noncommittal.

"I went to check on the temperature and there you were, savoring and sipping. Nary a drop went on the lamb chops."

"And what was the temperature when you checked?" I asked.

"Twenty-five," she said.

"Well there you go," I said. "Twenty-five. That's four below zero, Celsius. Obviously, the cognac was for medicinal purposes. Warming me up."

Maria rolled her eyes, reminding me of Elizabeth. Not to mention myself.

"I can't remember you ever needing to be warmed up," she said.

"Hmm," I said.

Chapter Forty-Three

Major el-Shahawi's mobile phone's alarm trilled at 7:15. He awoke at once. At his side, Laura didn't budge as he shut off the alarm. Her left breast was exposed. He felt like kissing it or licking it but knew what would happen if he did. And, this Monday morning, he could not afford to be late at the embassy. He sighed and quietly worked his way out of bed as Laura continued to snore softly.

He showered and shaved and donned his dark-blue civilian suit. The suit went over a white shirt with a spread collar and a pale-blue checked tie. He re-combed his short hair and thought that he looked somewhat American. Or Italian when he donned his sunglasses. His Cuban driver was waiting for him when he stepped out of the apartment block at 7:45 a.m. The December morning air was pleasantly devoid of the summer humidity.

Twelve minutes later he was in his embassy office. Tariq, also dressed in western civilian garb, brought him a Turkish coffee. *Orta.* Medium sweet. Major el-Shahawi took off his suit jacket and hung it from a coat rack in the far corner of his office. Sipping the coffee, he listened as Tariq answered the phone and grunted a couple of times before hanging up.

"Communications Center," he said. "Special communications. I'll run up and pick it up."

He stepped out of the office suite and returned in a few minutes with a bright red folder.

"A communiqué from America," he said. "From *Saladdin* in Virginia. Forwarded by our ambassador in Washington."

El-Shahawi took a final sip of the thick, rich coffee and opened the red folder.

[Most Secret]

From: Yemeni Embassy, Washington, D.C.
Saladdin in place. Martyrs in place. Vengeance day
19 December on infidel/Christian calendar. Sefir
(Ambassador) sends.

[Most Secret]

El-Shahawi looked at his desk calendar. The nineteenth was seventeen days hence. There was a post-it note stuck to the message copy.

We need to discuss this, it said. The calligraphic signature was that of the Yemeni ambassador to Cuba. El-Shahawi's boss. Nominally.

He dialed the ambassador's office. Fatima, the ambassador's secretary, answered.

"Good morning, Fatima. This is Major el-Shahawi. May I speak with Ali, please?"

"Certainly, major. One moment, please."

El-Shahawi heard a few clicks, and then Ali came on the line.

"Good morning, major. How can I help you?"

"Good morning, Ali. You probably already know how you can help me. The old man said he needs to see me about an inbound message," el-Shahawi answered.

"Ah, yes, major. Are you free now?"

"Yes. Of course. I'll be right up."

El-Shahawi took his suit jacket from the coat rack and donned it again.

"I'm going to the old man's office," he said to Tariq. "I have no idea how long this will take."

Ihsan Mohsin Hamdi, the Yemeni ambassador to Cuba, wore English suits of fine quality and spoke Spanish like the nobility of Spain. He was five-feet, four inches tall and weighed one hundred thirty-two pounds. His manners were exquisite. When Ali showed el-Shahawi into his office, Hamdi arose from his desk, came around and shook el-Shahawi's hand.

"Thank you for coming, major," he said. "Have a seat. Ali, would you be so kind as to call down for some tea?"

"Yes, Excellency. Immediately."

El-Shahawi and the ambassador sat down in comfortable, straight-backed chairs facing a table inlaid with mother of pearl. Ali returned immediately and took the third seat at the table. By the time he was seated, a small man in a white jacket and black trousers was placing three glasses of tea and a small crystal bowl of sugar cubes on the table. He added tiny linen napkins and vanished. The ambassador used a small pair of tongs to put three cubes of sugar into his glass of tea. Ali gestured to el-Shahawi to help himself. He did and added four cubes. Ali added one cube to his glass. The ambassador sipped and el-Shahawi and Ali followed suit.

"This individual, this 'Saladdin,' he came through Cuba? Do I have that right?" the ambassador asked.

"Yes, Excellency. He did. With the approval of our Ministry of Foreign Affairs. As well as the *Muhkabaret,* the Intelligence Department. As you know, Excellency."

The ambassador took another sip of tea.

"My memory is not as good as it once was," he said. "But I do seem to remember you telling me about 'Saladdin' coming from Germany to orchestrate attacks against the American infidels."

"Yes, Excellency. *Saladdin* came to Cuba with three comrades. We spoke of it. I have a paper—"

"I'm sure you do," the ambassador interrupted. "Did those three people accompany this *Saladdin* to America?"

El-Shahawi saw no reason to lie. At least not a total lie.

"No, Excellency. One of them met with an unfortunate accident and was lost in the sea off the coast of *Palizada.*

"Allah, Allah! Do the Cubans know of this?"

"No Excellency. Saladdin and the two martyrs know. They were there. Sergeant Tariq from my office knows. That's all. Besides us. The Cubans know nothing of the plan nor of the accident."

"I want to emphasize the necessity that there be not a trace of Cuban fingerprints on these attacks. Not one iota. If the Americans see el Qaeda or Hamas or Hezbollah or Iran behind the attacks—or even Yemen, their ostensible ally—that is potentially embarrassing but acceptable. No problem at all. We're in a war. The Americans know that. We know that. Even though we're supposed to be allies. They also know that Yemen is seething with lowlife evildoers—both outside and inside the government. But Cuba—there must be no connection with the Cubans. No connection whatsoever."

"Yes, Excellency. We launched *Saladdin* from Palizada to Florida. Clandestinely. There is no indication that the Americans made that connection. The explosives in the martyrs' vests come from Cuban artillery ammunition purchased clandestinely here. That will all be gone the instant the explosives detonate. So no trace to Cuba."

"My worry—an old man's worry, admittedly—is that one of our martyrs will be intercepted before he blows himself or herself up," the ambassador said. "And hence the Americans get a vest. That is loaded with Cuban artillery propellant. Their laboratories will determine the Russian and Cuban connections within hours. Our Cuban hosts will have egg on their faces, to say the least."

"Excellency, there is no reason to believe that the attacks will not succeed. And even if one or two does fail—a most unlikely prospect— there is a 'Plan B' for detonating the explosives. Besides there are literally tons of Russian artillery ammunition in Iraq and Afghanistan. Virtually every improvised explosive device that blows up American soldiers almost daily is made from Soviet artillery ammunition. The vests will not fall into the hands of the Americans. But even if they do, there will be no Cuban connection."

"So you say, Major el-Shahawi. So you say. But you and I both know that these vests are now in the hands of Allah's children. And that introduces an element of what our Greek brothers of antiquity once called 'chaos' into the equations.

"And even more worrisome is the Cuban connection," the ambassador continued. "If memory serves, you were to hire a Cuban jet boat to take the *shahids* to America. Suppose a member of that boat crew goes to the authorities?"

"Your Excellency, we've been over this before. There's no way the boat contractor will go to the authorities. Neither he nor his crewmembers want to trade a pretty good life for a stinking prison cell. Besides, the crew has returned after delivering the martyrs safely to Florida. And now they— the martyrs, that is—are safely in Virginia."

"Very well, Major el-Shahawi. I guess it's out of our hands now anyway. The matter is in Allah's hands now."

The old ambassador stood up and Major el-Shahawi did likewise. The ambassador reached for his hand and the two men shook hands.

"Thank you for coming, major," said the ambassador. "Please keep me posted on *Saladin*'s progress."

Major el-Shahawi felt an uncomfortable sensation of uncertainty, a sense of a partial loss of influence over the success of the mission. Once on the ground floor of the embassy, he opted for a visit to the embassy garden rather than returning to his office. He found a shaded bench, sat, and lit a cigarette.

The old fart, he thought. *He must think he's somehow in partial control.* 'Keep me posted,' *indeed.*

But then, the conspiratorial side of el-Shahawi's brain kicked in. He recalled that the message had come from the Yemeni Ambassador in Washington. *I hope Saladdin doesn't spend much time communicating with the embassy in America. And that our Washington embassy doesn't try to communicate with our embassy here in Havana very much. Every fucking electronic communication is susceptible to intercept. Every code is breakable. The Americans, the Russians, and the Cubans will learn of the plot if there's too much communications on the airwaves,* he mused. He stubbed out his cigarette on the sole of his shoe and carried the butt out of the garden and into the sunshine, where he tossed it into the gutter of the Havana street.

Chapter Forty-Four

The snow crunched underfoot when I took Cory on her morning walk and again when I walked into work early. When I arrived, Judy was there and coffee was made. I poured a mugful, played at the white board for a few minutes and then sat down at my computer. Thinking of my thoughts of yesterday—including "simultaneity" and "four vs. one," I fiddled with the numbers a bit. Then I typed up a two-column list with "our" new numbers. I changed the numbers on the white board accordingly. Darps and Sammy might well screech like gut-shot panthers when they saw what I'd done to the probabilities that we'd discussed yesterday. But what the hell. I'm the captain. I get to drive the ship. At least once in a while. I was sure that *Cheetah* remembered our chat yesterday, so I didn't feel like I needed to put anything additional in by way of explanation in a blurb to him. The numbers had wobbled a little, but that was all.

I saved the table to a thumb drive and wandered back to Judy's office.

"Morning, neighbor. Have you heard from Luke or Mike this morning?" I asked.

"Yes. Both. They should both be here within a few minutes."

"Well, they can flip a coin. One of 'em will have to ride the train this morning. For a briefcase swap."

I held out the little flash drive.

"Got it," she said, taking the drive. "I'll have them set it up and keep you posted."

Darps showed up about fifteen seconds later.

"What's up, shipmate?" he asked.

"Simultaneity," I said.

"What? Have you turned into the sphinx or something? What are you talking about?"

"Simultaneity. The quality of two or more events happening simultaneously. At the same time. I did have a thought or two yesterday afternoon that caused me to revisit the probabilities that we kicked around yesterday," I said. "And, yes, the issue of 'simultaneity' surfaced then as well."

"Care to elucidate?"

"Sure. It was a non-random thought going all the way back to nine-eleven."

"Wanna get the German-Arab team together?"

"Yeah. But let's let everybody read their email, check the news, and meet in the Big Kahuna at zero-nine."

"Nine it is. I'll have Sammy there as well as either Luke or Mike. Now tell me about simultaneity."

"Okay. This isn't something I spent a lot of time pondering. But I did spend a little time grazing on the Internet. Consider the nine-eleven attacks. The first hijacked jet, American Flight Eleven, took off from Logan at 0752. The fourth plane to take off was United Flight Ninety-Three, which left Newark at 0842. That's a total of fifty minutes separating the launches of all four hijacked airplanes. Then there are the impacts. American Airlines Flight Eleven struck the North Tower of the World Trade Center at 0846. United Flight Ninety-Three hit the field in Pennsylvania at 1003—a total of an hour and seventeen minutes between first and last impacts. And that interval would probably have been shorter if the heroes of Flight Ninety-Three hadn't fought with the terrorists and caused the plane to miss its intended target and crash in Pennsylvania. The bastards wanted those targets hit at—or close to—the same time. For maximum effect. Maximum terror. Simultaneity.

"Then we have four people in the green Jetta. Assuming al-Husni is the puppet *meister* and won't soil his hands by blowing himself up, that leaves three passengers. Kehoe advised that the green Jetta was spotted by Virginia cops heading south yesterday. One driver, all by himself. That leaves two *shahids*, one male and one female. Two martyrs suggests two targets."

When I entered the Kahuna, there was a fair amount of chatter that seemed to be a response to the locations and probabilities listed on the white board.

"Okay, everybody. Here's where we are," I said. The chattering stopped. People found seats. "Yesterday, Sammy, Darps, and I decided to hang out here to give *Cheetah* thirty minutes to answer our email. You'll remember that our message told him that, based on the Israeli professor's study, it would probably be from two to four weeks before the dirt bags tried to blow anything up here. We also said it was of paramount importance to figure out the 'where.' While we waited for a response from the man, we began looking at the 'where' here on our favorite Smart board. The targets as listed are from the terrorists' computer in Germany, refined by us. We agreed that the German-Arab list need not be all-inclusive and that it could be dangerous to consider it so. So we added, 'Elsewhere.'"

I pointed to 'Elsewhere' with a laser.

"We also knew that the probabilities couldn't add up to more than one—or 100 percent. So we basically pulled probabilities out of thin air and came up with a list that added up to one. We jacked up the 'Burbs/ Stafford' probability to point-three, based on that cell phone call from South Carolina to Stafford, the FBI's spotting of a suspicious vehicle with shady-looking guys in South Carolina heading north, and our spotting of what is probably the same vehicle—we think—coming into the local area.

"Oh, and that's another thing. The Virginia State Police spotted the green Jetta south of Richmond. Right license number. Yesterday. Heading south on I-95."

"*South?*" Ashleigh interjected. "How many people were in it? Was it the same car?"

"One and yes," I said. "The driver was alone."

"That must mean that he dropped his riders off and turned around to go back to Florida," Ashleigh said

"When did the police see the vehicle?" Samantha asked.

"About twenty-four hours ago—the first time," I said. "That's what made me jack up the Burbs/Stafford probability another ten percent to point-four. And the Jetta stopped at South of the Border last night and left there at seven-thirty this morning. Still heading south and still with just a driver. He must have dropped his passengers somewhere around here. And then, earlier this morning, I separated the Burbs and Stafford probabilities. Here's what the new probability matrix looks like. And by the way, *Cheetah* never did call back yesterday."

Target	Probability
Mall	0.2
Stafford/Chestertown	0.3
Other Suburbs	0.1
USNA, Annapolis	0.2
M&T Bank Stadium	0.05
Pentagon	0.1
Elsewhere	0.05
TOTAL	*1.00*

"Originally, we gave the Mall and the Arlington area double the priority of the Annapolis and Baltimore targets because they're higher-value, more spectacular targets."

I put up an infamous nine-eleven slide showing the North Tower of the World Trade Center ablaze and the second jet about to crash into the South Tower.

"The nine-eleven terrorists wanted 'simultaneity' in their attacks," I continued. "For maximum shock value. Maximum terror. The first three targets were all hit within a fifty-one-minute timeframe. The jet with the 'Let's roll' heroes crashed in Pennsylvania about twenty-six minutes after American Seventy-Seven struck the Pentagon."

I took a slug of lukewarm coffee.

"I thought about that for a while. I thought about the multiple targets listed on the computer in Germany and the fact that there were four people in the Jetta coming up the east coast. I wondered if these clowns wanted to take down multiple targets around here. Simultaneously. So I pursued that thread. I looked at event schedules, pro sports, colleges and universities, political events. I looked at college basketball games and hockey games. I went to local colleges' websites. Then I went to public school districts. Private schools. I looked at so many websites that my eyeballs ached. Looking for simultaneity. Stuff happening at the same time. Congress is gone. On recess. The Redskins are at Dallas on the 17th but home against the Giants on the 23rd. The Ravens are away on both the 17th and the 23rd. So I knocked down the probability of an attack in Baltimore to five percent. Ditto for 'elsewhere.' One of the sites I went to listed the Naval Academy Calendar. It's in Maryland—which was on the terrorists' computer in Germany. I found that the Naval Academy goes on Christmas leave at approximately 10:30 a.m. on December 19th. Which is a Thursday. I bumped up the probability of an attack in Annapolis to point-two. And those numbers are going to the man this morning."

"So you're saying Stafford-Chestertown area is a likely bombing target? On 19 December?" Darps asked, his voice a bit more strained than usual with excitement.

"I'm not ready to bet the ranch on it. Yet. Thirty percent is thirty percent. Point-three. But that's what our latest probability matrix looks like right now. And what we *are* saying is that there's a probability of *point-eight* that the Mall, the Naval Academy, or the Stafford/Chestertown area will be attacked. And by the way, 19 December is two weeks and two days from today, putting it well within Professor Fleischmann's two-to-four-week window for 'martyr prep' time," I added.

"There are a couple of problems with that matrix," Ashleigh said. "*Suburbs* is too vague. It includes all kinds of territory around the metro area. And 'elsewhere's' probability is way low, if you ask me."

"Both points are valid. That's why I pulled 'Stafford' out from 'suburbs' and made it a separate category. And re-allocated probabilities. The 'elsewhere' issue is a bit different. More difficult. If we raise that probability, we have to lower another. Or others. They still have to add up to exactly one-point-zero. And we do have positive intelligence pointing at Stafford and a few flimsy indications that Annapolis is a target."

I decided that this would be an excellent time for me to shut up. I sat down.

The Big Kahuna chatter fairly erupted. I let it run for a few minutes, stood up again, and held my hand up. If I'd had a whistle, I would have blown it.

"Ahem," I said, instead. Somewhat loudly.

"I just made a decision. It's not frivolous. But well considered. I want three papers by noon," I announced. "One from Darps, One from Sammy, and one from Ashleigh. Three pages, each, max. Anyone can provide input to any or all three papers. No ego issues here. Give your input to Darps, Sammy, or Ashleigh. Whether solicited or not. Feel free to share your thoughts with all three principals. Or one or two. Their papers are to be recommendations on what the National Command Authority needs to do with the threat as we see it. Now. No arm waving, no bullshit. Definite timelines and courses of action. We'll take the three papers as a group and see if we can use them to draft a single paper that we'll send up the road. And, once again, we're jumping off the reservation. The man may tell us to take whatever we give him and stick it up our asses sidewise, but that's his prerogative. But step one is I need three papers from you. By noon. We'll hammer them together into one single paper and we'll send it up north. Secret service needs to prime the pump for a fifteen hundred run up to the big house. And by the way, we'll have an in-house working lunch. On the house, so to speak."

I tapped my watch.

"Let's go."

Chairs rattled and shoes clicked. In less than thirty seconds, Kahuna was empty except for Judy and me.

"Well, neighbor," I said. "What do you think?"

"A pretty tall order," Judy answered.

"We have a pretty tall problem," I answered.

Chapter Forty-Five

Major el-Shahawi began to clear his desk. It was 1545—3:45 in the afternoon. The embassy closed at 4:00. He was putting several folders into a safe when he heard the office phone chirp and Tariq answering. He heard Tariq say "Okay," and hang up the phone. Tariq's head popped into el-Shahawi's office.

"The basement has something for us. I'll run down and sign for it," he advised and disappeared. Irked, Major el-Shahawi glanced at his watch.

"The basement" was a special communications center with which the embassy maintained secret contact with official Cuban government and military intelligence services. The connection was via an underground, fiber-optic cable. Both the Cuban Government and the Yemeni Embassy believed it provided totally secure communications. It by-passed the embassy's normal diplomatic communications center. El-Shahawi hated it when the basement sprung something on him at the end of the day. *I wonder what sort of grenade those bastards are throwing my way this afternoon,* he thought. This evening was supposed to be free—a rare privilege, an escape from the seemingly non-stop gamut of diplomatic social functions that oftentimes included intelligence assignments. The latter were the only thing that made the evenings interesting. Sometimes. This evening, however, he was supposed to be free. He had arranged to meet Laura at a restricted-access Havana club for cocktails and dinner. Afterwards, they'd planned to go to Laura's flat for what she'd described as a "special treat," whatever that was. It couldn't be bad.

Tariq was back from the basement within three minutes. His eyes had a "you're not going to like this" look as he handed el-Shahawi the red folder.

"Maybe you'd better sit down, Major," he said.

El-Shahawi took his advice and sat in one of the two visitors' chairs in his office. He opened the folder. It contained a single sheet of printout.

[Most Secret]

Allied communications intelligence has noted a sharp upswing in the volume of police and military radio and mobile telephone communications   along the I-95 corridor along the U.S. East Coast and in particular in northern Virginia and eastern Maryland.
Destroy by 240019 December.

[Most Secret]

"Allah, Allah!" el-Shahawi muttered. "The Vengeance of Muslim Martyrs cat may be out of the fucking bag."

The office phone rang, and Tariq went to answer it. "I'll bet a hundred dollars it's the old man," el-Shahawi mumbled, half to himself.

"It's Ali," Tariq said.

"I *knew* it!" el-Shahawi hissed, getting up and walking to his phone.

"El-Shahawi," he barked.

"Yes, Major," Ali's silky voice oozed through the line. "Can you please come upstairs? His Excellency would like to chat with you for a few minutes."

"Certainly, Ali. I'll be right up."

"Let's meet in room two-sixteen, Major."

"Of course. I'll be right there."

El-Shahawi hung up the phone, grabbed a notebook and the red folder and headed for the door.

"Don't leave until I get back. I'm sure the old man got the same Russian advisory we just got and is now pissing his pants about the Americans making a Cuban connection. *Inshallah,* this won't take long," he said. "But who the fuck knows?' he asked, rhetorically. El-Shahawi's brain started calculating as he walked out of his office.

Who knows? he asked himself, mentally. *Are the Cubans witting about 'Vengeance'? No fucking way,* he told himself. *If they knew that Yemen had a hand in launching a terrorist operation against the United States of America from Cuban soil, neither the ambassador nor I would be going to a meeting in room two-sixteen here in the embassy. We'd both be heading for some stinking pesthole like Djibouti or Ulan Bator, if not prison. If not a bullet in the brain.*

How about the Russians? he asked himself as he headed up the stairs. *Maybe. Maybe not. Those swine have a thousand ways of getting information. Even if they do know about Saladdin and Vengeance, there's probably no harm. They certainly won't tell the Americans. They certainly did not tell their Cuban comrades. Most likely, they'll just watch and wait. The Americans? Probably not. They may smell a rat and be suspicious. If they really* knew *about the operation, there'd be more than just heightened chatter on the east coast military and police frequencies.*

El-Shahawi turned out of the stairwell and turned left toward room two-sixteen. Ali was unlocking the door to the tiny conference room, which the Yemenis believed to be immune from any sort of bugging. Most embassy staffers referred to room two-sixteen as "the safe room." As Major el-Shahawi approached, Ali pulled the door open.

"Let me turn on the lights and the air," he said. "His Excellency will be along presently."

El-Shahawi stepped into the room and immediately began to sweat. The temperature must have been more than 40 degrees Celsius. He stepped out and decided to wait for the ambassador in the corridor. He heard the deep hum of the air conditioner kick in. Ali stepped out of the room.

"I'll tell his Excellency you're here," he said. "The room should be comfortable in a few minutes."

"*Inshallah,*" el-Shahawi muttered. He had visions of Laura and him feasting on *ceviche* and Champagne. Followed by visions of Laura naked. He saw Ali emerge from the ambassador's office down the hall, followed by the ambassador, buttoning the jacket of his five-thousand dollar English suit. Ali was carrying a red folder. El-Shahawi stepped inside the safe room. It was still warm, but not murderously uncomfortable. He stood and waited for the ambassador.

"Ah. Major el-Shahawi. Thank you so much for coming up. Shall we sit?"

"If you please, Your Excellency."

They shook hands and sat. Ali closed the door. There was a hiss of air pressure changing.

"Our Cuban hosts tell me that the police and military communications on the east coast of the United States between Florida and Washington have suddenly become very active," the ambassador intoned. "I have to wonder if that has any connection to Saladdin's travels. What do you think?"

Major el-Shahawi chose his words carefully.

"Yes, Excellency. I'm fairly certain that our Cuban hosts received the intelligence from the Russians. The Russian satellites are like giant vacuum cleaners in the sky. If indeed American police communications are more active, certainly the Russians would know. But there could be various reasons. The approach of the Christmas holiday. Holiday traffic. Contests between American universities in what they call football.

"It's even possible that they have a suspicion about Saladdin and Vengeance of the Muslim Martyrs. I doubt that, but even if they do, I don't think it's a problem. The operation will go forward as planned."

"I don't understand, Major. How can the Americans being suspicious not be a problem? Suppose they arrest one of our donkeys with Cuban explosives?"

"Suspicions are different from knowledge, Excellency. The Americans usually don't arrest and detain—at least on American soil—based on suspicion alone. Our operation has been totally secret. The Americans can have no knowledge. Our martyrs are out of sight. They will remain out of sight until they burst forth and wreak death and destruction on the infidels."

"I hope you are right, Major," the ambassador said. "I'm still worried. If one of our martyrs mistakenly blows himself up in a sewer, fine. No problem. If an American policeman shoots one of them and he or she blows himself or herself to bits, no problem. But if the Americans can arrest one of them, take him alive and take the vest intact, we have major problems."

Visions of Djibouti and Ulan Bator flashed through al-Shahawi's brain for a split second.

"I think we needn't worry, your Excellency," al-Shahawi said. "That will not happen."

"You mentioned a 'Plan B,' Major," the ambassador said. "Perhaps it's time to start thinking of a Plan C."

The short, wizened man in the expensive suit rose to his feet and held out his hand.

"Thank you again for coming up, Major," the ambassador said.

El-Shahawi rose and shook hands with his ambassador.

"Always a pleasure, Excellency," he said.

He waited until the ambassador left, looked at his watch, and left Ali to turn off the lights and lock the room. Tariq was waiting for him downstairs in his office.

"How bad was it, Major?" he asked.

"Civilian swine have no balls," he muttered. "No balls at all. But it could have been a lot worse. The ambassador's spine is quivering, as only that of a professional diplomat will do. He's pissing his pants about the Americans finding a Cuban connection to the Vengeance operation. Fuck him. Let's get out of here."

Back at his apartment, Major el-Shahawi took off his jacket and tie, unbuttoned his collar, and poured himself a stiff scotch. He sat in his favorite chair, sighed and sipped.

I can't help but wonder why the old bastard is so interested in Vengeance, he thought. *He usually wants to keep some distance between nasty operational details and himself.*

He took another sip of scotch. He felt a vague twinge of unease.

Chapter Forty-Six

I had Judy call Fat Harry's for a fairly eclectic mix of sandwiches and told her I'd pick them up myself, in person, to pay and to check on Hafez. We added a bunch of bottled water, soda, and beer to the order.

There was a lot of trotting around the halls from office to office. A lot of buzz. I guess that was what I'd started and what I'd wanted. At 11:40, I went out into the wintry day to make the sandwich run.

Hafez seemed a bit distant when I entered the restaurant ten minutes later. I paid for lunch with my own credit card. Lunch and drinks were in six large shopping bags. Harry took three and I took the other three and headed outside for the Explorer.

"How's Khalil?" I asked. "Is he ready for full-time teaching?"

Harry put the heavy shopping bags on the floor of the passenger side. He stood up and frowned.

"Alan, I don't know what to tell you. I hardly ever see him in the last couple of weeks. After he moved to Stafford a year and a half ago, he would stop by the restaurant once or twice a week. Or more. He'd talk about things—the teaching, the girlfriend, and movies, whatever. Then, he started getting phone calls on his mobile, which he'd take outside. I figured it was the girlfriend. And he wanted some privacy. No problem. Then he stopped visiting here. He was in here yesterday—but just for a couple of minutes. And that was the first time in a couple of weeks. There was a scruffy-looking old guy with him. An Arab. Egyptian, I think. From his accent. I called Khalil's apartment a couple of times but I just got voicemail. I was starting to worry, but then, he did drop by yesterday, so I guess he's okay."

"Well tell him I said, 'hi,' the next time he drops by," I said, putting the other shopping bags into the shotgun seat.

"*Inshallah*, that'll be soon," he said, with a thin smile.

"*Inshallah*," I repeated.

I was back at Ripley Hall by 12:05 with the shopping bags, which I brought into the Kahuna conference room.

"You're *not* going to serve lunch out of plastic shopping bags," Judy advised primly. "Give me a few minutes to arrange things."

She had a stash of napkins, paper plates, plastic cups, and such. Even a couple of paper tablecloths. Darps wandered in with a couple of coolers.

"I just picked up some ice," he said and started loading the beer and sodas into the coolers.

Judy put little piles of wrapped and labeled sandwiches on several paper plates. The room started to fill up.

"Help yourself—dig in," I announced, "Enjoy the lunch. We'll start kicking the papers around in about thirty or forty minutes."

I reached into one of the coolers and pulled out a bottle of Michelob Amber Bock. Judy took a bottle of water from the same cooler. We both poured our beverages into clear plastic cups. Judy probably because she's prim and proper, me because I like to look at Amber Bock almost as much as I like to drink it.

"How was your buddy—Fat Harry?" she asked

"Preoccupied," I said. "He seemed to be worried about his nephew, Khalil. Have you met him?"

"No. At least not that I know of. He may have been there, but I know we've not been introduced."

"Nice guy. In his twenties. Wants to be a teacher."

I took a swig of Amber Bock. Something about Hafez and Khalil was rattling around in some deep recess of my brain.

I unwrapped a sandwich that was labeled, "Steak Bomb," and took a bite. It hit the spot, as always.

Ten minutes later, I crumpled Fat Harry's white sandwich-wrapping paper and finished the last of my Amber Bock and looked around. People were finishing their lunches just as I was.

"Ten minutes," I announced, glancing at my watch. "Darps, you're up first. Sammy will follow you, and Ashleigh will finish. Then we'll put all three of the papers together."

Darps was ready and gave me a thumb's up. He hooked a laptop to the Smart board and sat down to wait. I used the break to retrieve my laptop and check email. Three minutes later, he put up his first slide.

Vengeance of the Muslim Martyrs, it read.

"Time, ladies and gentlemen," I announced. I nodded at Darps and he stood up.

"We think this is the code word of a terrorist operation against the homeland of the United States of America," he began. "There are a few minor pissing contests among interpreters as to whether the correct word is 'Vengeance' or 'Revenge,' but we don't think that matters."

His next slide was a map of the Middle Atlantic states, including Maryland and Virginia. The latter two states were outlined in green.

"Data retrieved from a terrorist cell's computers in Hamburg—the cell that apparently executed the bombing of the night club in Kaiserslautern—contained *Google-Earth* hits on various locations in Maryland, Virginia, and the nation's capital.

"A suspected terrorist—one Mehmet al-Husni—is believed by German authorities to have 'directed' the suicide bombing of the night club in Kaiserslautern. Al-Husni is a German citizen of Egyptian origin. There is no hard, actionable evidence linking him to the Kaiserslautern bombing. So they can't take him to court.

"German authorities advised us that al-Husni traveled to Cuba several days ago.

"The Coast Guard advised the NCTC that a small craft—possibly coming from Cuba—entered Marathon in the Florida Keys early Friday. It left almost immediately and headed back for Cuba—we think. We're guessing that al-Husni may have been aboard and disembarked in Marathon.

"Then we have an FBI report of a green Volkswagen Jetta heading north with four guys—or three guys and a woman—after spending the night at the South of the Border complex in South Carolina. One of the 'guests' was a scruffy-looking old guy with a description matching that of al-Husni."

Darps' next few slides were a series of maps that went into the construct of a montage. The first slide showed Cuba with a highlighted spot on the north shore. The next one showed the Florida Keys and a highlighted spot on Marathon, a little more than halfway from Key West to the mainland.

A highlighted line connected the two dots. The following slide showed a zoomed-out map of Cuba and the east coast of the United States with a squiggly line following the Florida Keys and I-95 up the southeast coast to a dot in northern South Carolina. The final map showed a line through North Carolina and Virginia connected to another dot in northern Virginia.

"The northernmost sighting of the green Jetta was by us—Ashleigh, to be specific—here in Thornburg on Saturday. The vehicle had four occupants—genders undetermined. Then, the Virginia State Police spotted the same vehicle yesterday, heading south. With a lone, unaccompanied driver. Who spent last night at South of the Border and continued south this morning. Still unaccompanied."

Darps went to the slide with the headshot of al-Husni.

"This is Mehmet al-Husni. As I said, a guy matching his description stayed at South of the Border in South Carolina Friday night. According to the FBI, he and three companions left South of the Border Saturday morning. One of the three 'buddies' was a female.

"Our feeling is that Mehmet and one of his pals are planning to conduct a suicide bombing somewhere on the mall in D.C. Our bet is either the Lincoln Memorial or the Washington Monument. Maximum shock value. Old Mehmet was probably the director or puppet-master as Sammy says, of the Germany suicide bombing. One of his comrades was the martyr. We believe he will try to execute this CONUS bombing within the next seventy-two hours."

Darps sat down. A number of people gasped. The image of the stubble-faced Mehmet al-Husni remained on the Smart board. People started jabbering.

"How can an Egyptian become a German citizen?" somebody asked.

"German mother," Willi said.

"Why don't the cops pick up the driver of the green Jetta?" someone else asked. "Sweat him for a while and find out who and where his friends are?"

"I'm not sure, but my guess is that the Feebs don't want to let on how much we know," Luke said.

"Sammy," I said. "You're up."

Sammy stood up.

"We agree with Darps on most of the run-up to the planned attack. Including the name of the operation—*Vengeance of Muslim Martyrs* or *Revenge of the Islamic Martyrs*. We disagree on the timeframe and the targets."

Sammy put up a slide that said: *Targets: Chestertown, Virginia, and National Mall.*

"Chestertown? Virginia?" I asked. "Whiskey-Tango-Foxtrot? What's up with that? Are they going to bomb City Hall? Or the City Park? Or us?"

"That's where we flamed out. But we figure that al-Husni is here. We also figure that he apparently came up here with two or three other guys or maybe two guys and a woman, so that there are at least two targets. Probably three. One of them has to be the Mall in D.C. The second one is probably here. We couldn't narrow it down more than that. The third target is anybody's guess. My totally subjective guess is the Naval Academy in Annapolis. It's a popular tourist attraction. That courtyard is packed with midshipmen and officers at the noon formations. On December 19th, the noon meal formation will be lined with parents waiting for their sons and daughters. Incidentally, the formation will be early that day. 10:30. The Brigade and a fair number of parents will be ready to depart on Christmas leave. And the usual quota of tourists will be there. A fat target. So that's my personal guess. As a group, we came to a consensus on the Mall and Chestertown. No consensus on Annapolis. And no consensus on where in Chestertown.

"As for the timing, since I'm betting on the last formation before the Brigade of Midshipmen goes on leave—December 19th—I'm betting on that date for the other two attacks as well. But that's just me. We couldn't find consensus there, either."

He sat down. I finished my note taking.

"Ashleigh?" I said. "Your turn."

She stood up, fooled with the computer for a few seconds and another *Vengeance of Muslim Martyrs* slide splashed up on the board.

"We also differ only in our description of the planned attacks. We also tied pretty subjective probability estimates to what we think will happen. We used the latest *BIAS* probability matrix as a point of departure.

"In that matrix, we showed a probability of an attack on the Mall, the burbs, including Chestertown, or the Naval Academy having a combined probability of eighty percent. Since al-Husni and his henchman and henchwoman arrived in town on Saturday morning and it's now Tuesday morning, we've re-evaluated the probabilities in the matrix. This is what we've come up with. For starters, we zeroed out the probabilities of the attacks in Baltimore, Arlington. and elsewhere, making the probability of an attack on the Mall, the Naval Academy or Chestertown combined at 100 percent. That means zero for Baltimore, the Pentagon, or 'elsewhere.' Here's half our bottom line."

Ashleigh went to her next slide. It was a now-familiar table. But the entries were different.

Target	Probability
U. S. Naval Academy	0.25
Lincoln Memorial (Mall)	0.25
Martha Washington University*	0.50

"Here's what that asterisk with Martha University means," she said. "We're pretty well agreed that al-Husni has (a) communicated with Stafford/Chestertown, (b) has come to the Stafford/Chestertown area, and (c) has been the subject of communications from or to Chestertown. Ergo, there's a target here. We felt the biggest target was the university. December 20th is their last day of classes."

She changed to a slide that showed a calendar page for December.

"Here's the other half of our bottom line," she said, tapping the mouse.

On the December calendar page that came up on the screen, all thirty-one days were displayed. Eight days in a row, starting with the 4th were tinted yellow. Ashleigh tapped the mouse again. The next seven days— December 12th through the 18th—were now tinted pink.

"One more time," she said and went to the mouse. December 19th turned blood red on the calendar.

"T-Day," she said. "That's our best guess."

Ashleigh sat down. There was a short interval of silence and then a dozen conversations erupted at once.

Chapter Forty-Seven

"Okay," I said to my rabble. "Take ten, get organized, and at 1:30, we'll start synching these three papers into one for the man."

People starting trashing sandwich wrappers, water bottles, and beer bottles. That's when I heard the explosion. It sounded huge. Much more than what one might hear in a normal suburban environment. I went to the front door and looked around and immediately saw dense clouds of black smoke rising from somewhere down near the river. The smoke dissipated in the northerly breeze quickly. I turned back into Ripley Hall.

"What the fuck was that?" I asked.

Luke was already on a mobile.

"Wait one," he said.

Thirty seconds later, he hung up the cell. I heard sirens.

"Explosion of 'unknown origin' the cops say. On River Road. Apparently, no vehicle involved. That's all they know, as of now," Luke said.

My little tribe of smart people was already hunched over computers or phones or both. I'd have to wait a little to see what sort of information they would harvest. I had every confidence in them. It would only be a matter of time.

I walked past Judy's office. She was on the phone and she waved me in. I stood in her doorway.

She mouthed the word, "Maria," as she pointed at the receiver. Then she said, "He's standing right here. Shall I put him on?"

I gave her a thumbs up, stepped across to my office, and pressed the blinking button on one of the phones on my desk. Judy went scurrying out of her office.

"Hi, Love. What's up?" I asked.

"You probably heard the explosion," she said.

"Oh yes indeed. I could even see the smoke. Luke called a friend on the CPD. 'Unknown origin,' his source told him."

"Well, maybe it's not unknown anymore. I just came from there. I was coming home from a meeting. The police are putting up crime scene tape. Around an absolutely *huge* area."

"Hmm. Maybe they're worried about more explosions. I'm guessing Elizabeth's still at school," I said.

"Yeah, I'm sure. But I think I'll call All Saints and tell them I'm going to pick her up, rather than let her ride the bus. We just don't know what's going on and I'll feel better if she's with me."

"Me, too," I said. "Give me a buzz when you leave and when you get back home. Please."

"Will do. Keep me posted on whatever you can," she said before we said our goodbyes.

I hung up. Darps jumped through my door like a bald, bearded version of Kramer on a *Seinfeld* episode.

"It appears that some clown blew himself up across the river," he said. "It's really weird. From what I hear, there were no other casualties. This dipshit was walking along River Road and all of a sudden disappeared in a burst of flame and smoke. Pieces of him scattered all over the road and the riverbank. A guy walking his dog on our side of the river saw it happen and called the police. The cops have taped off a huge crime scene."

"Jesus Christ," I said. "Exploding people. Whiskey tango foxtrot?"

I immediately started wondering about connections between the explosion on River Road, Revenge of the Martyrs, and Saladdin. But nothing was making sense. I got up from my desk and started wandering around Ripley Hall. My smart people were flogging away on their computers. The TVs were showing fragmentary morsels about a heretofore-unexplained explosion in Chestertown. The news media were still saying 'unknown origin.' No mention of casualties. I donned my raincoat, told Judy I was going for a walk, and headed for the door.

"Don't forget your phones," she called after me.

I went back to my office and grabbed the two phones. She knows me too well.

"Let's delay our meeting by fifteen minutes," I said over my shoulder.

I already had a pair of binoculars from my desk hanging around my neck.

I got down to the river in about five minutes. The Rapp is a generally south-flowing river, but here in town, it flows from west to east. River Road is on the north bank. I was on the south bank where I frequently walked Cory. I could see Chestertown Police Department officers across the river and could see the yellow tape. I took out the pair of seven-by-fifty binoculars, leaned against a lone oak tree and scoped out the scene across the river. I saw a guy with an expensive looking digital camera walking around and taking photos, mostly, it appeared, of stuff on the ground. Then I saw several—I think there were four—pairs of guys in black coveralls. One guy in each pair was carrying what looked like white plastic bags. Both guys were wearing white gloves. A couple of guys had some sort of big tweezers or small tongs. I followed one duo with the binoculars for several seconds. One of the guys bent down and picked up something and appeared to put it into one of the white bags that the other guy held. He made a couple of notes with a pen and seemed to attach part of the note to the white bag. Then his partner took the white bag and deposited it in the back of a silver-gray panel truck. The logo "Chestertown Medical Examiner's Office" was stenciled in black on the side of the panel truck. It seemed like Darps's assessment was right on target. But what the hell did it all mean?

Chapter Forty-Eight

Havana
December 3
Tuesday

They dined in fine style at *El Club Caribe*. The *ceviche* was excellent. They'd washed it down with cold *Freixenet*, a bubbling wine from Spain, and followed that up with steaks and an excellent *Malbec* from Argentina. When they returned to Laura's flat, the temperature was quite warm. She'd poured them each a cognac and started the ceiling fans. They sipped cognac and kissed.

"It's hot—even with the fan. Let's shed some clothes," she said.

She stood and unbuttoned her dress and let it slide to the floor.

El-Shahawi made short work of his tie and shirt. Laura looked at him expectantly. He removed his shoes, pulled off his socks and slithered out of his trousers.

"Isn't that better? With the fan blowing on our skin?" she asked.

She giggled. She walked across the room and inserted a DVD in the player under the large, flat-screen television. She bent over to pick up a remote. Her ass was magnificent in the thong panties. She pressed a button on the remote. "Now you have to watch this. Before you have another cognac."

The video commenced.

El-Shahawi couldn't understand the language the on-screen couple was speaking. They were both in their underwear. There were English subtitles, but he had difficulty taking his eyes off the man and woman in the video, so he missed most of the dialog. The man was in an obviously aroused condition. When the woman in the video began tugging at her partner's briefs, Laura moved to follow suit with el-Shahawi. At that moment, his mobile rang. He cursed in Arabic and groped for his pants and the phone. Laura cursed as well. In Italian.

He answered the phone. In Arabic.

"I must go to the embassy," he croaked, reaching again for his trousers. "There is something that I must look at. Now."

"Goddamn it, Faisal!" she snarled. "This was supposed to be a free evening. A special treat. Now you're running off to your fucking embassy like a whipped dog."

"It's duty, Laura. Sworn duty. I am a soldier. I have no choice."

El-Shahawi was buttoning his shirt.

"Duty my ass, you worm. Speaking of which, you'd better find yourself another 'friend' with an ass you like. This ass is leaving the picture."

She stood up, went to her closet, and pulled on a dressing gown. When she looked at him, there were tears in her eyes.

"Go to your fucking embassy. I'm having the locks changed. *Arrivaderci!*"

Allah, Allah! he thought. *I'm getting fucked without getting fucked every time I turn around. I need to find an understanding, compliant Arab woman.*

Tariq was waiting for him at the embassy. Holding a red folder.

"It's bad," he said.

"No shit. It's already bad, and I don't even know what's in the goddamned folder."

"Take a look," Tariq said, handing him the folder. "Ali is on his way in. He'll decide whether or not the ambassador needs to come in."

El-Shahawi took the red folder, opened it, and read.

"The fucking imbecile!" el-Shahawi hissed. "The worthless asshole!"

He closed the red folder.

"How could he be so fucking stupid?" he asked, rhetorically. He paused. "But then, perhaps it's not as bad as it looks at first," he continued.

"If this report is accurate, then the moron blew himself to bits. With virtually no collateral damage. No American injuries, let alone deaths. Presumably, al-Husni instructed him to travel without ID. So pieces of his worthless corpse will sit in freezer bags in a refrigerator somewhere in Virginia. Unidentified. The police will scratch their heads. But that's the only thing that will happen as a result of this bloody fiasco."

They heard the buzzer at the outer door of the military attaché's office space.

"Ali," Tariq said. "I'll let him in."

Seconds later, Tariq and Ali entered el-Shahawi's office. Ali's eyes were still swollen from sleep.

"How bad is it? Do I need to call the ambassador?" he asked.

"It looks worse than it is. One of our intrepid *shahids* accidentally blew himself up in Chestertown, Virginia. At least, I assume it was accidental. Apparently, there was hardly any damage. And no injuries except our gallant *shahid* who is now in Paradise. That's an assumption, too, obviously."

"But that's terrible. Terrible."

"Well, it is and it isn't. We lost the *shahid*. But that was going to happen anyway. There will be one less target on Vengeance Day. But there was no compromise of the operation."

"I'll call his Excellency," Ali said, taking out his mobile.

"That's not necessary. Don't disturb him. Just schedule me for five or ten minutes first thing when he gets in tomorrow."

"Are you sure? It'll be my ass that he'll tear a piece off when he finds out."

"Ali, you recall the last time we talked. His Excellency's only concern was that the connection with our Cuban hosts is not discovered. That isn't going to happen here. I'll make sure he understands that."

El-Shahawi took the red folder from Ali and handed it to Tariq.

"Lock this up," he said.

"I'll be in by 7:30," the major said to Ali. "Call me as soon as the old man is in and I'll come right up. Perhaps you should open room two-sixteen and turn on the air conditioning when you get in later. Now, I'm going home to bed."

He got up wearily and glanced at his Movado. 1:55.

"We'll have to sleep fast," he said and went out to his car.

He was nearly home when his mobile strummed. *Sweet Allah*, he thought. He glanced at the phone's screen. It was Laura.

"Allo," he said.

"Are you still at the embassy?" she asked.

"No," he said. "I'm in the car. Almost home."

"I'm sorry I blew up when you had to leave. I was just so disappointed...."

"Okay. I understand."

"I haven't changed the locks."

"Good. I'm home now. And exhausted. I have a meeting with the old man first thing this morning. I've got to go to bed."

"I understand. Sleep well. Call me later."

"I will."

Major el-Shahawi unlocked the door to his flat, closed the door, and stripped off his clothes before collapsing on his bed. He was exhausted but it still took him a long time to fall asleep.

Chapter Forty-Nine

When I got back to Ripley Hall, the chatter was almost overwhelming. The explosion had really set the cat amongst the pigeons. Once again, if I'd had a whistle, I'd have blown it. But I didn't. Instead I walked through both floors of Ripley.

"Kahuna! Five minutes," I called, using my best parade-ground voice. "Everyone is welcome. Five minutes."

In around four minutes, the principals and everyone else were assembled in the big conference room. I tossed them a bone about the explosion across the river.

"Some rocket scientist apparently blew himself or herself to pieces across the river," I said. "At this point, we have no way of knowing whether this incident is connected to the D.C. area terrorist threat. We have to wait for more information.

"Meantime, we need to put together what Darps, Sammy, and Ashleigh gave us in a semi-coherent paper for the man. Spelling out what we know, what we suspect, and what we think he should do about it."

I stepped to the Smart Board. Picked up an electronic marker and listed three headings in red:

Darps   *Sammy*   *Ashleigh*

Then I went to the left of the board and picked up the blue marker and wrote the following notes, aligned with the red headings:

	Darps	*Sammy*	*Ashleigh*
Target:	Mall	Mall & Chestertown	USNA (.25)
		USNA (?)	Mall (.25)
			C-town (0.50)
Date:	Dec 5th	Dec 19th	Dec 19th

203

"Okay. Even though I usually mistrust consensus intensely, you guys think well enough for me to discard that mistrust. The National Mall is a target. The Naval Academy is a target. Chestertown is a target. The latter is pretty big and pretty widespread, target-wise. Ashleigh's group suggested the university. If I had to pick a target in Chestertown, that's probably where my pencil would land as well. There's a pretty hefty probability assigned by Ashleigh's group. Fifty percent. In the paper that I send to Cheetah, I'm going with the Mall, the Naval Academy, and Martha Washington University, each with a probability of 0.33. Then I'm going with Dec 19th."

A bunch of hands jumped up and chattering started. I pointed at Samantha.

"Samantha? Your comment?" I asked.

"You're taking 'elsewhere' off the table?" she asked.

"Yes, ma'am. I want to give the man a definitive call. I know there's some risk of being wrong that creeps in, but I want to give him a clear, uncluttered estimate. So 'elsewhere' is indeed off the table," I said. "Besides, in the info we have so far, there's nothing to support an attack elsewhere. And God knows what he'll get from the NCTC. If anything."

She nodded her head slightly in reluctant agreement.

"Alan," Darps said as the chatter subsided. "I'm not comfortable with saying the boom-day is the 19th of December. Alone. And it's not just because my group came up with a much earlier date. Which we did. Because al-Husni is here. Now. But if we tell POTUS the bombs are going off on 19 December and they go off on the 15th or on Christmas Day, *BIAS* credibility takes a major hit. I think giving him a date range, say from the 17th through Christmas Day would be more useful. Even if we said the highest probability date was the 19th."

Ashleigh and Samantha were both nodding their heads. Darps's argument made sense.

"Okay," I said. "I'll go along with that. But I am thinking along the lines of 19 December being a high-probability date. As in 0.6. Then we taper off on either side. Like 0.1 on the 18th and the 20th. Then maybe 0.05 on the 17th and then taper off some more on either side. Thoughts?"

"Makes sense to me. If that means that we're predicting the attack will occur between the 15th and 22nd, I think that's a good call," Darps said, leaning back in his chair.

I looked around the room. Sammy, Ashleigh, and Samantha all were nodding their heads. We were ready to go to press for the leader of the free world.

> Keys,
>
> Subj: BIAS bottom line
>
> Here it is. We believe "Saladdin," aka al-Husni, is in CONUS, most probably in the Chestertown, VA, area now.
>
> We believe he is intent on carrying out three terrorist attacks, using suicide bombers. Our analysis strongly suggests that the targets are one, The National Mall between the Capitol and the Lincoln Memorial (Probability 0.34); two, The Naval Academy at Annapolis (Probability 0.33); and three, Martha Washington University in Chestertown, VA (Probability 0.33.)
>
> We believe these attacks are planned for 19 December (Probability 0.6) but could occur on 18 or 20 December (Probability of 0.1) with the probability of attack tapering off before and after those dates. But we do feel the attacks will be nearly simultaneous and will occur between 15 and 22 December. We also agree that all three attacks would most likely take place in mid morning.
>
> As of now, we have no knowledge of any connection between the person who blew himself up in Chestertown and this plot beyond the obvious geographical one. But we're going to look at that some more. Will advise.
>
> That's our bottom line for now. We think you should get FBI and/or state/park police into position on the National Mall, around MWU in Chestertown, and around USNA in Annapolis by 15 December latest.
>
> We'll keep you updated as more information comes available. As always, we'll be grateful for any crumbs of info you can toss our way.
>
> Loose

Everyone in the room followed my clumsy typing as the memo popped up on the Smart board. Willi and Mike made a 'thumbs up' sign; Ashleigh nodded and said, "I think you nailed it."

"Classification?" asked Judy.

"UNCLASS," I said. "The only thing that's classified with this paper is that it comes from us. Let's get it up the road via the special briefcase route."

"I can get it there in an hour from now, Alan," Mike said. "Six o'clock."

I thought about that for about a microsecond.

"Save it on a flash drive and give the man a briefcase," I told Judy.

Three minutes later Mike was out the door.

A huge letdown washed over me like an eight-foot wave. It was five till 6:00.

"Okay, let's shut it down for tonight. I think we gave it our best shot. Thank you all. I intend to have a few swallows of an adult beverage, sleep for ten or eleven hours, and then try to figure out where we go from here. And pray that these bastards don't try anything tonight."

Chairs scraped, low voices blended. I was startled to see Darps lip-synch the word, "Emergency," and quickly figured he meant the Dewar's in the file cabinet. Very quickly, *BIAS* was down to a staff of three—Darps, Judy, and I.

"I'm going to get the leftovers into the fridge unless you guys want to take some home," Judy said, busying herself with straightening up.

"Would you like a scotch, Judy?" Darps asked.

"No thanks. I want to keep my head clear for setting the alarm since something tells me you two are having one. Besides, I don't like scotch."

"Well, in that case, don't throw away the ice till I've got a couple of glassfuls," Darps replied.

Darps poured and the two of us helped Judy with the clean up as we sipped. We talked a bit about the poor wretch that had blown himself up across the river. We agreed that this one-man explosion had to have been an accident unlike the nightclub bombing in Germany. It was cold and dark when we locked up, and I let Judy talk me into accepting a ride home.

"It's on my way," she said.

"Thanks. And sleep well," I said as I climbed out of her Toyota in front of fifteen-oh-six Prince Henry.

Chapter Fifty

Next morning began as a "normal" morning, whatever that is. People came to work, began their day with a quick scan of email and news. I did the same thing after checking in with Judy and Darps. I ran my eyeballs over a copy of the memo we sent to the president yesterday. It still looked okay.

I went to Luke's office.

"Can you find out if the cops have any more info on the person who blew himself up?"

"Just got off the phone. There is more, but very damned little."

Luke glanced at a notebook.

"It was a male. No ID. Probably Mediterranean. No matches on fingerprints. No dental match. No DNA match. *But*, get this. The guy had some sort of anti-anxiety med still in his system. Could have caused him to fuck around with the bomb, setting it off by mistake. More later.

"No clothing labels. Shirt probably manufactured in Vietnam. Pants and underwear in China. Shoes in Thailand. Wristwatch was a Seiko. No cell phone. He could be from anywhere. Except here. Cops said he had a cheeseburger and a beer for lunch, coffee for breakfast. FBI Lab might be able to tell something about his long-term eating habits, but that'll take a few days. Bomb contained a few fairly common, low-grade explosives. Most of it was Russian—but there were German fuzes and caps and American detonating cord as well. Plus a lot of crude, homemade shrapnel. Screws and nails and suchlike."

"Could you put all that in an email? Send it to everybody on the Arab/German team. I'd like to kick it around and see if we can tie this clown to Saladdin and his buddies," I said.

"Sure," he said. "I'll have it out in less than fifteen minutes."

I went back to my cage and tried to get caught up with stuff that I'd been neglecting for the past couple of weeks. Judy popped in frequently to nudge me toward particular items that I needed to eyeball and/or sign. I walked home for lunch and realized that lunchtime walks weren't an acceptable substitute for real runs, but I enjoyed my lunch with Maria nonetheless. We had tomato and basil soup with grilled Swiss cheese sandwiches on pumpernickel bread.

"How goes it with the New York Regiments in the Union Army?" I asked.

"It's amazing how much they helped the Union," she said. "And it's amazing how many of them there were. Two hundred infantry regiments alone. But there's lots of other fascinating stuff as well."

She took a dainty bite of her sandwich.

"Did you hear from Kehoe about the paper?" she asked.

"I did not. I kind of expect the second shoe to drop this afternoon. If he doesn't respond, I'll start to think he's blowing off our stuff. Even though we really exceeded our charter with that paper."

"Do you actually have a charter?"

"No. Not in writing."

"That's what I thought," Maria said, smiling.

She finished the last of her dark brown sandwich and wiped her lips daintily with her napkin.

"What time do you have to be back?" she asked.

"Um, no special time. I'm the boss."

"Goody," she said "That's what I thought.".

Cinq a sept amour is supposedly very good. I can tell you that *une a trois* is pretty damned good as well.

When I got back to Ripley Hall at 3:15, Darps popped into my office.

"A nooner, you sly dog," he muttered, with a grin. "But we have to look at the exploding man and ask ourselves if that might cause changes to the conclusions and recommendations we sent up the road."

"Sounds good," I said. "Round up the team. Ten minutes."

I'm not sure, but I think I heard a few groans and curses as Darps wandered through Ripley Hall announcing the meeting. A lot of people I know would have launched an immediate email announcing the meeting ten minutes hence, but Darps likes to do things the old fashioned way. By looking people in the eyeballs.

Ten minutes later, we were in Kahuna with Luke's email on the Smart board.

"Okay, *mes enfants,* we now have some more info about the guy who went up in smoke yesterday." I said. "You all have Luke's email about what he learned from the local cops about the incident. The question is: do you see anything there that should make us change our memo to the man? Like altering targets, probabilities, or dates?"

Answers ranged between "no," "I dunno," and "let us get back to you after we digest Luke's email."

"Okay. Any target changes?" I asked.

"If the guy was one of the bombers, his explosion could make for one less target," Sammy said, echoing the thought that was on everybody's mind. "One bomb, one bomber gone."

"Which target goes away?" Samantha asked.

"I don't know," Sammy said. "My guess is that they'd scrub the hardest target. The Mall. That leaves Annapolis and beautiful downtown Chestertown still alive."

"Okay. We're playing guessing games now. Which is fine. But maybe it's time to give it a rest. See if anything else surfaces overnight. Let's pull the plug and reconvene at 0800 tomorrow."

We were finished till 8:00 tomorrow morning.

I walked home. I had an inexplicably uneasy feeling. About going home. A lot of Chestertown homes and shops were sporting Christmas lights. There was a guy at the corner of Prince Henry and Queen Street, standing under the streetlight playing Christmas carols on a violin. He was into *Adeste Fidelis* as I approached. A few snowflakes were descending slowly through the light. There was an open violin case at his feet. A few crumpled dollar bills and some change lay there gathering a little snow. I pulled out my wallet. It held three twenties and a ten. I pulled out a twenty and dropped it into the case. The violinist segued into *God Rest Ye Merry Gentlemen* and murmured "Merry Christmas, sir."

"Merry Christmas," I said.

It was easy to stay in the Christmas spirit when I got home.

"We bought a Christmas tree," Elizabeth announced. "It's in the back yard."

"Well, we better bring it in or someone will steal it," I said.

"Would someone really steal a Christmas tree?" Elizabeth asked.

"Let's hope not, sweetie. But let's not take the chance. I'll put it in a bucket of water in the mud room and we can put it up and decorate it tomorrow."

I could see a covered skillet on the stove and smelled something winey, earthy, and delicious.

"Excuse me if I drool. What have you got going on the stove?" I asked Maria, after kissing the nape of her neck.

"*Coq au vin,*" she said. "With roasted potatoes."

"I need to prepare my stomach," I said and retrieved the scotch bottle. There was Christmas music on one of the TV music channels. I took a sip of scotch and went out and retrieved the fragrant fir tree from the cold yard and stood it in a bucket of water in the mudroom. Life was good. But I did say a quick Hail Mary, praying that Saladdin and his minions wouldn't attack tonight.

Chapter Fifty-One

Major el-Shahawi arrived at his office at the Yemeni Embassy at 8:15. Sergeant Tariq presented him with a small cup of *orta* Turkish coffee along with the morning folder of message traffic. The first message was a summary of the account of the imbecile who had blown himself to bits in Virginia.

Allah, Allah! he thought. *How could this fucking fool make it so far and blow himself to pieces? Which target is taken off the board?*

"Did you read this drivel, Tariq?" he asked. "Which one of those morons do you think it was?"

"Of course I read it, major. If I were betting, my money would be on that whining slime-dog that was here. Farouk. The one that yowled like a kicked cur about the one that you shot. The old man was smart and tough. So was the woman. But that slobbering fool that was sobbing over the moron you killed would be my guess."

"That would be my bet also," el-Shahawi said. "The idiot was a spineless turd. I just wonder whether he blew himself up on purpose or by a stupid accident. I guess it doesn't matter at this point. But now two of the so-called soldiers in this four-man vengeance operation are dead."

He turned back to the folder.

"There's nothing in here about the Americans and what they know or don't know," he said.

"That's probably because they don't know much of anything," Tariq said.

"*Inshallah,*" muttered el-Shahawi.

Their office phone rang. Tariq stepped into the outer office and picked it up.

"Office of the Military Attaché. Sergeant Tariq speaking," he said.

"Yes, *Signorina*," he said. "One moment, please."

"I think it is the Italian woman," he whispered.

"Allah, Allah," muttered el-Shahawi. He and Laura had agreed never to telephone each other through the embassy phone system.

"Allo," he muttered.

"*Mi dispiaci,* I'm sorry," she said. "I just saw a cable saying someone blew himself—or herself—up in Chestertown, Virginia. Do you know anything about that?"

"No," he lied. "And we need to hang up immediately."

He hung up the phone.

What's up with that? he asked himself mentally. *Why in the name of Allah would Laura break security so outrageously to ask about an imbecile blowing himself or herself to pieces in Virginia?*

He thought he knew the answer to his question, but he didn't like it. At all.

Chapter Fifty-Two

Chestertown
Thursday
December 5

I walked in to Ripley Hall the next morning. Skies were gray and low; the temperature was in the mid twenties. The college student traffic seemed to have thinned out a bit. Judy had the office opened and had started the coffee jugs brewing. I said "Hi" to her, poured a mugful of fabulous-smelling coffee, and went to my desk. There was a blinking bar on my monitor. An email. From *Cheetah*.

> From: Keys@LISound.com
>
> To: Loose@BIAS.gov
>
> Subj: Explosion
>
> That clown that blew himself up in Chestertown has GOT to be connected with this fucking plot. What do you guys think?
>
> I am having DHS arrange for extra law enforcement on the three sites—Mall, USNA, and MWU in Chestertown beginning 15 December, open-ended. For your eyes only, I'll pull them off 2 Jan unless the shit has hit the fan before then. They tell me park police will cover the Mall w/ uniformed Secret Service reinforced around the House. Virginia State Police will cover Chestertown. Maryland State Police will cover Annapolis outside the Yard; Marines will be in the Yard.
>
> This a.m.'s Intel Brief said Italian source in Cuba claims Yemeni connection with bomb plot is "real."
>
> Keys

Well.

The exploding martyr was our first order of business this morning, so I should be able to get back to the man within a couple of hours. The

213

extra security on the three sites was comforting. Somewhat. The "Italian source's" reappearance was interesting, as were his/her observation that the bombing threat was real and Yemeni-based. I wondered if my boss and the Israelis might be hatching a plot to bomb Yemen. Or mount a number of drone strikes. Yemen is nominally our ally. Not sure how Jerusalem feels about the Yemenis. They probably don't trust them as far as any one of them could throw a Mirkava tank. There are a lot of evildoing cucarachas crawling around the place. Which I gather is a pesthole of the rankest sort. But dropping bombs on Yemen is way above my pay grade. My job was to focus what comes *out* of Yemen—not what goes in. Ditto for Germany.

I went into the Big Kahuna conference room alone with my coffee and went to the Smart board. My intention was to wrap up what we knew about the lone Chestertown bomber and any connection to the D.C.-area plot. I listed a heading and three subheadings in red, followed by my notes in blue.

CHESTERTOWN EXPLOSION

BOMB	SCENE	BOMBER
Unknown origin,	No vehicle,	No ID, no prints,
Russian explosive	Large!	No DNA, Internt'l
Some US & German	CPD bagging evid.	clothes, Burger &
mat'ls, crude shrapnel	CS tape	beer for lunch;
	No add'l casualties	Mediter orig? Male

I stepped back from the board and looked at it. People started straggling into Kahuna. It was scrub time. Somehow, we had to overlay the Chestertown explosion with what we had constructed for the overall attack. And make sense out of the whole mess somehow. I stood by the Smart board and waited till everyone had found a seat.

"Good morning, everybody. Here's a summary of what we have on the exploding man across the river," I said, gesturing at the Smart board. "It's *all* we've got. Luke obtained the info from police sources. This is it. What we need to do now is figure out the connection between the exploding guy and the D.C. metro-area bomb plot—if said connection exists. If we agree that there probably is a connection, then we need to ascertain the nature of the connection. And we need to nail down whether this guy and his explosion change the info that we sent to *Cheetah* yesterday. If it does, then we need to make the necessary revisions."

"Upon reflection, I think it does. Change the info," Darps said. "I think the explosion means one fewer bomber and one fewer target. Two instead of three. I can't imagine that these bastards would have a backup plan for one of their martyrs blowing himself up by mistake. And that's what this fiasco seems to be."

"Amen to that," added Samantha. "We're down to two targets. The question is 'which two?'"

"Not so fast," Sammy said. "Even though the proximity to the White House would mean tougher security for the National Mall, and the evildoers surely realize that, I don't think that fact zeros out the likelihood of an attack there. It may degrade some probabilities somewhat, but none of them to zero. In my opinion, the Mall is still a live target, probability-wise, even if there are, ultimately, only two bombing attacks."

Ashleigh, Willi, Luke, and Mike all agreed. As did I. I started to type. The words popped up on the Smart board.

Keys:

BIAS is adjusting our probabilities due to this clown blowing himself up in Chestertown. The bombers are minus one bomber and one bomb. They've got to realize that the Mall is a harder target because of your presence nearby but also more lucrative for the same reason. We dropped the probability of a hit on the Mall to point-two. Twenty percent. MWU in Chestertown and USNA in Annapolis are also still live. Forty percent probability for each.

Loose

"Um," Ashleigh said. "How about we make USNA and MWU thirty-five percent each and throw 'elsewhere' back into the mix at point-one. Ten percent. That way, the Academy and Chestertown are still high, but if one of these martyrs blows himself up at the Pentagon metro station, we won't look like morons."

"Ash, you have a soft spot in your heart for 'elsewhere,' but your point is well-taken."

I made the changes.

"I don't want to send this via email," I said. "But it needs to get up the road to the man."

Luke and Mike looked at each other and at their watches.

"I'll take it," Luke said. "Drive it all the way. We don't need to waste time with the train-metro cutout at Reagan National. I'll have it there within an hour and a half."

I glanced at my watch.

"Maybe two hours," I said. "It's only 8:30. I-95 is still constipated. Maybe The VRE/Metro swap is faster."

"I'll check the schedules and also check with the big house. Whichever way is quicker, that's what I'll use," Luke said.

I tapped out a short text on the phone.

Keys: Update memo inbound WH via Luke. Should b there by 10:30 latest

I nodded to Judy and she saved our memo on a flash drive.

"It's ready to go," she said to Luke.

"Okay, guys. It's back to business as usual. Sort of. This D.C.-Saladdin thing is obviously on the front burner. But let's not forget the rest of the world, either. At least not totally."

I almost felt like I should be crossing my fingers behind my back, but I didn't. What I'd said was mostly true. Mostly.

Chapter Fifty-Three

Darps and I walked a few blocks toward the river, turned right, and headed for J. Brian's pub. The sky was dark and low, and an occasional flake of snow drifted and spun slowly through the damp air. It was nice to step into the warmth of the crowded and Christmas-decorated pub. We both ordered pints of Guinness and Reuben sandwiches.

Darps took a pull at his Guinness, licked the foam off his mustache, and set his glass down.

"I don't have a good feeling about this fucking situation, shipmate," he said.

"For what it's worth, I'm not real comfortable with where we are, either," I said. "But I think we've given it our best shot."

"You're right. Let's enjoy our sandwiches. What do you think about taking a trip to the country this afternoon? For some secure brainstorming."

"Good idea," I said as the waitress brought our sandwiches and French fries.

We ate our sandwiches and fries, drank our Guinness, and traded observations on the appeal—or lack thereof—of various females who came into the restaurant. A couple of middle-aged dirt bags fantasizing about still being twenty-one-year-old midshipmen.

After lunch, we returned to Ripley Hall, checked our email, and headed out together to the little dive of a house in the Wilderness. The snow, still not heavy, was a bit more serious than when we were at lunch. Darps unlocked the little farmhouse annex and did something with the thermostat that started a low roar and a welcome blast of warm air. He then went to a cupboard and hauled out mugs and a foil bag of *Mystic Monks - Midnight Vigils Blend* coffee.

'What say, shipmate? Coffee?"

"Yeah," I said. "A cup of coffee would hit the spot. Judy's catered coffee is fine, but there's nothing like *Mystic Monks.* "

"You got it," he said and seconds later the coffee maker was moaning, and the *Midnight Vigils* aroma was wafting through the warming air of the hovel.

Minutes later, we sipped.

"I'm not comfortable with our—*BIAS*'s—posture," I said.

"What do you mean?"

"Well, we've got two or three or four terrorists roaming around and getting ready to blow something—or some things—up. And we're sitting on our asses, waiting for it to happen."

"Well, we *did* go a little active, looking for the green Jetta. For which action you got your knuckles rapped. And you're probably lucky that *Cheetah* didn't throw your ass in jail," Darps said. "Besides, we just don't have the assets to collect the kind of info to tell us when or where."

We both sipped more coffee.

"I'm not talking about sending people out on the street," I said. "I don't think that would give us anything anyway. Too much street and not enough of us. But I do think we need the store open and the wheels turning until this hairball is resolved. As in round-the-clock operations. I'm thinking we need to put together a watch bill."

Darps stood up, walked to the sink, and rinsed out his cup.

"To what purpose?" he asked, drying his cup with a dishtowel.

"A couple. First, to have at least a pair of eyeballs and a pair of ears monitoring the Internet and the phones for any morsel or two that might come zinging—or floating—our way. I'm just not comfortable turning our backs and walking away from what's going on in the world for fourteen or fifteen hours every day. Or night."

"For what it's worth, I agree. What else?" Darps asked.

"Faster, more responsive communications. With the White House. After all, Kehoe's driving the ship. If we—*BIAS*—learn something that makes any sort of preventive action necessary, we've got to let *Cheetah* know so he can set things in motion. For example, if a *BIAS* watch officer learned that a target was the Pentagon Metro station rather than Chestertown, Kehoe's the only one with which we have contact who can move the cops to the Pentagon," I said. "And we can't fiddle-dick around for thirty or forty minutes getting him the word."

"You've convinced me. Let's go back to Rip. Judy and I can cobble something together for you to take a look at."

"Sounds good," I said and washed and dried my coffee cup.

Chapter Fifty-Four

When we returned to Ripley Hall at four o'clock, the snowfall had intensified. The office was like Dunkirk early in World War Two. Everybody there seemed to have a shell-shocked, whipped-dog expression. I understood immediately that the folks were in an info-starvation mode. There was simply no new information. None. The data flow on the D.C. area suicide bombers had flat-lined. No new clues. No new information nuggets. No morsels from DHS, NCTC, FBI. I was tempted to go back to *Cheetah* and re-ask for permission for *BIAS* to fish in home waters. But the timelines were growing short. Tomorrow was the sixth. I was sure that Kehoe would tell me to go fuck myself, and even if I could turn him around, that probably would take a few days. After that, there would be a few more days hiring or reassigning people, getting our hands on the necessary money. By then, the bombs would probably have blown and Americans would be dead.

I decided against another big meeting and decided to try and turn things around the hard way. One-on-one. I went to Sammy's desk first.

"Darps and I had a meeting. We're thinking we need to produce a watch bill so we can go over to twenty-four-hours-a-day operations. At least until this D.C. bombing threat is resolved."

Sammy perked up.

"Well, from the sideline, I think that's good. I'm not at all comfortable closing up shop and all of us going home in the evening to watch TV with these bastards running around loose. Especially, here in good ole Chestertown."

Ashleigh had just popped into the room.

"There's another angle. It's possible—likely, even—that these people have rehearsed their attacks. Their suicide attacks. And would *not* be inclined to change targets. And the puppet-master might be reluctant to depart from the script as practiced. Remember, these guys aren't known for their flexibility and their ability to segue into *ad hoc* operations."

"Good thoughts. So we need to try and get into the chatter as deeply as we can and see what turns up. We also really need to narrow down the timelines."

"Samantha is listening to and looking at a lot of Arabic-language stuff on the web. I'm pretty sure she hasn't found anything having to do with a D.C. area suicide bombing," Ashleigh said.

"No surprise there. The bombers and their minders no doubt have a total blackout on info related to the operation. We need to keep looking. Or listening. Or both."

Bugging anybody's phone or email was, of course, off the table. But the Internet was in the public domain. One never knew what one might find out there.

I continued to wander through the building. At least people were thinking. Samantha was fishing, had a line in the water. She hadn't had any recent bites, though.

I went by Judy's office. Darps was already there. It sounded like he'd already broached the idea of going to round-the-clock operations—at least for the time being.

"What would you have them do?" Judy asked me as I stepped into her office. "These twenty-four-seven watch-standers?"

"Monitor everything they can understand on the Internet. News feeds. Any and all sites they can make sense of. Especially those associated with radical dirt bags. Hack and listen where they can. Watch email and phones for anything from our folks overseas. I haven't really thought it through. That's why I need your help—to help me think things through."

Darps scribbled furiously on his graph paper.

"Sounds like you *have* thought things through," Judy said.

"A little," he said. "Alan and I tossed a few softballs around out at the ranch. And it was pretty random. On the fly. And we didn't even touch details like numbers of people, numbers of hours, and suchlike."

Darps turned to me. "Tell you what, shipmate," he said. "It's almost five and snowing. Let's shut down here. Everybody goes home including you. Except, Judy and I stay a while and build a strawman of a watch bill, which will be in your email when you come in in the morning."

"Works for me. Don't spend a lot of time picking the fly shit out of the pepper. That means 'don't stay too late.' Email it to me, and we'll kick it around tomorrow."

I walked through the building sending people home. Then I put on my jacket. I could hear Darps's and Judy's voices. I decided to leave them alone and not say "good night."

I had to wonder why the hell NSA and CIA still weren't getting the same kind of info that we at *BIAS* were getting. Or had been. Maybe it was because we were a lot closer to the ground. Now, of course, *nobody*— including us—was getting anything.

Chapter Fifty-Five

Iwas whupped when I stepped out the door of Rip at 5:25. Darps and Judy still had their heads together. Outside, the snowfall was steady, and the snow was starting to stick on the sidewalks and the lawns. The cold, damp air seemed to pick me up a little as I walked. I stopped in Lucille's Pan Asian Delights place and picked up a quart of pho, a couple dozen tiny barbecued spare ribs, and a large container of pad Thai. If we had extra mouths to feed, we could handle that. If not, there would be yummy leftovers tomorrow. I didn't feel quite as horsewhipped as I had when I left Ripley as I let myself into the mudroom at fifteen oh-six. A light cacophony of female voices wafted out from the family room.

There was a piquant aroma of the Far East coming from the cardboard containers I set down on the stove. Perfect for a snowy Thursday evening in December.

The five women who frequently hung out in my house at cocktail time were there. Maria was tapping away on her laptop. Elizabeth and her chums, Esmé and Tala, were on the floor with another laptop. Cory was in their midst and thumped the floor with her tail a couple of times when she saw me. For once, the TV was off. So all the female voices were natural. A fire blazed merrily behind the glass fireplace doors. There was Christmas music on the stereo—it sounded like an English choir.

"Hi Love/Dad/Mr. El!" rang through the cozy air. It doesn't get any better than that.

"Hi, ladies, and isn't this nice. Gently falling snow outside in the dark. A cheery fire, and Christmas music inside. And a bunch of lovely women to welcome the hunter home from the hill."

That claptrap got me a couple of eye-rolls and a couple of moans and one finger-gagging sign.

"Okay, okay. A bit over the top, I admit. But it truly is nice to come into this atmosphere, especially after the day that I've had."

"I guess that means you need to fix yourself a cocktail, Mr. El," Esmé chirped. "And a glass of sherry for Mrs. El. I'll get apple juice for the rest of us."

I raised my eyebrows in puzzlement.

"Esmé built the fire," Elizabeth said.

"Do you need a loan, Esmé?" I asked. "Perhaps some intervention with your parents?"

"No, Mr. El. Just some old fashioned Christmas spirit at work."

"Well, God bless us every one," I said.

That got more groans from the ladies. I went and found the scotch and sherry bottles.

"How bad was it?" Maria asked when I sat down.

"Well, you know about the guy blowing himself up the other day. We think—and the boss man agrees—that it's got to be connected with the D.C. area bomb plot. But we don't know how. I left Judy and Darps in at Ripley putting together a watch bill, which will keep BIAS open and working twenty-four/seven. I think we're flying into the danger zone."

I sipped scotch.

"Well it sounds like you're doing everything you possibly can to deal with it," Maria said.

"Maybe so, maybe not," I said. "Lord knows, we're trying. But there's a shitload of unknowns."

The girls on the floor pretended not to hear my vulgarity.

"I just finished another chapter of *The New York Regiments*," Maria said.

"Way to go," I said. "At least one of us is making progress."

"I'll bet you're making progress, too, you just don't recognize it yet. What's for supper?" she asked.

"Mixed bag. Vietnamese, Chinese, and Thai. Enough for five, if need be."

She turned to the girl-pack.

"If you girls take Cory for her evening walk, you'll be welcome to stay for what appears to be Asian takeout," she announced. "I'm sure that Alan will be happy to share his world-class hot sauce."

"Well that settles it," Esmè said, springing to her feet. "Where's the leash?"

We had a nice dinner and nice conversation, although I thought for a few seconds that the Sergeant Major hot sauce was going to put Tala down for the count. At nine o'clock, Elizabeth, Cory, and I walked the two girls home. The snow had stopped and the air was cold. After we saw Tala to her door, we headed for home.

"Dad," Elizabeth squeaked. "Are you scared?"

"Not scared, honey," I replied. I'm her dad, after all. "But I am worried. Very worried."

Chapter Fifty-Six

Saturday in Havana. Major el-Shahawi arose and went to the toilet. The time on his wristwatch was 7:15. Saturday. He dove back into the bed. He could easily bag himself two more hours of sleep. He was about fifty percent of the way back to oblivion when the phone shrieked.

"Allah, Allah," he muttered and groped for the phone. "Allo. El-Shahawi," he growled.

"Good morning, my sweet," purred Laura. "Will you be around your flat for another twenty minutes?"

"Yes. Of course. For you? Always."

El-Shahawi cradled the phone and glanced at his watch. Stripping out of his boxer shorts, he stepped into the bathroom and started the water in the shower. Its pressure was feeble but its temperature was warm.

After a barely sufficient shower, El-Shahawi stepped out of the stall and toweled himself semi-dry. He then stepped into a clean pair of boxers, followed by a fresh pair of jeans. He applied American deodorant and followed with a blue Miami Dolphins t-shirt. He was brushing his teeth when he heard the doorbell screech. He hit the *Open* button and heard the ground floor door open.

"Why the fuck doesn't she just use her key to let herself in?" he asked himself. *"Like she does every other night after I'm asleep?"*

He heard the downstairs door slam shut, followed by high-heeled footsteps in the stairwell. It had to be Laura. She never used the lift. He went to the door of the flat and opened it. Laura came through the stairwell door at the same moment.

"Cara mia," she muttered, striding into the flat.

"Ciao Bella. Che succede?" he asked. "What's going on?"

"I don't know," she said. "The Americans' chatter has changed."

"What do you mean? What does that mean?" he asked.

"I don't know. Their communications *tempo* has changed."

"Well, someone will sort that out. Either the Russians or the Cubans."

"I don't think the Cubans have a clue," Laura said.

"You're probably right. But you can bet your sweet ass that the Russians have noticed the change," El-Shahawi said.

Laura nodded.

"*Senza dubito*," she said. "Without a doubt."

The shrill ring of the phone startled them both. El-Shahawi picked up the handset.

"Allo. El-Shahawi."

He rolled his eyes.

"I'll be there in ten or twelve minutes," he said, hanging up the phone.

"That was Sergeant Tariq. From my office. Something's come up and I need to go to the embassy. My guess is that it's the Americans' communications anomaly."

"Will you be long?" she asked.

"Allah knows. My bet is that the Ambassador is pissing his pants again and needs to be stroked. But I shouldn't be long. The old man usually plays tennis at 11:00 on Saturdays. As you know. You're not playing with him today, are you?"

"No. I'll stay here and wait for you. I'll make coffee."

"Good," he said. "I'll see you in about an hour, Inshallah."

He let himself out the door.

Traffic was light. He reached the embassy in eight minutes. Sergeant Tariq was waiting for him inside the main door. He wore a t-shirt and jeans.

"H.E. is on the way in. Ali is already here and is pretty sure the old man will want to talk to you," he said. He pointed at the floor in front of them with an index finger.

El-Shahawi took that to mean "downstairs," and nodded.

Together they headed for the military attaché's office suite. Tariq keyed in the code to unlock the door and held it open for his boss. He let it close and picked up a red folder.

"You're right, Major," he said. "Downstairs. A little bit weird."

He handed the red folder to El-Shahawi, who flipped it open.

[Most Secret]

04Dec. Allied sources advise that American military, naval, and air force as well as police communications have spiked to new highs in terms of volume unprecedented in recent years. Frequencies are live and traffic is extremely heavy. But there are bursts of even higher-volume comms. Neither Allied sources nor headquarters has an explanation for the sudden wild fluctuation in traffic levels.

[Most Secret]

The office phone trilled as El-Shahawi finished reading the brief note. Tariq answered.

"Yes, sir, he's here. You may speak with him," he said. He handed the receiver to El-Shahawi and mouthed "Ali" silently.

"Good morning, Ali. Let me guess. Room two-sixteen in five minutes?"

Ali chuckled.

"Ten minutes will be fine, Major," he said.

When El-Shahawi reached the safe room, the door was open. Ali was inside fooling with the thermostat.

"His Excellency will be here momentarily, Major," he said. "I'll go get him."

He scurried out. El-Shahawi sat at the large, glass table. The air conditioning seemed to be sucking the atmosphere out of the little room. Two minutes later, His Excellency Ihsan Hamdi, Ambassador of Yemen to Cuba, appeared in the doorway of the safe room. Ali followed him in. He carried a red folder. As El-Shahawi stood, the two other men sat down at the table. Feeling awkward, el-Shahawi sat down again.

The ambassador tapped his tiny fist on the red folder in front of him.

"What do you make of this, Major?" he asked. "The Americans' communications craziness?"

"I'm not sure what to make of it, Your Excellency. I only just learned of it a few minutes ago. Perhaps the Americans are having an exercise or a drill. They do that, every once in a while."

"God *Damn* it to hell! Don't you see a connection between our Vengeance operation and the Americans' communications spike?"

The old man slapped the glass-top table. Sharply.

"No, sir," Major El-Shahawi said softly. "I see no connection whatsoever. If the communications surge is not part of an exercise, then it probably has to do with some sort of Russian or Chinese military activity. If the Americans had some inkling about our planned attacks, there would be an upsurge of back-channel communications traffic, not a burst of operational traffic. The Americans aren't about to start moving aircraft carriers or ballistic missile submarines around because of a terrorist threat. My guess is this jumping around has got to be in response to some heavy-handed moves by the Russians or the Chinese."

Major El-Shahawi could have sworn that Ambassador Hamdi had bared his fangs at him as he made his statement.

"So," the ambassador snarled. "Vengeance of the Martyrs continues. The Americans have no clue. Even with one of the shahids blowing himself to bits in their front yard. And their communications maxing out means nothing."

"Your Excellency, we can't know everything. The shahids are in Virginia. They have been briefed. They have their bombs. They are ready to go. They're like a football team. It's time for them to start knocking the ball around and time for the coaches to sit down and watch the game."

"As long as the Americans—or anyone else, for that matter—don't make a connection between the bombings and Cuba, we're fine," The ambassador said. "But, if somebody somehow connects the dots and a Cuban connection emerges, the shit will be in the fan. And Allah only knows where we'll end up."

The ambassador stood up and left the safe room. Without shaking hands.

"I couldn't have said it better myself," el-Shahawi muttered, thinking of Djibouti. The heat. Or Ulan Bator. The freezing cold. He left the safe

room. Downstairs, he turned to Sergeant Tariq. "Lock the red folder up in
our office, secure everything, and have a good weekend," he said.

   "Yes sir," said the sergeant, taking the red folder.

Chapter Fifty-Seven

I slept later than usual, waking up, and putting my feet on the floor at 7:11. I stretched and thought that my slumber had been rock solid. I'd read somewhere that sleep can be a defense mechanism against a variety of psych disorders—stress, fear, PTSD, grief, anxiety, or whatever. In my case, I think I've got my PTSD pretty much under control. Probably not so with the stress-anxiety combo, what with suicide bombers running around Chestertown and Washington, D.C. I pulled on a ratty pair of Augustine Washington High School sweats and an old pair of running socks and grabbed a pair of running shoes from the closet. Cory was waiting for me at the foot of the stairs, tail a-wag. I gave her a scritch behind the ears and did a quick outside recon. Sun was out, temperature was a dead-even forty. I pulled the newspapers in and put on the shoes. Then I grabbed a jacket and a leash, hooked up the hound, and headed out for our morning constitutional.

There was skin ice on the river's surface close to shore. It wouldn't last long with the temperature in the 40s and the sun full out. Steam was rising from the melting frost on the brown grass along the riverbank. I unhooked Cory, found a stick, and started throwing. After about twenty minutes of stick chasing, she came and sat down in front of me, grinning expectantly. I figured canine starvation was beginning to set in, so I hooked her up again, and we headed back to Prince Henry. By the time I got there, Maria and Elizabeth were rustling around in the kitchen. I fed our starving animal and then slapped a half-pot of coffee together.

"You seem to be running later than usual," Maria said as she poured soy milk onto Honey Nut Cheerios.

"No doubt," I said, opening a package of English muffins. "I probably slept an extra forty minutes. I'm sure Cory was convinced that she was about to expire from starvation."

I looked at the clock. Five till eight.

"We still have plenty of time to make 9:30 Mass," I said, starting the toaster. The women of my life said something like "mrmph" and continued with their breakfast and the Sunday newspapers. I chortled a bit as I grabbed the jar of orange marmalade from the second shelf of our reefer. The toaster sprang, and I slathered butter and marmalade on my English muffin halves. By that time, the coffee was done, so I poured a mugful for Maria and another for myself. I trolled through the discarded portions of the two Sunday newspapers and was able to collar the New York Times magazine section and the local rag's sports section. That would do for starters.

A few minutes later, Maria and Elizabeth parked their breakfast dishes in the sink and headed upstairs. I refilled my coffee mug and was gathering up other parts of the newspapers when the phone rang. It was Darps.

"Good morning, shipmate," I said.

"Hi," he said. "How fast can you get to the Woodbridge Rest Area on I-95?"

"Half an hour, give or take."

"See you there in thirty minutes. I'll look for you at the south end of Northbound."

"Roger. Thirty," I said. So much for 9:30 Mass. I trotted upstairs, made a uniform-race change into jeans and a sweatshirt, and popped open the bathroom door. The shower was thundering, and Maria was naked under the streaming water and the steam. She always looks so good in steam. Naked.

"Gotta run up the road and meet Darps," I hollered. "I'll catch a later Mass."

"Okay. Drive carefully," she said from the steam.

I was out the mudroom door, into the truck and onto the highway in very short order. I wondered what was up with Darps. With him, one never knows.

His Saab convertible was parked in the southern end of the rest area as I pulled in. There was an open parking place about five or six spaces past his vehicle, which I took. By the time I'd turned my engine off, Darps was opening the passenger side door.

"Got a minute, shipmate?" he asked.

"Of course," I said. "I'm here."

I climbed in.

"Remember my old buddy, Ray Smiley?" he asked.

"Of course," I said. "The squash player…"

"That's the one. He came by the house again. This morning. They got a cell phone call hit into Chestertown from parts unknown. It said quote, Revenge of Martyrs, unquote. And then quote, *[three seconds of static]* Thursday. Unquote."

"What's up with the 'static?'" I asked.

"Unintelligible. Totally. Ray said they enhanced the shit out of it but that was the best they could do with that call."

"Jesus Christ," I said. "Did Smiley know where the call originated?"

"They think offshore, near Key West, Florida. But they're waffling on that. They've got coordinates of a point fifteen miles south of Key West, but the CEP^2 is huge. It includes both Havana and Miami. So it's pretty imprecise."

"What language?"

"Arabic."

"Anything else?"

"Nope. That's it."

"Jesus. Now I gotta figure out a way to let the old man know in such a way that he doesn't have me taken out and shot. Or the two of us taken out and shot."

"Change the probability calendar. Goose up the probabilities on the Thursdays in the window. Don't give him a reason. Say, 'We've revised our estimates of the likelihoods of the attacks,' or some such arm-waving bullshit."

"Roger. I'll think of something."

The dashboard clock said 8:45 as I rolled out of the rest area. I should be able to catch up with Maria and Elizabeth at Saint Katherine's in time for the 9:30 Mass.

I envisioned a December calendar page. Today was Sunday, the eighth. That meant this Thursday would be the twelfth. And the other Thursdays

---

2   Circular Error Probable. Radius of a circle containing 50% of probable emission locations.

would fall on the nineteenth and twenty-sixth. The nineteenth was looking like an awfully strong candidate for Boom Day.

Father David, one of the deacons and three altar servers were lined up in the rear of the church when I slipped in. I espied my two beautiful, dark-haired women in a pew about halfway down a side aisle on the left and was able to slip down there before the Entrance Hymn started. Dressed as I was, I felt like a bum sitting with them but I figured the Lord would understand.

"Hi," I whispered as the opening notes of *O Come, O Come Emmanuel* kicked things off.

I thought about getting the revised probabilities to Kehoe. Securely. I knew that he and Franny would be going to Mass this morning—unless they'd gone to a vigil Mass last evening. I knew he liked to float and go to Mass at different churches. At different times. The Secret Service probably liked that too.

After Mass, we schmoozed out in front of Saint Katherine's. Elizabeth, Tala, and Esmè magically found one another and began an animated exchange of the latest All Saints and Chestertown intelligence. Maria found a Martha Washington history professor with whom she liked to trade ideas. I started worrying again about a suicide bomber in the area and then saw Judy. We caught one another's eyes and I approached her.

"I got a call from Darps this morning," I said. "We met for a few minutes at a rest stop on I-95 in Dumfries."

"Let me guess," she said. "He had a visit from one of his weird friends."

"You win the prize," I said. "It changes the probabilities that we sent up the road. Pretty drastically, I think."

"Are you going to send the new ones up?" she asked.

"I don't know. The logistics are a pain in the ass because it's Sunday and I don't know where the man is. But he should know. The new numbers are a real game changer. If I have it figured right, a live probability kicks in today. It's small, but it's greater than zero."

"Well, then. Let's figure something out. Do you have your keys?" Judy asked.

"Of course," I said and re-located Maria.

"Judy and I are going to the office for a few minutes," I said. "If you'll drop me at Rip and take the Explorer, I'll walk home from there and be home for lunch."

"Works for me," she said.

By the time she dropped me outside Ripley Hall, Judy was unlocking the door. I went inside and turned on the heat while she disabled the alarm.

"Do you want coffee?" I asked.

"Not unless you do."

"I've had enough," I said.

We sat down in my office.

"Here's what Darps and his friend hit me with," I said. "There was a telephone call into Chestertown that contained the words, 'Revenge of Martyrs,' and, 'Thursday,' separated by three seconds of static. They couldn't make any sense out of the static. Or of the call, for that matter. My intuition tells me that the probability of a suicide bombing on Thursday has just gone up. And I think there's a finite probability of an attack today."

"Just out of curiosity, what makes you think that?" she asked.

"Intuition. Plus the fact that 'Revenge of the Martyrs' was mentioned this morning."

"Mother of God," she said. "Do you have a fail-safe comms link with *Cheetah*?"

"The only one is the 'face-time' email that I use when I need to see him," I said. "I suppose I could use that for a message. It would probably get through."

"Okay. Tell me what to send. I'll send it," she said.

I thought for a few seconds. Judy fired up her computer.

"Okay. Here goes."

TOP SECRET-SHADOW

From: Allewellyn@Bias.gov

To: Keys@LISound.gov

Subj: Face Time/Changed Probs (TS-S)

(TS/S) New stuff. Changes to Thursday's numbers: 08/.01, 09/.01, 10/.02, 11/.03, 12/.10, 13/.03, 14/.02, 15/.01, 16/.01, 17/.02, 18/.05, 19/.30, 20/.05, 21/.02, 22/.01, 23/.01, 24/.02, 25/.03, 26/.20, 27/.03, 28/.02.

Loose

TOP SECRET-SHADOW

I hated sending out classified stuff from *BIAS*. Oftentimes, the classification tended to obfuscate the message. Of course, the classification restricted access, meaning the message might not get through to the people who needed it the most. In this case, I hoped that my classmate and running mate, Jim Kehoe, would (a) get the message and (b) figure out the first number in each term of the series I'd sent was the December date and that the second was our estimate of the probability of a suicide bombing attack on that date. Hence, the initial 12 was 12 December (this Thursday) with a probability of attack of point-one zero or ten percent; 19 was 19 December (a week from Thursday) with a probability of attack of point-three or thirty percent, and 26 Thursday had a probability of twenty percent. These numbers were based on Darps's buddy's report of the phone call linking 'Revenge' with 'Thursday.' The numbers—probabilities—on all the other dates were way low, compared to the Thursday probabilities. All probabilities were 'soft' numbers, which I had just pulled out of my ass. But my intuition had been well groomed at Monterey years ago.

Probably the biggest concern in my message was the threat start date—today, 8 December. The probability of an attack was low—point-zero one—but it was more than zero. Maybe he'd want to get back to the park and state police as well as the Marines and start the watch earlier than the fifteenth. Like today.

Surely he'd figure this out. He graduated from Holy Cross after all. A Jesuit school.

Chapter Fifty-Eight

We implemented our new watch bill starting today at 5:00 p.m. Two people manning the phones and a computer. One pair between 5:00 and midnight, another pair from midnight till 7:00. The five-till-midnight pair got to come in at noon the next day. The midnight-till-seven pair got the whole next day off following their watch. I thought that schedule was a helluva lot easier than a one-and-three watch bill onboard a Navy ship. Darps and I would be in before 7:00 every day and would handle the daylight hours on the weekends.

Kehoe moved up the protective details in Annapolis, the Mall, and MWU and put them in place starting at 1800 this evening.

Once again, someone turned the information spigot off. We weren't getting anything. Our folks overseas had nothing. The Italian source in Cuba was mute. None of the big guys in D.C., including NCTC, had anything. At least anything they were willing to share. Supposedly, they had drones up twenty-four-seven. It was like the whole issue had gone away. I was a little edgy all day on Thursday, but nothing happened. Nothing blew. A little after four, the hotline rang with its distinctive ring tone and startled the piss out of me. It was *Cheetah*.

"Let's run tomorrow morning. LZ Hornet at 11:00. Short and slow so we can shoot the shit," he said.

"Works for me," I said. "How long?"

"How does five clicks sound?"

"Perfect," I said. "See you at 11:00."

Weather next morning was delightful. Sunny, no wind, and forty-two degrees when I left Ripley Hall for Quantico. I'd spent three hours in the morning looking at websites and prowling around Ripley Hall like a caged beast, and it was a relief to change into running clothes and head for the wooded side of the base. There was extra security on the gate, but the Marines had my name on a list. I drove to the LZ where a Marine MP directed me to a parking spot at the side of the road. Luke met me as I climbed out of the Explorer. He wore a hooded sweatshirt. "Park Police" was stenciled on it.

"I'm told that you and the man are going to run slow enough that I can stay with you," he said.

"He said, 'short and slow,' and I'm taking him at his word," I said. That's when the *whump-whump-whump* sound of the choppers kicked in. Two white-tops landed in the middle of the zone. A Marine clambered out of the first one to land and then *Cheetah* got out. He wore Holy Cross purple sweats and a Yankees hat. Luke and I jogged out to meet him.

"Know a turnaround point about a mile and a half from here?" he asked.

"More or less," I said. "We'll just run for thirteen minutes or so and then turn around."

"Sounds good as long as we keep the pace gentlemanly," he said and we headed out of the LZ at an easy jog

After a few minutes of quiet running, he said:

"Here's my problem. All this fucking silence. Nary a word in the last three or four days. You can't see 'em, but we've got drones all over the air space between the Atlantic and the Blue Ridge Mountains and from North Carolina to Delaware. Calm before the storm. It keeps making me think that the shit is about to hit the fan. Any minute. That chopper," he said and jerked his head skywards. "is keeping an eye on me and will land to pick us up if something blows up."

"If it's any comfort," I said, "My whole crew is going bonkers. For the same reason. The silence. My guy in Germany keeps sending in negative reports every twelve hours. Darps's weirdo friends are off the radar. Your national guys are mute. I'm keeping a minimum of two people on the phones and the computers twenty-four-seven and *nada*."

"Here's something," Luke said, startling both of us. He tapped the ear bud in his right ear. "From Mike. Now. The FBI has just confirmed that the turd who blew himself up in Chestertown last week was an Egyptian. They and the Germans think he was a guy who had a student visa in Germany. In Hamburg. Apparently the German cops were keeping an eye on this guy and he disappeared. He may have been with the foursome that went to Cuba. If so, he traveled on a bogus passport."

"That's not much, but it's something," I said. "Here's our turnaround," I added, looking back and crossing the road.

"A possible tie-in with the Hamburg bombers," I added. "A possible trip to Cuba. Coming to Chestertown from Cuba. Going *boom!*"

"That doesn't make me any less edgy," Kehoe said. "I still feel more nervous than a cat covering up shit. If anything, that morsel on our Chestertown Unabomber coming here from Egypt via Hamburg and Cuba ties the indicators more closely to the D.C. metro area and the present time for a big explosion. Fuck!"

"Well, at least, you've got the cops and the Marines in place. Let's hope we've got the targets covered," I said.

"That's the problem. We don't *know* if we've got the targets covered. We have cops on the Mall, at Martha Washington, and cops and Marines in Annapolis. But we have no idea whether these assholes might have picked out a Metro station in Maryland or the National Cathedral in D.C. to pull off their suicide bombings."

"Limited resources," I said, sounding lame, even to myself. "We can't cover everything—either intel-wise or security-wise. We've just got to do the best we can with what we have."

"Okay. Tell your people to keep the faith. Keep looking and keep calculating. DHS will keep the drones flying."

We were approaching LZ Hornet. The chopper that seemed to be following us landed and the other started spinning its blades. Cheetah gave a little wave and ran toward the lead helicopter.

At first, *BIAS* literally *feasted* on the morsel from the FBI about the Hamburg Egyptian. We were delighted to get a headshot photo of one Ismail Baradi, a bearded, rodent-faced young man with wild eyes. But then, the info seemed like a mid-morning sugar buzz one got from a jelly donut and sweetened coffee that folded a half-hour later as one nearly collapsed with sudden fatigue. All *Cheetah's* words of encouragement not withstanding, *BIAS* and I seemed to slip back into the black hole of dispirited ennui.

Friday afternoon, I called in a pickup order for antipasto and a large Stromboli to Fat Harry's. One of his Pakistani cooks manned the phone and took the order. Nothing unusual about that. When I stopped at the restaurant to pick up the order, Hafez wasn't there. I pulled out my wallet and asked the Pakistani cook, "Where's Harry?"

"He was here this morning, took a call and left just before noon. Very strange," he said.

I'd been buying pizzas, Strombolis, and Steak Bombs from Fat Harry's for ten years. Fat Harry closed on Thanksgiving Day and Christmas Day. Otherwise, he was always there. Always. Except today. Like the Pakistani cook said, it was "very strange." Very strange indeed.

"Please add a dozen wings to my order," I said.

"Of course," he said.

I didn't count but I would have bet only twelve wings dropped into the foil bag. Fair enough. I paid for everything and rounded up the total for a tip and headed home.

Surprise, surprise! Only Maria, Elizabeth, and Cory were hanging out in the family room. Mutt and Jeff were absent. I had mixed feelings. I missed Elizabeth's friends. (After all, why had I bought the wings?) But it was nice to have my girls all to myself.

"There's antipasto, Stromboli, and wings," I said. "I'll take Cory for a walk. Help yourself to the chow. And I intend to have a scotch when I get back."

"Ouch!" Maria said. "Sounds like you had a rough day."

"I shouldn't whine," I said. "It wasn't all that bad. I'll be back in ten or fifteen minutes."

I headed out into the dark with Cory. In about twenty minutes, we were back. I unhooked the dog and took off my leather jacket. The packaged pizzeria food was still stacked on the stovetop, in its wrappings.

"Alan, Darling. When you build your dark scotch, be so kind as to pour your wife and daughter a pale sherry and an apple juice. And then sit with us."

Minutes later, I was sitting with the two most beautiful women on the planet whilst sipping a very dark amber scotch. It doesn't get any better than that.

"Elizabeth and I decided that you need to relax. You're too hot-wired. So sit and enjoy your drink and enjoy our company. I'll dish you up some antipasto in a few minutes. I probably won't massage your feet, but maybe Elizabeth will."

"Eww!" said Elizabeth. "I think I'll feed the dog."

"Thank you," I said and took a sip of scotch. It was pretty stout. Hit the spot.

When I headed for the rack a little before ten, the tiredness was morphing into sleepiness, which was a good thing. Maria stayed up for the ten o'clock news. As my head hit the pillow, I said two prayers. One was that the bombers wouldn't strike tonight. The other was that they wouldn't strike ever. But for the latter prayer to come true, *BIAS* would have to get a whole lot more information. Lately, we hadn't been getting any.

Thanks to Maria, Elizabeth, and the scotch, I fell asleep immediately.

Chapter Fifty-Nine

I walked in to Ripley in the dark and, following Navy custom, arrived to relieve the watch a couple of minutes before 0645. Ashleigh was one of last night's watch-standers. I was amazed at how fresh-eyed she looked.

"The silence is deafening," she said. "There may have been a satellite phone call from offshore Florida into Stafford, but we got no content whatsoever. Nobody else is reporting it. We're not even sure of the endpoints."

"Hmm," I muttered. "Maybe some phone traffic from Cuba to Stafford. Content unknown."

"That's about it, boss."

Darps showed up a minute later. Ashleigh was putting on her jacket and I was making an urn of *Breakfast Blend* coffee. I told him about the blank phone call.

"All the more reason to be concerned about the bastards targeting Stafford or Chestertown," he said.

"Say that again," I said.

He did.

"We haven't even mentioned a target in Stafford," I said. "Until now."

"Yeah, I know. But it seems like there's been a fair amount of communications traffic into and out of Stafford. We've assumed that's meant a target in Chestertown, next door. I'm starting to wonder if that's a good assumption."

Darps and I relieved the watch. Ashleigh and an analyst named Doug headed for home.

"Stafford," I said. "What the hell would these bastards want to bomb in Stafford?"

Darps poured two cups of coffee.

"I don't have a clue," he said. "But I do know that we've had comms traffic into and out of Stafford. We're pretty sure we had evildoers' vehicle traffic into Stafford. Ergo, it's not unreasonable to think that the bastards have their eye on something in Stafford."

"Well what the hell could it be?" I countered.

Darps sipped coffee.

"Beats the shit out of me," he muttered. "Quantico? The southern edge of the base is in Stafford County. Stafford Courthouse? Fat Harry's? One of the county schools?"

"I think Quantico is unlikely," I said. "It's a hard target. Six or seven months ago the Marines shot and killed some asshole that tried to run one of the gates in a vehicle. Our guys prefer soft targets. Like night clubs and pizza joints."

I thought for a moment.

"Holy Christ," I whispered. "There are a shitload of public schools in Stafford. It's a big, growing county."

I scrabbled around on my keyboard.

"Looks like about thirty schools," I said. "Let's see if I can get a look at the calendar."

I scrabbled some more.

"They all have a two-hour early release on the nineteenth," I said.

"What does that mean?" Darps asked.

"Maybe nothing. But it synchs with the Naval Academy's winter break start," I said.

"So what are we going to do? Call the man and tell him to pull the cops off Martha Washington University and put teams at all thirty schools in Stafford?"

"No. We're flailing here. We don't have a morsel of evidence that Stafford's public schools are a more likely target than the university in Chestertown. Not a smidgen," I said.

Chapter Sixty

Chestertown
Thursday
December 19

Today was the Red Day. Boom Day. The high-probability-of-attack day. I walked in to Ripley again, arriving at five. Sammy and Samantha were on watch. Judy and Darps showed up within the next two minutes. Great minds.

"I knew you guys would be arriving early, so I brewed a fresh batch of coffee. Help yourself," Sammy said.

"Thanks, Sammy," Darps and I mumbled, reaching for our mugs. Judy took a bottle of spring water from her purse.

"Let's sit and have the night shift and the day shift brainstorm a bit," I said. "I confess to a certain elevated degree of edginess. Today is 'der Tag,' as we said. Anything cooking?"

Sammy and Samantha exchanged glances.

"Nothing really," Samantha said. "We got negative reports from Annapolis, the Mall, and Martha Washington University at 0400, a little over an hour ago."

"Nothing from either our guys downrange or the big boys at NCTC since 1800 last evening," Sammy added.

"We're not leaving," Samantha said. "Even when our watches are over. We decided a couple of hours ago that we'll hang here until 1800 or when things start blowing up. Or stop blowing up. Grungy clothes and all."

"Amen," Sammy said. "I will make a bagel run to Einstein's for Samantha and me and anyone else who is hungry."

We placed orders with Sammy and he was off to Einstein's in the dark. He was back in less than thirty minutes with a bag of bagels sporting various food groups.

My bagel was heinously unhealthy but it hit the spot. It was a plain, toasted and buttered number with two scrambled eggs and three slices of bacon. I doctored it with a few drops of Sergeant Major hot sauce that I kept in my desk.

Ripley Hall seemed dead. The morning dragged on. *BIAS* seemed to be generating a low-frequency hum. The TV's were on low volume. There were no shouted curses from the desks. No exclamations of shock or surprise. And very damned few telephone calls. The noise level picked up for a while as the bulk of the team arrived and then subsided again. Until a few minutes after ten when the White House phone rang.

"Damn," I muttered and grabbed the phone.

"*BIAS.* Llewellyn," I answered.

"This is Staff Sergeant Mancuso at the White House Communications Agency. I'm calling to inform you that Maryland State Police have just apprehended a woman wearing an explosive vest between the Navy-Marine Corps Memorial Stadium and the main Naval Academy campus. She is under Maryland State Police control and the explosives have been removed from her person. She was walking toward the Yard when she was intercepted. Initial observations suggest that her ethnicity is Arabic, probably Egyptian. Sir."

"Thanks for the heads-up, Staff Sergeant," I said. "Anything else?"

"No sir. Not at this time."

"Okay. Thanks Staff Sergeant," I said again before hanging up the phone and turning to Darps.

"Maryland State Police just picked up a woman with an explosive vest walking toward the Naval Academy," I said. "Looks like the ball is in play."

"No shit," he said. "Sounds like the evildoers just made the first serve. Whatever happens next is going to happen soon. Like now or in a few minutes. The question is 'where?'"

The phone rang again. This time it was the outside landline. I heard Natalie, one of our admin assistants, answer the call.

"Bureau of International Affairs Studies. This is Natalie."

Pause.

"Please hold, sir. I'll connect you."

My phone chirped. I picked up.

"Llewellyn."

"Alan! Alan!"

It was Hafez. He was screaming.

"What's up, Hafez?" I asked, trying to inject a note of calmness into a conversation that already sounded like it was going off the rails.

"Alan! Khalil! He's gone crazy! Insane! Like we talked about! Crazy!"

He sobbed.

I felt a jolt of ice water in my system, clawing its way to my heart.

"Calm down, Hafez," I said, ridiculously. Even I could hear the tremor in my voice. "Tell me what's happening."

"Allah, Allah! It's Khalil. He's gone to the school! Wearing a vest! And he's got a gun!"

He sobbed again.

Jesus Christ.

"Vest? What are you talking about?" I asked.

"A fucking suicide vest! With *plastique* and nails!"

"What school?" I shouted.

"Where he teaches!" he screamed. "Your old school! Wearing the vest!"

"When did he leave?" I yelled.

"Two—three minutes ago. I don't know..." He was still sobbing. "Those children..."

I slammed down the phone and ran for Darps's emergency locker. I grabbed both weapons—the M-1 rifle and the .45—and two clips of rifle ammo plus two magazines of .45-caliber handgun rounds from the locker. I seem to remember a Marine staff sergeant from long ago telling us that "combat elevation" on the M-1 sights was twelve clicks. I ratcheted the rear sight down to zero and up to ten. There was zero windage on the weapon. There seemed to be no wind outside so that was good.

"Stay here and man the phones," I shouted and ran for the door.

"Alan! What the hell?" Judy screamed as I raced past her office.

"Later!" I shouted over my shoulder. I tossed the M-1 and the Colt .45 as well as the ammo onto the front seat, jumped into the truck. and left in a hurry. I had absolutely no fucking idea what I was going to do.

I took a couple of deep breaths and slowed down to within fifteen miles an hour of the speed limit. That put me at fifty in town. Fat Harry said that Khalil was heading to his school—"where he teaches." That would be Augustine Washington High School. My old school. If he'd left two minutes before me and had left from Stafford—two big ifs—he wouldn't be all that far ahead of me. Whatever, I needed to get to the school in a hurry. Fat Harry said that Khalil was wearing a vest that was loaded with explosives and nails. That meant it was designed to maximize lethality in a crowd when detonated by a suicide bomber. A crowd containing a bunch of kids and teachers that I knew. I had no idea what sort of "gun" he was carrying.

Mother of God!

I edged the truck up to eighty-five as I got on I-95 north, speed-dialed Judy on the cell and told her to call the cops and tell them that a suicide bomber was heading to Augustine Washington High School. I hoped they wouldn't shoot me. I was doing ninety-five when I had to hit the brakes for the exit. When I swung into the school parking lot a couple of minutes later, everything seemed quiet. I circled the building, looking for Khalil's gray Prius. Nothing doing. I left the parking lot, turned left and left again to Asian Pear Avenue that bordered the woods on the south side of the campus. The gray Prius was parked on the side of the road. License tag read *TCHR MN.* No doubt. Khalil's wheels. But where the fuck was Khalil?

There was a narrow, twisting creek that crossed under Asian Pear Avenue through a pair of culverts and then flowed parallel to the road. Between the road and the creek there was a dirt trail. It led back toward the high school. Khalil had to be heading that way. I drove around a bend in the road and caught sight of a pudgy figure in a burgundy-colored jacket jogging ahead of me. I lowered the window.

"Hey!" I yelled. "Khalil!"

The figure stopped and turned. It was indeed Khalil. Probably looking pudgy because of the explosive vest underneath his Washington Redskins jacket. And a submachine gun. Like an MP-5 or an Uzi. I jumped out of the truck.

"Khalil!" I shouted again. "Stop! Ditch the vest."

He stared at me uncomprehendingly for a second before turning and breaking into a clumsy run toward the school and away from me.

I grabbed the rifle and a clip of ammo and started running.

This was no eight-minute-per-mile lope like I was used to. I hammered out a half mile in probably less than two-and-a-half minutes and gained a few yards on him. But I was wheezing like it was the end of the world.

"Hey!" I yelled, between gasps. "Khalil!"

But I was very close to running out of gas. The good news was that I knew exactly where we were. From here, it was a steep, uphill jog to the school's practice fields and the loading ramp right behind the cafeteria. I took a glance at my watch—11:04—right in the middle of second lunch on an early-out day. My breath was whistling in my throat as I headed up the hill. Khalil was no more than a hundred meters ahead of me, and I was closing. The trail turned to the left about twenty meters ahead of him. In a few seconds, he would be out of sight. I made a quick decision and dropped to my knees and then to a prone position, bracing my fall with the butt of the rifle.

"Khalil!" I shouted. "Stop! Halt!" I yelled, hoping that one of the words would get through to him.

He looked back, briefly, stopped for a second, and hosed off a five-round burst that rattled the foliage around me. I couldn't believe it! The prick had shot at me! He turned and started running again. I jammed an eight-round clip into the M-1 and let the bolt slam home. Lining up the front and rear sights on his back, I held my breath and slowly squeezed the M-1's trigger till the rifle barked and kicked. Khalil stumbled and then disappeared in an ugly, horizontal sheet of flame that dissolved instantly into a burgeoning mass of greasy-looking black smoke. The sound washed over me like a giant wave and was followed by a rain of debris—dirt, small stones, twigs, and leaf fragments. Maybe human body fragments. Khalil had disappeared in the blast.

I stood up and automatically looked for the spent cartridge case. It was lying in the middle of the trail a couple of feet below me. I pocketed it, put the M-1's safety on and headed back down the dirt trail. I was still gasping for breath. I turned and looked back up the hill. There was no sign of Khalil except for a couple of blackened, smoking shapes on the trail. There were several small fires burning in the woods on either side of the trail and heavy, gray smoke everywhere. It was a scene from hell. I couldn't believe what had just happened—what I had just done. I'd shot Khalil in the back, causing him to blow himself to bits. But that was in the woods. He was intending to blow himself—and a bunch of kids—to smithereens in a Virginia high school.

By the time I got to the bottom of the hill, my breathing had returned to something close to normal. I shouldered the M-1 upside-down under my windbreaker, hiding it in a somewhat half-assed way. I turned and started to jog the few yards to my truck. I could hear sirens in the distance, getting closer. I was carrying a rifle that had just been fired and a spent cartridge casing in my pocket. Not to mention a bunch of live ammo. I needed to get the fuck out of Dodge. Immediately.

Chapter Sixty-One

I was heading down the ramp for I-95 south when the cops hit the opposite ramp going north and heading west to Augustine Washington. Usually, zipping along with the I-95 traffic didn't make me feel secure, but this time it did. I felt anonymous and more or less hidden in the southbound traffic swarm and that made me feel relatively safe. Even with a rifle that stank of cordite. I also felt an enormous relief about the kids in the cafeteria at Augustine Washington High School. They were safe. And probably unwitting that they had been about four or five minutes away from being blown to pieces. But I was fucked to a fare-thee-well at what I had just done.

I think I've mentioned before that I'm absolutely paranoid about putting close-hold stuff out on the air. Telephones, email, and secure phones, whatever—I consider it all to be more or less in the public domain. But I should let my office and my boss know what happened. I called Darps.

"I'm coming in, shipmate. Be there in less than ten minutes. Shit's in the fan. See you in a few."

Darps met me at the front door of Rip and took the M-1.

"Careful. There's a clip and seven rounds still in there," I said.

"Seven? So you fired it?"

"It was the only way I could blow up the fucking bomb before he got it into the school," I said.

"So that means you blew up what's his face—the bomber?"

"Khalil. Fat Harry's fucking nephew. I had no choice. It was either shoot him or let him go into the school with the bomb. When I shot him, the bomb blew," I said.

"Luke's listening to the cops on his scanner. I don't think they mentioned a shooting. They're all over a second guy in the Chestertown-

Stafford area blowing himself up, but nothing about a shooter. Let's check with him."

We did.

"I haven't heard anybody say anything about gunfire," Luke said. "Apparently somebody in the school called nine-one-one when they heard the explosion and saw the smoke. If anyone had said anything about shots fired, the cops would be worried about a shooter in those woods. And they'd be talking about it. But they're not. They did find a damaged Uzi, which they assumed, was carried by the bomber. But nothing about another shooter."

"I figure we need to get a cleaning rod through this baby right away. Do you have the spent brass?" Darps asked.

I pulled the cartridge case out of my pocket and dumped it into his palm.

"The rifle will be as pure as the driven snow in a few minutes. The brass will disappear from the face of the earth. Meantime, you need to go home, dump your clothes in the washing machine, and start it going. Then spend some time under the shower making GSR disappear from your filthy bod and well down the drain."

"You're right, shipmate. Let's make it all happen right away. Be careful with the rifle. There's a round in the chamber and a partial clip on board. Safety is on. But it sounds like the cops won't be busting their balls to find the rifle or the shooter. I'll be back in an hour or so."

I walked home and let myself in.

"Mother of God," Maria said. "What's wrong with you?"

"It's a long story," I said. "Let's start with running these clothes through the washer and this bod through the shower. Then we can talk."

I went to our little laundry set-up in the basement, stripped off all my clothes and dumped them in the washing machine. I figured the shoes were probably clean, but used my polo shirt to wipe them off, tops and bottoms. Then I dumped the polo shirt on top of the other clothes, added a little cup of detergent on top of the clothes, closed the lid, and started the machine. Maria was looking at me like I'd turned green and grown scales.

"Now for the shower," I said, and headed upstairs, naked as the proverbial jaybird.

The shower was good. Hot and forceful. It helped with the awful tension about lining up the M-1 sights on Khalil's back and squeezing the trigger. Somewhat. I shampooed my short hair and soaped everything below it mightily and savored the hot water sluicing over me. I got out, dried off, and donned a blue Oxford shirt and a pair of LL Bean blue jeans. I carried an old pair of loafers and a pair of black socks downstairs and poured myself a neat scotch.

"You still look horrible," Maria said.

"I just killed Khalil. Shot him in the back. He exploded. He was trying to suicide-bomb Augustine Washington."

"Oh good Lord," Maria said.

I took a fairly hefty slug of scotch and started putting on socks. Then I picked up the mobile and punched in Darps's cell number.

"Yo," he said.

"I'm clean, the clothes are in the wash, and you've got the deck and the conn. I'm not coming back in till tomorrow morning."

"Understand. Everything here is cleaned up and the phone only rang once. *Cheetah*. A minute or so ago. You'll probably be hearing from him. Within seconds."

My other cell phone chimed.

"There he is," I said, pushed the *End* button, and answered the other phone.

"What the hell is going on down there in Virginia?" he yelled.

I told him. Everything. Well, almost everything. I told him I'd been chasing Khalil based on a tip from his uncle. That the bomb had detonated prematurely.

He said, "Jesus Christ!" Several times.

Then he said: "The big question is: are they finished?"

"Jesus Christ," I said, mimicking my boss. "Lemme call you back in fifteen or twenty minutes."

I put my half-finished scotch on the table, stood up and grabbed a Navy windbreaker.

"I've got to go in to Ripley," I said. "Inshallah, I won't be long. One or two loose ends."

"That's the first time I've witnessed you telling a lie," Maria said. "To the President of the United States, no less."

"No it wasn't," I said. "Everything I told him was true. I simply omitted a detail that he doesn't need to know about."

I drove back to Ripley Hall to save time and called Darps as I drove.

"I'm on my way in," I said.

I went immediately to Darps's office. He was on the phone. When he looked up at me, an almost-tangible expression of relief flooded across his bearded face.

"Okay. Got it. And thanks," he said and hung up the phone.

"They got Husni. CPD. The slime ball is in custody. You already know they got the chick wearing the explosive vest in Annapolis. The Maryland cops turned her over to the Feebs. As you know, the other bomber in Stafford blew himself up near the high school. With your help, I might add. Sounds like he was Khalil. Fat Harry's nephew.

"The guy who drove Husni and company up from Florida was unwitting. Husni paid him two grand to drive. He appears to be some Arab asshole in the Florida Keys who may be a 'facilitator.' The Feebs are looking at him. But this episode has ended," he said. "There's nothing out their flapping in the breeze that we know of or suspect. Am I right?"

"Yes. You are. And it was Khalil. Without a doubt. I think we've got this baby shut down," I said.

I texted POTUS:

Game over. Completely. Loose.

His text came in about three minutes later.

That's what I'm hearing. Come for lunch @ CD tomorrow for a wash-up. Be @ MCAS Quantico @1115 for helo p/u. U'll b home by 1430. Keys.

I walked home and finished my scotch. And then I poured another.

Epilogue

The little "Christmas Break" was fabulous. We'd had our Christmas party at *BIAS* the day before Christmas Eve. Judy had arranged for catering. I bought scratch-off lottery tickets for everyone and enclosed them with their Christmas cards. Ashleigh won twenty-five dollars. We had a ten-dollar max on Secret Santa gifts, resulting in a lot of pens and fast-food gift cards. Except for one mystery gift. For me.

"That came in the mail," Judy said. "I know the Postal Services examines parcels, but I asked Luke to have the secret service check it anyway. It's fine."

It felt like a book. I unwrapped it and, lo and behold, it was a book. The title was *The Guest Book at Harry's Bar - A Novel of Hemingway in Venice.* The author was one Laura Marino, who, from the dust jacket, appeared to be a spectacularly attractive woman. I flipped open the front cover. The title page was inscribed: *To Alan Llewellyn, Recommend you read* La Floridita - a novel of Hemingway in Havana *when it comes out. Ciao, Laura M.*

"Hmm," I mumbled, puzzled.

"Could it be from one of Darps's weird friends?" Judy asked.

"I dunno," I answered truthfully. "But that's certainly a possibility. I've never heard of the book or the author. But it and she pique my curiosity."

"Could it be from Darps?" she asked quietly.

"I don't think we'll ever know that," I said.

I'd decided that testing my theory about sleep being a defense mechanism against stress, depression, and PTSD was a worthwhile strategy. Hence I was getting nine to ten hours of sleep every night. And loving it. I wondered how long it could go on.

I'd gone to Camp David and given Kehoe the lowdown on the *BIAS* side of the operation as instructed. I'd continued to omit the part about the

M-1 and Khalil. He actually seemed grateful. We'd shared eggnogs before the fire prior to lunch. Normally, I hate eggnog, but his was excellent. He mixed it with some sort of apple schnapps and a hearty sprinkling of nutmeg and the combo hit the spot. Franny and Cham were there too. I got another chaste smooch on the left corner of my mouth from Franny when I got off the HMX-One chopper and a tail-and-body wag from Cham like she recognized me. Maybe she recognized the scent of her long-lost cousin Cory.

At home, everything was good. Maria was closing in on finishing her book. Elizabeth's report card from All Saints' Academy was replete with As.

The three of us went to 9:30 Mass on Christmas Day. Saint Katherine's did a beautiful job with the liturgy and a not-half-bad job with the homily, for a change. After Mass, the outside schmoozing had a new dimension. Judy was there; Tala and Esmè were there with their parents and immediately got together with Elizabeth. Then I noticed Luke, looking our way.

"Merry Christmas, Luke!" I said. "I didn't know you were a Papist."

He laughed.

"I used to be. I read somewhere that you can't stop being Catholic any more than you can stop being black. I'm starting to believe that. So here I am.

Merry Christmas."

"You're welcome to swing by the house for a Bloody Mary," I said.

"I'd love to, but I need to run to First Baptist to pick up Louise and Billy and we're having coffee with her parents. The bouquet of Bloody Mary's on Christmas Day would probably be a hard sell."

I understood. Our little family returned to 1506 Prince Henry. I fixed up an artfully spiced-up Virgin Mary for Elizabeth and a pair of Stolichnaya Specials for Maria and me and we exchanged gifts. I gave Maria an iPad and an antiquated, original copy of the impossibly titled *History of the Service of the Third Ohio Volunteer Veteran Cavalry in the War for Preservation of the Union from 1861 - 1865.* Santa Claus gave Elizabeth a mixed bag: several Young Adult novels, a DVD of the movie *Sarah's Key,* and some frilly adult-looking underwear. (Maria picked out the latter. I averted my eyes.) I got a classy-looking All Saints polo from Elizabeth and an expensive-feeling leather passport holder/wallet from Maria.

The Bloody Mary helped a little with the PTSD. I'll never stop seeing the sheet of flame flaring into the woods after I'd pulled the trigger on the M-1. Christmas dinner helped as well. We had a standing rib roast that must have cost a small or medium fortune, accompanied by horseradish, oven-roasted potatoes, and green peas with pearl onions. Dessert was mince pie with vanilla ice cream. I almost swooned.

I'll never forget Khalil. I'll never wander into Fat Harry's pizza joint without feeling a stab of guilt. I'll never tell him about the part I played in his beloved nephew's demise. I haven't been in there since the horror show. But sooner or later, I'll have to go. Life goes on. I'm lucky to have Maria, Elizabeth, and, yes, Cory, in my life. When we walk at night, I talk quietly to the dog. She seems to listen. And who knows what the New Year will bring?

The End

Acknowledgements

Special thanks to my eagle-eyed editor, Karen. Thanks also to John (God rest his soul), Lori, Chuck, Pete, Nick, Carol, and Tom for showing me the ropes of "special intelligence activities" a while ago. And special thanks to Betty, the love of my life, for putting up with me whilst I try to spin these tales.

Other titles in the *Alan Llewellyn* series by Walt Breede:

Snow on the Golden Horn

Altar Stone

Sanity Check

These great reads and others can be found by visiting our online catalog at
http://www.signalmanpublishing.com

258

www.ingramcontent.com/pod-product-compliance
Lightning Source LLC
Chambersburg PA
CBHW060541260626
47161CB00003B/1005